About the Author

Gudeta Urgessaa Bayissa, a journalist, interpreter, translator and a playwright, is originally from Ethiopia, now a Norwegian citizen residing in Bergen. He has a Bachelor degree in cultural and social sciences and a Master degree in social anthropology from The University of Bergen. Gudeta Urgessa Bayissa has published earlier a book entitled *Transformed Oromo Lives and Secularization of Identity - Oromo Narratives from Norwegian Context*, based upon his anthropological fieldwork. *Institution Child – The Beginning* is the first book of the novel he has planned to publish in three books.

Institution Child – The Beginning

Gudeta U. Bayissa

Institution Child – The Beginning

Vanguard Press

VANGUARD PAPERBACK

© Copyright 2023
Gudeta U. Bayissa

The right of Gudeta U. Bayissa to be identified as author of
this work has been asserted by him in accordance with the
Copyright, Designs and Patents Act 1988.

All Rights Reserved

No reproduction, copy or transmission of this publication
may be made without written permission.
No paragraph of this publication may be reproduced,
copied or transmitted save with the written permission of the
publisher, or in accordance with the provisions
of the Copyright Act 1956 (as amended).

Any person who commits any unauthorised act in relation to
this publication may be liable to criminal
prosecution and civil claims for damages.

A CIP catalogue record for this title is
available from the British Library.

ISBN 978 1 80016 875 6

*Vanguard Press is an imprint of
Pegasus Elliot Mackenzie Publishers Ltd.*
www.pegasuspublishers.com

This is a work of fiction. Names, characters, businesses, places, events and
incidents are either the product of the author's imagination or are used in a
fictitious manner. Any resemblance to actual persons, living or dead, or
actual events is purely coincidental.

First Published in 2023

**Vanguard Press
Sheraton House Castle Park
Cambridge England**

Printed & Bound in Great Britain

Dedication

To Genet
    Yannet
   Natoli

      With Love!

Acknowledgements

I feel obliged to thank Mr. Jon Bordal for being willing to be the first person to read through the manuscript of *Institution Child – The Beginning*, and to encourage me to send it to publishers without hesitation.

I also thank Mis Synnøve Eide, the CEO of Bergen Internasjonale Kultursenter, for the heartfelt assistance she granted me in my search for publishers inside and outside Norway, and for her promise to do whatever she could in promoting *Institution Child – The Beginning* in the future.

Huge thanks to Elaine Wadsworth at Pegasus Publishers for giving *The Institution Child – The Beginning* a chance, and to all the people at Pegasus Production Team and the talented proofreaders.

Finally, I would like to thank my wife, Genet Dadi Senbeto and my children, Yannet Gudeta Urgessa and Natoli Gudeta Urgessa for their unwavering support to make this book a reality.

1

He yawned, yawned, and yawned. Slowly, he helped himself up and came out of his bed. He checked his alarm clock. It was still early: seven a.m.

"That is why it didn't ring, huh." He smiled.

It was his foster-mother who woke him. She had knocked on the door to his bedroom three times already. At first very slowly; then a bit harder; and at the last round strongly, accompanying her knock with her usual whisper call, "My boy."

He smiled again. It felt amazing to him the way he grew fond of her. The first time he had been placed under her care, he simply levelled her with those who were his custodians before her. He ignored her charm and scrutinised all her bearings, day in and day out, based upon his experiences so far. He had advised himself to stop trusting the people from the institution, and he wasn't thinking to start trusting her either. People before her, they all took him with open arms at first. They all promised to give him what he needed. Until, at the end, he figured out, or thought to have figured out, that what they were weighing up was the income that followed his placement. 'That is the way it is,' his child-brain concluded for him. That was then.

Through time he learned, though reluctantly, that she was different. Both her words and deeds happened to be very straightforward. He registered, as time went by, that she never tried to impress him, but just continued to be whom she was and is. He observed day after day how determined she was to help him. She made him see that the thing she wanted most was that he learnt to do things correctly. She didn't want him to get in trouble with the accepted norms and values. He also realised, hesitantly at first, that she didn't want him to change at all. She wanted him to adjust and to tune to his surroundings in his search for his own identity. She wanted him to understand himself and to see that he was different. She wanted him to get rid of the habit of munching the idea of retribution towards people he thought might have hurt him. She wanted him not to get accustomed to and identify himself with the bad stamp he got so early in his life. She wanted him to expel prejudices and invest his extraordinary energy in something positive. She talked to him constantly, never giving in to his bursts and shouting, never getting discouraged by his frustrations and his violent reactions. She wanted to know him by making him know her. She never forced him to tell her his story, but she told him hers, partly laughing, partly crying. She respected and listened to his opinions and wishes, but strictly reminded him about the limits in the real world. She talked to him as if he was her equal, without letting him forget that he was a child. She made him understand that she wanted him to see her concerns about him by deciphering his shortcomings. She won his heart and mind by not raising her voice, even when he was trying to provoke her.

Those before her, he disliked them. They made him think and draw a conclusion that they were not there for him. They seemed not to care about his feelings, about giving him security and comfort. As to him, they were there to serve a system. They were out to tame him, he believed. It seemed they wanted praise and recognition from the institution that placed him with them. Taming him the way the institution wanted, meant more assignments and more income, he thought. And therefore, he resisted their taming influence. Most of their activities and behaviours reminded him time and again that he was doomed to be an institution-child. They had no ears for his story, his fantasy, and his dreams, nor for his opinion. They defined him as they wished. People of various attitudes were assigned to watch and report on him round the clock. He was only six years old, but they described him as aggressive, selfish, and manipulative.

He labelled them, too, in silence, and became enveloped in his loneliness. For example, the woman with that always-undone hairstyle, he called her 'haadha budeenaa' – which in his mother tongue contextually means stepmother, but he used it literally for the 'food mother'. Her only concern, he thought, was that he get his belly full and then left her alone. He remembered how she jokingly kept telling him again and again that many children in his age, especially in the country he came from, were always in search of something to eat, and slept with their stomachs empty most of the time. She seemed to always be happy when he shut his mouth and held distance from her. She felt upset whenever he rushed to her with his stories and fantasies. She made him think that he was nobody and was unwanted.

That old woman, the one who took the responsibility for his parenting after his relatively long stay at one of the institution's foster-homes, he called her 'gaararraa' – chameleon. He thought her mood changed so swiftly that he couldn't catch up with her, harmonise with her, and therefore he failed to maintain any possible human contact with her. In a moment she smiled, and he thought she was in a good mood; then she turned angry and complained about every spilt milk, unfinished bread slices, and undone bed. One moment she praised him, the other moment she accused him of everything.

There was this man who used to follow him to various activities, and whose nature he usually enjoyed a lot. He called him 'gowwaa' – the fool. He never said 'no' to him. However, often he frustrated him with his endlessly used word 'but'. This man was a kind of person that measured and weighed strictly beforehand anything a child wanted to do. At the end he said 'yes' and asked for assurance that the child would not do otherwise. "Okay; but we have to have an agreement first that you shouldn't choose the other way." His concern was more not to be manipulated than to give comfort and security to the child he was assigned to take care of.

The one he called 'mortu' – witch – was the woman he despised most. He always thought she was more than willing to punish him as hard as she could. He observed her cruelty starting from the first day he had been placed under her care. It seemed to him that she felt amused whenever she got an excuse to deny him watching the children's programmes on TV. She wrote down what he was supposed to do and examined strictly what he managed to do and not. Then she started with her amusement, denying him what he loved most.

He used to watch them, all of them, the way they watched him. He erected his own premises and thinking grounds in the middle of a guttered and trenched attitude of those working for the institution. Sometimes he wondered whether his brown eyes saw things differently compared to those blue eyes of these people trying to shape his destiny. For him, the matter was always about sharing, about non-calculating love, about negotiating his wishes, about flexibility, about attitudes. As a child, he expected love and tolerance, not punishment. He wanted admiration for his extraordinary energy, not isolation.

But, for those who took control over him, he thought, it was all about control, about structure, about doing or not doing that which was expected of him. They had convinced their conscience by saying that they followed principles. Principles they wanted to impose on a child like him. They never seemed to take into consideration that they might err. As to him, they happened to feel that they were always right, and that he was always wrong. Such a stance scared him. There were nights when he sat in his bed and sobbed. He felt so lonely. He felt so empty. He felt ashamed of himself and cursed the day he concocted that story he told his teacher to come away from his parents' home. There, with his parents, he used to negotiate his wishes. They did all they could to please him. He used to get hugs and love, despite his misdeeds and wrongdoing. It was him who used to push them to the edge. It was him who was violent and disrespectful. However, he reported on them as if they were mistreating and abusing him. He remembered how dreadful they felt the day those people from the child welfare institution came home to them, accompanied by the police, and accused them of child abuse and of caring inability. He remembered how powerless his parents felt right in front of him; how difficult it was for them to express their position because of the language barrier; how devastated they felt when he was taken away from them. He remembered how he enjoyed their helplessness, how he laughed triumphantly when his parents and his siblings cried for him not to be taken away from them.

All through his sojourn at various foster-homes, he looked for something that would constitute an excuse for what he had done. He looked for something that would make him feel complete and give him a new identity. He looked for sympathy for his rebellion against his parents and accordingly freedom of action. But he never came that long. He felt rather stranded and trapped. Both the children he met at foster-homes and those caretakers and concierges, he thought they were not there for him. His child-mind told him that they had constituted danger to him. He was constantly pushed around, being continuously reminded about the importance of abiding by rules and regulations he thought were so strange and careless. He had been confronted with more structure and a relentless and inexorable taming process. His denial to join the familial relationship at the foster-homes resulted in his isolation. His volatile reaction to the treatments he received from his tutors had generated another inescapable and thorough plan of action from the side of the institution. He missed warmth. He missed love. He couldn't sleep. He believed there was no one ready to listen to his worries.

That was then.

Now, everything had changed.

She knocked on the door for the fourth time. "Yes, yes, I am up." He smiled.

"Breakfast is ready."
"I need fifteen minutes to wash."
"You got it."
He followed her footsteps with his ears.

2

Ingrid Gullestad was in her late thirties. She was married once, to a teacher at a secondary school in her home village Sørreisa, a small town named after its district, having about three thousand inhabitants in the middle of Troms County, in the northern part of Norway. He was ten years older than her when they married. He died of cancer. She was so badly in love with him that she declared to herself she would not open her heart to another man after him. She found consolation in her work at the police station in the town of Finnsnes, some fifteen kilometres away from where she lived. She was assigned as the head of the immigration office at the police station a few months before her husband died. Alongside her necessary education, the life she spent in France was one of the advantages in the field of experience that made her score well in the competition for the post. This then helped her to add French proficiency to her well-accomplished knowledge of English and German languages.

At that time there were few asylum seekers in the entire Troms County. The first duty she was involved in was to help process the family reunification of

African refugees who came to Norway as UN quota refugees and get resettled in the city of Finnsnes. They were the first people of African descent resettling in the city. She was so excited to help them reunify with their families. One of the reasons for her excitement was the stories she was reading in the local newspaper, in one of the Saturday columns produced by a newly arrived refugee journalist. The reports and deliberations of this refugee journalist presented in this Saturday column that kept coming at two-week intervals were intended to inform the local population about the real situations of the refugees.

She wanted for so long to read reports and near-to-the-ground information representing different perspectives. She was eager to hear about stories not modulated to fit to the home audiences' ears. She wanted something that negated the fears she happened to share with her fellow citizens. Accordingly, the writings of this refugee journalist sometimes satisfied her eagerness and sensitivity.

Reading those newspaper articles made her laugh at herself, her ignorance, and her negligence of looking for the right information. She laughed at her fears. She laughed at her well-guarded scepticisms and generalisations with such a strong belief in what she assumed while she was reading the article entitled 'When do you go back home?'. This happened to be the question asked by each member of the hosting society. It was indeed the famous question refugees with various backgrounds were equally confronted with. She loved the way this journalist told his story to his readers, advising them not to worry about the newcomers of his type. For one thing, most of these refugees never had intentions to be in this part of the world, he pointed out. Many had lost their loved ones and were victims of bloody wars and brutalities before somebody sent them here. Some were badly traumatised and distressed because of what they went through. They never thought and wanted, he underlined, to be intruders in someone else's territory. It had been decided by someone for them to be here, away from all they knew, belonged to, loved and cherished. Although full of expectations, these were frightened people, mesmerised and captivated by the goodwill of those who sent them here and of those who received them with open arms. One thing these people kept thinking about when they went to bed and came out of it, was how on earth it was possible that their own government chased them out of their country and these foreign nations gave them accommodation and a new chance to life? They did not even know the rules of the game here, let alone to steal the welfare benefits of a modern world, he underlined. These were people, some of whom, all their life long, only knew a government and government officials who were disposed to terrorise them. Therefore, they were very grateful for being given a new chance in their life, the life that had been devastated by meaningless skirmishes and unexplainable brutalities. These were people who lost trust and now were trying to encourage themselves to trust again. These were people who really needed help, not avoidance.

Then there was a niggling opinion she was hearing from various sources that the asylum issue was highly relating to human trafficking issues. Cases were concocted and histories were made up to exploit wickedly the opportunities the asylum institutions of various countries were offering to those people in need. Dream worlds were created overnight by those heartless criminals and sold to those willing to pay whatever they had to get away from the impoverished life they were facing on the home front. Parents sent their children into the unknown, expecting a better time ahead, not valuing the risk of losing them forever. Boys and girls, women and men from various lifestyles and occupations, from different corners of the world, were driven by the wish to join this dream world called the First World, and many perished painfully on the road towards it.

She, in a way, felt proud of the job the politicians of her country were doing by rescuing these refugees. She thought of herself proudly as a citizen of a constitutional democratic country and promised to herself to be able to tolerate and help these people to realise their integration. She decided to be part of the undertakings that were on the move to give these people back the hope and the motivation they were robbed of.

One Wednesday afternoon, while she was at the office, somebody was talking to the receptionist on duty. The door to her office was open and she overheard the matter. She immediately came out and saw the person who was asking for information regarding family reunion. He was gorgeous in a way. His dark face was full of life and his physique seemed very strong. When she met his eyes, she thought they were on fire. She recognised him: she had read his articles a couple of times. The newspaper people always published his writing accompanied by his picture, placed in the middle of the column. She gave him a broad smile. He looked at her with caution. She invited him into her office.

"Well, I know you!" she said, after he sat in the chair in front of her desk.

"Finnsnes er et lite sted. Alle kjenner alle" – 'Finnsnes is a very small place. Everybody knows everybody' – he commented.

"You learn quick, man!" She looked into his fiery eyes, smiling big and wide.

"Thank you!" he said, trying hard to avoid her eyes.

"I really mean it. How long have you been here?"
"Six months now."
"Amazing!"

She gazed at him, unaware of how fiery her own eyes became. She followed his eyes without knowing that she seemed to be hunting his soul. He felt cornered and stared back at her for a moment. Suddenly, she felt her heartbeat growing faster, and she wondered why.

When he turned his eyes away, she registered his shyness. She smiled.

"By the way, I read your articles, all of them, in our local newspaper. You are very courageous. I liked your deliberations very well."

"Oh... thank you."

"You really gave us a lot of stuff to think about."

"Hmm..."

"I mean it. This last article of yours; after I read it, I laughed at myself. I laughed at my misperception of the refugee situation in my country."

"You know, I just wanted to share with my readers how weak the position of the refugees is and that nobody needs to be frightened of them."

"You have succeeded in doing so..."

"I don't know that..."

"You have indeed. You have won me, for example."

He blushed. He started sweating.

She smiled and pointed her finger at him, without knowing how much she was making him uncomfortable.

"I meant you win my support. I am telling you that I have been convinced."

He sighed. He looked at her for a moment and looked away.

"You are very kind!" he said. He inhaled deeply and added a comment in a very low voice. "You are very beautiful, too!"

"What…?" She opened her mouth wide and stared at him.

"I mean it!" he said.

She swallowed hard. She knew her colour was reddening. "Now, let us talk about your problem."

She tried to find her poise.

He looked at her and smiled. He breathed somewhat irregularly in and out. He tried hard to compose himself.

"Well, before I start telling you my problem, you have to assure me that you are not going to be bored and shut me off before I finish."

"I am not such a rude person."

"Thank you! You are very likeable!"

She stared at him with wide eyes. He felt uncertainty.

"Sorry!" he said.

"Hmmm, are you going to tell me your problem or what?" She stared at him again. She decided not to smile.

He tried to catch his breath.

"You know, I hadn't thought when I came here that I was going to meet a person like you, who would drive me out of my equilibrium. I do hesitate whether you are aware of what you could do to people like me with your kindness and lovely smile."

She didn't let him finish. "Stop!" she said.

As if he had been hit by a hard blow, he stopped talking. He stared at her.

"Look, I only want to help you. I am sorry if you understood me wrongly. I am truly interested to help those refugees in my country who are in need. Therefore, please, stop bullshitting – sorry for my word – and tell me what your problem is."

He smiled. "Okay, I will tell you!" he said.

He told her about his family, and how much he missed them. He told her about his four boys and his wife. He told her what it meant to be a refugee in surroundings where those grave injustices never seemed to disturb the so-called long arm of the law. He told her how hopeless it felt when one ended up being 'nobody', just because of crossing the border that constituted a national arena of both power and misery. He told her the burden of not knowing the code of conduct and the rule of the game in a foreign constituency and waiting for someone to decide for one's life to be cursed or blessed. He told her about the pressure one was exposed to in surroundings where everybody was trying to survive. He told her how many lives he watched perish while he himself was waiting in agony for what, at any possible moment, could confront him and how this kept him awake night after night. He told her about his country, calling it a police state. He told her how the people in his country tried hard to keep away from the police and security forces because of their cruelty and lawlessness. He told her how it felt when one ended up being the victim of mass arrests, gang-raping, and torture for no wrongdoing other than, maybe, simply asking what wrong one had done. He told her the helplessness of heads of families confronting the security forces who seemed to enjoy belittling and physically assaulting them in front of their children.

She kept listening to him, wooing him sometimes. As a person who was born and grew up in a humane and justice-oriented society, she couldn't imagine the magnitude of the experiences he was sharing with her. She had never been threatened by social injustices and political harassment. She never needed to fear people in power in her country. She simply couldn't imagine such brutalities that this man was talking about. She lived all her life in a society where people didn't need to turn and look over their shoulders now and then, fearing that they might have been followed by those who wanted to cover and protect their wrongdoings. She lived all her life where most of the population did not see it as necessary to lock their doors when they were away or when they were asleep, except, of course, when she was in France. That was another story. But here, she couldn't remember when she was worried about her security.

Or did she?

She thought about it while she was listening to him. Of course, she felt some sort of uneasiness at times, observing so many foreigners roaming so many places here and there. Her travels to Oslo on short sojourns had somehow impacted these feelings on her. She had worried about her security, whether seriously or not, when she met various refugees in places she never expected them to be. There was a time, of course, when she told herself that the old space configuration where one could meet only the 'Ola' and 'Kari' of Norway on the train, on the bus, in the restaurant, etc, had gone forever. She had registered long ago the fact that the colours of neighbourhoods were changing dramatically, breeding scepticism all the way. However, she didn't remember any incidence where she was extremely worried about her security and as a result decided to lock her door, let alone to run away from her country.

She watched him while he was trying so hard to hold back his tears. She watched him, with an overwhelming feeling of solidarity, while he was sharing with her all his pains and worries. In between, she wondered how she ended up listening to this man she had neither seen nor spoken to before. She moved herself right and left in her chair and settled her eyes on him now and then and tried to scrutinise him. Then, suddenly, he stopped talking. He stood up and looked down into her eyes. His tears kept running down his cheeks. After a while, to her relief, he took out his handkerchief. He dried his face and blew his nose as soundlessly as possible. He sat down again.

"You know, I have never been like this before. I used to be very strong in controlling my emotions. I was brought up learning not to cry and not to give in to hardships. But this time around, it is not the hardship I am facing. It is about my family, and the problem I made them face. I cry because I did let them down. They are suffering because of my political involvement."

He dried the corners of his eyes once more and smiled.

"You know, under the cultural context I was brought up in, it is embarrassing to cry in front of such a beautiful lady like you. I don't know how it is here in Norway, sorry!"

This time, she didn't ask him to stop.

He let his lips go wide and smiled at her. It seemed a sincere smile. She responded, too, with a big and wide smile.

It took him a while to catch his breath and continue talking to her.

"You know, refugeeness drained out of me my energy and my hope. I only see the mud I have fallen in. Most of the time I think that I certainly have lost the fight. I am so worried."

He settled his eyes on her and seemed to appeal to her conscience.

"The reason why I came here today is this. I have been advised to contact the police to find out the person in charge of my case at the directorate of immigration, UDI. It is very important to me to talk to this person. I want to try to make her or him understand the urgency of my case, the dire situation my families are in. I want to tell them how my wife, my children are harassed because of me. I want to tell them how grateful I am for being rescued, and how it became meaningless for me to be in peace here while my family suffers."

He swallowed hard and stood up again.

She followed his movement with measured caution.

"Would you please help me?" He pleaded to her with all the body languages he thought she might understand.

Slowly, she came out of her chair and took his hand. She looked into his eyes that had turned blood-red because of his crying. She smiled. "I will try!"

She breathed deep. "But you should know this. I try not because of you, but because it is my duty. As a police officer I can help you to find the person in charge of your case. That is your right, in fact. Apart from this, the police have no way to interfere in the works of the UDI. I also want you to know the things your family must do. They must apply for reunification with you. You must tell them that they should go to the embassy of Norway and submit their application."

She smiled again.

"They have already done that. That is why I want to talk with the person who oversees my case."

"Then no problem at all. I will do my best to find out for you."

"When can I come back and…?"

He suddenly seemed as if he wanted to leave her office as fast as he could. She smiled again.

"You can come tomorrow, the same time as today. You tell the receptionist that you have an appointment with me, Ingrid."

"Thank you so much!"

"You are welcome!"

She followed him and showed him the way out.

That night, she dreamed double, a dream inside a dream. It ended up for her being a wet dream. First, she dreamt of calling him. She called him from her office and told him that everything had gone easy and well. She asked him whether it was okay for him if she paid him a visit. She told him that she was thinking to visit him together with her female colleague. They agreed about the time, and she suddenly felt restless. In the afternoon, she drove to his place of residence with her colleague. She rang the bell of his door, but he was not answering. She tried again and again. She looked at her colleague, the woman beside her, who was watching her silently. She saw in her eyes some signs of suspicion, a questioning language like 'Do you really need to do this?' She turned around and went back to her car. She started the car and waited for her friend to jump in. She drove relatively fast as to what is allowed inside residential areas. When she came to the main road, she saw him. He was cycling fast towards them. He saw her and pressed hard on the brake. She stopped reluctantly and rolled down the window on her side.

"We were at your place!"

"I know, I left a message that I would be back in a minute."

"Left a message?"

"Yes, with my neighbour. Didn't she tell you?"

"Aha..."

"I just wanted to buy something we enjoy while we talk. You see... beverages, soft drinks..."

He showed her the pouch he was carrying.

"Sorry, my time is over; maybe another time." She drove away without waiting for his answer.

She dropped her colleague at the police station and drove home to Sørreisa. She felt upset. When she came into her house, she found herself breathing fast. She tried to calm herself down. She took her clothes off and went to the bathroom. She took a quick, cold shower. She dried herself and went to her bed. The moment her side touched the bed, she was asleep.

Right after that, she heard this very soft knock on her bedroom door. "It is me, may I come in?"

"What?"

"It is me..."

She heard the door open.

He came directly to her and before she made to ask him what he was doing, he kissed her. At first, she felt like wanting to resist him. She couldn't do that. He overwhelmed her with his passionate kiss, and she started gasping. Before she knew it, he had invaded her entire body. He kissed her all over, everywhere, igniting a vibration deep inside her. She gasped and gasped. Before she knew it, he had taken her nightgown off her. She opened her eyes, and he was pulling down his pants. She saw his hardened jojo and opened her mouth in shock-like surprise.

"Oh..."

She huffed and puffed.

He came to her face, holding his gorgeous jojo in his hand. He touched her lips with the tip of it. She wheezed and opened her lips slightly. He ignored that and put it between her breasts. She gasped and tried to follow him. He ignored her again and put his mouth on her nipples. He kept biting her softly. He licked her smooth body down to her belly button. He went further down. She felt so ready and very stimulated. He stopped his move and took her hand.

He forced her to touch him. The moment she took him in her hand, he plastered his lips on hers. Before she knew it, he had pushed her hand slowly aside and guided his hardened and stiffened jojo to enter her wet body very deeply. She exploded immediately. His trust fully occupied her inside. Before she knew it, he turned her around and did the same from behind. She gasped high, shrilled. This time he made his trust with such gentility and caution that she exploded again. She wanted to control him but failed to do it again and again. At last, she left herself to his mercy. She liked and enjoyed the way he was doing it to her. She surrendered and obeyed, to follow his rhythm.

He broke the silence.

"Now, please, turn and lie down on your back!" he said.

She did as he told her, without any resistance.

"Now, please, watch me as I am doing it to you!"

"What...?"

She looked at him. He was on his knees between her legs.

"Look at it, watch, it is sweet, you will love it..."

She looked at it and started shivering. "Oh my God..."

She gasped high. He did it to her, at first slowly and gently, then harder and harder.

She exploded again.

He moved himself quickly inside her. She came, and came, and came, enjoying unbelievable climaxes repeatedly.

She screamed aloud.

"Please come; please... let me feel you come... please," she moaned and implored him.

Then, suddenly, he stopped moving. He disengaged himself and stood up. She stared at him with her mouth wide open. He put on his trousers, but they couldn't hide the bulge of his hardness. Before she knew it, he opened the door and walked out of her bedroom and disappeared.

"Ohhh... please..."

She gasped and turned to her side. Then she opened her eyes. The wild truth of the real world engulfed her.

"Oh my God! What happened to me...?" She touched herself.

She found that she was wet, very wet. She shook herself awake. She jumped out of her bed and opened the door. There was no one.

The next day, she felt uneasiness and discomfort at her workplace. She wanted to talk to somebody. Her friend was not at work. She gave her a call and asked her to come by. An hour later, they sat alone in her office.

"What happened?"

"He did it to me."

"What...?"

"Don't shout…!"

She opened the door of her office, stretched her neck out and checked the outside, in the corridor. There was no one around.

"Who did it to you? And what?"

"Oh my God…"

"What…?"

"I thought you knew…"

"What is going on…?"

"Well,… it is so silly."

"That is why you asked me to come here?" Her friend scrutinised her.

"You remember this African man I told you about…?"

"The guy you said you talked to the other day?"

"It was yesterday, yes!"

"And…"

"Just, he did it to me. You know…"

"You went to him, and he just did it to you?"

"We went together."

"With who?"

"With you."

"Stop the nonsense."

"Then he followed me to my place…"

"Okay…?" Her friend looked at her with suspicion.

"He just made it to come into my house."

"Without your invitation?"

"I was asleep. I just heard him remotely knocking on my bedroom door."

"What...?"

"Before I knew it, he opened the door; he took off my gown; he kissed me both shallow and deep; he made me wet and entered me hard; he did it to me. He made me explode in orgasm after orgasm, so many times; and then he went with his hardness bulging through his trousers; without a sign of relaxation."

"My goodness, Ingrid!... What are you talking about? I never heard you talk like this before. Where did you find all these sexy words? I hope you are not losing your balance."

"I am telling you about my dream, my wet dream."

"Oh... hmmm... that is something."

"Oh my God. What is happening to me?"

"Nothing!"

Her friend smiled; a little bit at first, then wide, then she started laughing, laughing high.

Ingrid joined her friend at last.

After some time, they looked at one another. Her friend asked her, "You like him, ha...?"

She kept quiet.

Her friend inhaled deeply. "You have not had sex for such a long time now, Ingrid."

"You mean that is why I dreamed about a stranger, a guy I just talked to a day before, invading me in my own house?... Ha!... Don't make me insane!"

"I don't. Hmm..."

"Don't laugh at me!"

"I don't."

"We have an appointment today. He will come here in the afternoon. How can I meet his eyes?"

"The way you did in your dream."

Her friend laughed. Ingrid threw a pen at her. "Damn you."

She became calm.

"Behold your wet dream as a good memory of adventurous but safe sex. That is a nice experience, I hope. He couldn't know about it unless you tell him. And talk to him the way you did yesterday; unless, of course, you want more."

"To tell you the truth…"

Her friend looked at her.

"You want to find out… ha? Your dream in reality…?"

"I thought about just something like that."

"You'd better take time. You will be disappointed."

"You know, I was so loyal to my husband for so long. Why is this happening to me suddenly with this unknown person?"

"The answer…"

"Yes, if you have one!"

"You are just reacting naturally. You wanted sex. And this man, he awakens in you the lust. Maybe, you found him attractive. Maybe, it was his talk.

Maybe, it is the colour of his skin. Maybe, you imagined his body while talking to him."

"Well, thank you for that summary."

"But don't fool yourself, my friend. Take your time. If you one day decide to make him do it to you, again, then I am more than willing to listen about your experience."

She left her with a smile.

He was sharp on time.
"Good afternoon...!"

She greeted him and showed him to her office. He seemed restless. She wondered why.

"Do you have any answer for me?" he asked her, while he was sitting in the chair in front of her desk.

She looked at him for a while. She picked up a yellow notice pad from her table, removed the upper piece and handed it to him.

"This is a person who is in charge of my case?" He asked her softly.

She nodded.

"I can make a call and contact him any time?"

"Her; she is a woman. You can call her on Monday, Wednesday, and Friday!"

"Oh... thank you so much."

"You are welcome."

He stood up. "You know what?"

"What?"

"I have made a very good dinner for two of us, spicy food, with a hope you will say yes. Would you mind coming to my place and tasting it after work?"

"What?"

"What? It is a friendly invitation. Am I committing some wrong here?"

"No... no, it just... I don't know."

"Please?"

"Let me think about it."

"Do that. Look, I am so grateful for all that you have done for me. You are such a good person. And..." He stopped.

"And what?"

She wanted to know.

"Forget it. I am not going to say it again. You will stop me. Remember, I'll wait for you. It is very spicy food that is waiting to be tested. I prepared it for you. Give me a call when you are on your way so that I get enough time to warm the food. I am very sure you will like it."

Before she knew it, he pulled her hand, kissed inside her palm, and left her office. It took her a while to assemble herself.

"Wait; let me follow you out..."

She talked to the empty office. He had long ago closed the door behind him.

She sat quietly in her office for almost all the working hours after he left her office. She thought about her dreams. She thought about him.

'How come he is getting my full attention so quickly?' she wondered.

'Oh my God, what is it that I am doing?' she asked herself again and again.

At the end, she laughed aloud and made her decision.

On her way out, she gave him a call. "I am on my way!"

She told him.

She thought she heard him gasp. She smiled.

It took her a little over ten minutes to reach his place. She was about to ring his doorbell when he opened the door wide.

"Welcome!"

He pronounced the welcoming word with such a big smile and a cheerful look. He was dressed in baggy shorts and a basketball singlet.

He looked gorgeous, she thought.

As she entered his house, he locked the door behind them.

"No!" she said. "Don't lock the door!" She became very serious.

"Okay, okay. It is just a bad habit. We used to keep our doors locked in my country. That is the extension of the habit of growing up in insecurity. Sorry...!"

He unlocked it.

She became cautious.

But something of this man was forcing her to loosen her guard. Part of herself was demanding of her to know him more first; the other part was pushing her to get acquainted with him in all possible ways without delay. While she was taking off her shoes, he went to the sitting room and came back to her, holding something behind his back.

"Since you are so kind and accepted my friendly invitation to eat with me, I would like you to put this on. It is an African woman dress. You will like it."

"Oh... you mean it?"

"Yes, I mean it." He showed it to her.

"Oh, so lovely! But..."

"But what? Look, I don't mean any harm, but you must take off all that you have put on and change to this."

"What? All?... What do you mean by that?"

"I beg you! Do that for me. Just take them all off and put on this."

"I think that's not..."

"Please..."

She couldn't say no. "I have to have on at least my..."

"No, please..."

"Are you crazy...?"

"I don't know yet."

She flushed. She looked around. She saw the bathroom. He pointed to his bedroom. She took the garment and went to the bathroom.

She took all her clothes off quickly and put on the cloth he gave her. She looked at herself in the bathroom mirror.

"Hmmm…"

She liked what she saw, but felt her nakedness underneath.

When she saw him in the mirror, standing behind her, she reflexively put her hand on her mouth. She turned and faced him.

"You see! You look fabulous. You look beautiful. Now, my friend, let us eat!"

She followed him to the kitchen. He pulled the chair and invited her to sit. After she sat down, he folded up her shoulder-long hair and kissed her gently on the back of her neck, and whispered, "Thank you so much for coming."

She listened with closed eyes. 'Why is it that I am not saying stop to this stranger?' She thought about it silently.

He came with the food he said he had prepared for her. The first dish contained shredded lamb meat roasted in garlic and white onion. The other dish contained rice roasted dry in a mix of water and olive oil, and topped by a stew of sweet paprika, raisin and chopped red onion roasted together in margarine. The sauce was something like hot-chilli sauce made with tomatoes and hot paprika powder from his country.

After he put the food on the table, he opened the wine, INCA. He had fallen in love with this wine the first day he tested it. It is The Wine of The Andes, from Argentina.

"I am driving!"

"I have two bedrooms. You can stay."

"How do you know that nobody is waiting for me?"

"I didn't. But I know now…"

He smiled.

She smiled, too.

He stood up and took his glass.

"Let us say cheers and wish this to be a beautiful beginning of a long-lasting friendship."

First, he served her, putting on her plate portion after portion of the food he had prepared for the occasion. Then he served himself and sat down.

He cut and picked up with his fork a piece of roasted lamb from his plate and asked her to close her eyes and open her mouth. She did. He first kissed her lower lip, then the upper, then put the meat in her mouth. She opened her eyes and looked into his eyes and sighed.

She started chewing on the roasted meat he had put in her mouth. "Omm… it is delicious."

"In my language, we call it 'waaddii'."

He put some more on her plate.

"Stop, please. The plate is full. It is too much. Let me finish this first."

"Very well, you are the guest. The guest is always right."

He stretched on his seat, facing her. He looked into her eyes. She investigated his.

"How old are you?" he asked her.

She blushed.

"Oh, damn me. Sorry for that. I am almost forty."

She looked at him suspiciously.

"I am a few years younger," she answered quickly.

"Honest?"

"Yes."

"You are not kidding me… or…?"

"No, I am not."

She put some more food in her mouth.

"So, it means we are matured enough."

"Matured enough for what?"

"To do what we feel is right."

"You think it is right to dine with someone you have met a day before, and be alone with him in such a private atmosphere in his house? Rather, it is so strange."

"I thought I heard you saying that you knew me before. You remember what you said in our conversation yesterday?"

She didn't answer.

They concentrated on their food for a while.

She was about to sip from her glass when he stopped her.

"Sorry, I forgot to make my welcoming a little briefer. I must say a word to cheer up our togetherness here and now."

He stood up and took his glass.

"First of all, I thank you for coming. I am so lucky for having met you. You don't know how I feel right now, sitting here with you. I want you to be my friend and a friend of my family in the future, when they come here. In case we, you and me, are going to do something that friends aren't supposed to do, then it is the fate we shouldn't fear. I love my family, to tell you the truth. But my heart was aching for you from that first moment I met your lovely and innocent eyes. I don't know how you feel, but I am so happy for having you with me. Cheers!"

She stood up and knocked her glass with his. They kept quiet for a while.

She looked at him. She inhaled long and deeply, before she uttered, "Everything is happening so fast. I met you yesterday. Of course, I read your articles in the newspaper earlier. It might be because of it that I am feeling at ease with you here and now. However, believe me, everything is happening so fast. I cannot say how I made it to accept your invitation to come here, to drop all my clothes and change into this one, to sit here nearly naked and dining with you, alone."

He smiled and asked her, "How do you feel?"

"You want to know the truth?"

"Yes!"

"I am terrified. I wonder what is going to happen between us."

"Why?"

"Look! You get me easily doing everything you ask. I say yes to everything you ask. That is crazy. I couldn't resist you. I don't know what is happening."

"Really?"

"Yes. Don't you see?"

He paused for a while.

"How long since you had sex for the last time?"

"What?"

"Just tell me. please, how long?"

She kept quiet.

"Please…"

"Almost six years now."

"I had sex for the last time three and a half years ago. That was with my wife." He smiled.

She abandoned his eyes for a while. She breathed deep and looked at him.

"I had it before my husband died. He died five and a half years ago."

"I am sorry."

"Don't be, it is an old story."

They kept quiet and ate their food.

He gently put down his knife and fork. He looked at her. She looked at him with tension.

"You know what?" he asked.

"What?"

"I want to make love to you right now, right here."

She suddenly stopped breathing. She swallowed hard and looked at him with wide open eyes.

He raised his glass. She hesitated. He waited for her. At last, she raised her glass, too. He sipped his drink and placed his glass back on the table. She did the same. He raised himself and stood in front of her.

"Look at me, please."

She saw it, his bulge. She gasped.

He took her hand and helped her up. He hugged her and pressed himself against her body. He dropped his baggy shorts and his jojo was out in the open. He kissed her. She responded. He buried himself between her gorgeous breasts. He whispered in her left ear.

"I liked you from the very moment I saw you."

"It was yesterday." She whispered, too.

"I know."

He gasped.

"I want you to sit on the kitchen drawer."

"Okay..."

She swallowed hard.

"Are you ready to take me in?"

"Yes, but be careful."

"I will."

He did it gently. She hung on him with her legs tightened behind his back, her arms clinging to his neck. He held her behind and lifted her up from the kitchen drawer.

She screamed.

"Please... slow down!" she whispered.

"Okay... I am trying." He gasped and gasped.

"Oh my God, I am coming, I am coming…"
"That is good."

He did it to her harder and harder while her responding body was chewing on him. Holding himself inside her, he put her down on the kitchen floor. He moved in and out, in and out.

"My God, you are killing me," she whispered into his ear.

He stopped moving and looked down into her eyes. He smiled. "You don't like it?"

"I didn't say that."

She bit his lower lip gently.

He kissed her and started doing it to her, very hard but controlled. He huffed and puffed.

"I am coming now…"

He exploded inside her. She did the same. She looked into his eyes. Surprisingly, she became aware of the fact that she wanted more. She pulled him down and kissed him deep.

After a while, he removed himself and stood up. He threw away his singlet.

She saw that he was still full-hard. He bent down and took all her body in his arms. He lifted her up and carried her away.

"I am taking you to my bedroom." He kissed her on her forehead.

She clung to him and buried herself under his neck. "Do whatever you want."

"I want you the whole day and night."

"No, you can have me only for the whole afternoon."

"Okay then, for the whole afternoon."

"You got me. I am yours."

He slowly put her on his bed and removed the African cloth from her. Before she knew it, he entered her. He touched her deep inside and she screamed.

He kept whispering while he made love to her.

"You know what?" he said.

"What?" she asked him.

"I dreamt about you yesterday."

"What...?"

She stopped moving.

"Yes... I made love to you in my dream." He continued his move inside her.

She kept quiet and resumed her move.

"You made me come over and over again, without yourself coming."

She hesitated for a while.

"What can I say...?" she said.

She moved fast and knocked him out of his rhythm.

"Wait... Wait! Let us finish together."

"Hurry up then!" she gasped. "Hurry..."

She came before him. He put her legs on his shoulder and made his thrust harder. She moaned. He moaned. After a while, he removed himself from inside her and burst all over her body. Then he collapsed beside her. They both panted.

"Do you want to hear more about my dream?" he asked her.

"Yes, please."

She turned her face to him.

"You came to visit me. We first sat in the sitting room. Then you went to my bedroom and came out with this dress on you. You were naked underneath. Just the way I asked you to be today. I was terrified by you. I thought I would explode before I entered you. You kissed me so wet and sent a devastating vibration throughout my entire body."

He paused.

"It seemed we made love all night long."

He looked into her eyes. Before she knew it, he turned her around and entered her again.

"Oh my God, I cannot take it any more...," she said.

He kissed her.

She kissed him back. He moved inside her gently. His hardness filled her. She thought it was painfully enjoyable. Suddenly, she came out from under him, pushed him aside and made him lay on his back. She sat on him and took control. She rocked him and felt him deep inside her. At first, she hesitated as she felt this sticking pain when she forced herself on him. Not long after, she felt it as heavenly delicious. She groaned.

"What a hell...," she whispered.

"What?"

She didn't respond.

She rode him wildly. She screamed. He turned her around.

"Oh my God…," she whispered.

"You like it?"

"It hurts…"

"Shall I stop…?"

"Do it to me… but gently."

He did it to her.

She thought she had never experienced a sex that was so coarse, so wild, and so sweet at the same time. She felt overwhelmed. She couldn't help following his rhythm. She couldn't help coming again and again. She thought she was falling in love. She thought she was not going to like it.

This time, they finished at the same time.

Half an hour later, she kissed him and left his bed.

She took a quick shower. She put on her own clothes. He followed her and took a quick shower after her.

They went back to the kitchen and ate in silence.

She thanked him very much and told him that she would call him. Before he knew it, she made herself ready to leave him.

He followed her to her car silently. She thought he read her mind. She saw that he wanted to give her a goodbye kiss, but she ignored him. She waved him goodbye while she drove away.

The moment she was out of his sight, she started crying. She wept all the way home. 'This is not right!' she told herself repeatedly. 'He loves his family. He cannot be mine. I cannot even borrow him,' she whispered.

She wanted to get home as fast as she could. But she needed to stop on the way now and then because her tears made her sight fuzzy.

She felt both ashamed and very happy. She acknowledged that she indeed enjoyed this sex after such a long time.

'He was so gentle and respectful,' she told herself.

'He knew what he wanted. He knew what I needed,' she concluded.

She tried to calm herself. But each justification she came up with failed to satisfy her. 'But how dare I let him do this to me?'

The question brought back to her the memory of the afternoon sex session she had with him. Her body responded quickly, and she knew she was getting wet. Although she felt so mad, she thought she missed him already.

She parked her car and hurried to her house.

She entered her bedroom and took down the picture of her husband from the wall.

"I am not loyal any more. I betrayed you," she whispered.

"Try to be yourself, madam!" She heard a voice.

"What?"

She was puzzled. She looked around. She heard it again.

"No need to be ashamed. Be yourself! Try to have fun and to live your life." It was a powerful voice.

She sat on the edge of her bed and sobbed.

When she came out of the bathtub after nearly an hour, she felt fresh and settled. She dried her hair and changed into her nightgown.

She took her phone and dialled the number of her friend. The moment she heard the response from the other end, she burst into laughter.

"You know, I did it again."

"My goodness, Ingrid... I told you to take your time."

"I did take my time. I talked to him for more than ten minutes."

"You are kidding me... ten minutes?"

"Yes, and he invited me for dinner to his place."

"And...?"

"What can I say...? It was..."

"You found out what you wanted to find out?"

"You bet I did."

"You are changed, my friend. How was it?"

"You want to hear?"

"Yes, I am dying to hear about it."

"Come here right away. I have a bottle of red wine."

"I will... and do you have an appetite for Cognac?"

"I hope so."

"See you then!"
"See you!"
She smiled broadly and hung up.

Suddenly, she felt cheerful. Deep inside her the good feeling started churning. It had never been like this before. She did not remember feeling like this when she was sharing with her friend the intimacy she enjoyed with her husband. She sat down on her Italian sofa and stretched herself. She examined her sitting room. The late summer sun had illuminated the room so strongly and made it so white that she missed the composition of the real colour of the room she had organised throughout most of her adult life. She stood up and pulled the curtains hanging over those huge windows of her hundred square metre sitting room that was facing the direction of the setting sun. She went to her player stand and picked up one of the CDs that were neatly and alphabetically placed on the CD shelf.

"Barry White, ha," she exclaimed.

She took her time evaluating the picture on the CD cover. She suddenly found herself trying to figure out the similarities.

'Please! Stop this nonsense!' part of her told her. 'Nonsense...?' Another part of her wondered. 'Is it really... nonsense?'

"I don't know..." she answered aloud to the whisper in her head.

She put the CD inside the player and made the player locate her favourite song.

"Which way is up..."
She followed the lyrics in her own way:
"Which way is up, what's going down?
I just don't know, no more
How about to turn around. Hmmm
Which way is up? What is going down?
The world is moving... too fast, too fast,
Enjoy the good thing, and make it last.
Make him last.
These days something new to learn.
New to learn.
Every day is a new way for what you learn..."

It took her a while to hear the doorbell ringing.

"Don't look at me like that?" she said, and shoved her friend towards the sofa.

"Wow, listening to Barry White? What is that song? 'Which Way Is Up'... you are crazy, my friend. Thinking how to make it last... ha?"

They looked at each other silently for a while.

"It is just unexplainable! I mean all of it."

"I am dying to hear about it!" said her friend, placing the Cognac bottle on the table and throwing her jacket to Ingrid. "Let us first make ourselves comfortable, my dear!"

Ingrid smiled and went to hang up her friend's jacket and to collect glasses and some snacks.

It took her a lot of courage to calm herself down and start describing her adventure to her friend.

"You know, I always thought the way I used to do it to my husband was safer and more enjoyable. This guy, he overwhelmed me and forced me to let him ride freely the wild feeling buried inside me. I tell you."

"Didn't he kiss you?"

"Yes, but I think he was already inside me when he passionately explored my mouth. I cannot even remember how I responded."

"He did it to you without you being ready for it?"

"My goodness, Solveig, it is unexplainable. He made me wet from the start. The moment he asked me to remove all my clothes and put on that African dress, I started shivering and feeling like bursting into climax."

"Oh my God, Ingrid, listening to you, I am losing my breath. I hope you are telling the truth."

"Don't you trust me? I swear to whatever you demand, I am not kidding."

Solveig swallowed hard.

"You know, since I left his bed and his house, I have been thinking and thinking. I couldn't stop thinking about him. There was no faking in his action, you know. He just did it to me as if I was used to having sex with him all the time. He didn't try to find out how I would be in bed. He rather made me enjoy the bed. He didn't bother how I was reacting when he asked me to sit on the kitchen work-bench and…"

"He did that to you?" Solveig covered her mouth with the palms of her big hands.

"Yes, he did. And he made me rather feel as if it was my suggestion and brought me to the climax again and again, which I already had given up and thought had gone for ever. My dear friend, this man, he didn't give me a chance to think about how painful it could be if he forced himself inside me, without me getting wet or ready to accommodate him. I didn't know how he even entered me; I swear to God, I was simply overwhelmed experiencing my entire body chewing on him while cherishing and enjoying the climax."

"My dear friend Ingrid, you know what? You talk P O R N O. I have never seen you like this before. You are changed. They are right. Once you go black, you will never come back to normal."

"Good that you mentioned it. I thought about it, too. Right now, I hesitate that I will find my way back."

"Haa, haa, haa. Don't make me laugh, my dear. Anyway, it is not me who has experienced it."

"Well! For one thing, he was very good; very, very good. It is not the size of his jojo, by the way. It was, let us say, normal. Rather, it was how he did it to me, how he touched my inside. He happened to be very self-confident. He was sure about the fact that he was a man and I was a woman. He was so willing to do it to me as only a confident man can do to his woman. He was stone hard when he dropped his baggy pants and exposed himself to me. He was equally hard when we finished the first round. He was as hard as one could get when he transported me to his bedroom. He never let me get down on him. He never went down on me either. All his style seemed to be rough, but I found it sweet. Oh my gosh, rough and sweet. Hmmm, believe me; I know now that I have fallen in love with this man."

"What if he is not feeling the same way? What if he...?"

"I don't know. The only thing I know is that he did say that he liked me from the first moment he set eyes on me. He also made it clear to me that he loves his family. I suspect he thinks ours is purely sexual."

"How that...?"

She stretched her arms and inhaled deeply. "He first asked me when I had sex the last time. I told him. And he told me, too, when he had sex the last time."

"You trusted him?"

"I did trust him on the spot. He trusted me, too, you know. He did not ask me to have safe sex, for example. That is because, I do believe, I told him I had sex the last time with my husband. He told me, too, the fact that he did it to his wife the last time. It sounded an assurance for both of us."

"Now, how do you think this will be in the future?"

"To tell you the truth, I am very scared. If he is going to do it to me one more time, I will fight to conquer him."

"Are you sure he will let you conquer him?"

"I know he loves his family. But he also is a man, and he cannot be immune against seduction." She smiled.

"I don't think seduction works on mature men like him. However, I do wish you would think about his wife. Have you ever thought about her?"

"Yes… enviously, for that matter." She breathed long and sharp. "I don't know what I am thinking. Honestly, I am dying to know when I will see him again. He is so likeable."

They looked at one another. It was Solveig who first sent a good portion of her Cognac down her throat, then Ingrid followed suit.

Placing her glass on the sofa table, Ingrid suspiciously looked at Solveig.

"What?" Solveig wondered.

"The first round, I made him finish inside me. I wanted to experience that feeling."

Ingrid sighed.

"Oh, you are afraid of … "

"Yes, but … you know. I had a problem to get pregnant with my husband. Truly speaking, I don't think I will be conceiving a child of this stranger so suddenly. However … "

Solveig smiled, took the cognac bottle and poured for both of them.

"No worries Ingrid. You have this talented GP. Talk to her."

'Imagine, Ingrid having a baby for this man.' Solveig thought and smiled big. Ingrid smiled too as if she was reading her friend's mind.

Three days passed since she discussed with her friend about her adventurous experience with this man, this mysterious man. She felt more attracted to him after she told her friend about the incident. She wanted to know more about him. She wanted to know about his personality, his background, his family, about every possible piece of information that could help to bolster her confidence to declare him likeable. As she was following her friend to her taxi that very evening, she told herself that she was going to give him a call next morning, right after she got to her office. That next morning, however, she hesitated. She thought she might send him a wrong message by calling him first.

'A wrong message...?' The words echoed in her mind.

She leaned back on her chair and smiled.

She knew she was dying to hear his voice and to confide in him that she was falling in love with him.

"So, why do I think about sending him a wrong message?" she thought aloud, and checked immediately if someone had overheard her. There was no one around.

Against her intense wish to call him, she decided to wait for his call. She waited for one day. She waited for two days. His call did not come. She became angry. She became restless.

"This son of a bitch, he gratified his urge and now he has no more need for me. How dare I let him do this to me?"

She wanted to curse him. Nevertheless, every second she was spending thinking about him, her mind kept reminding her how lucky she was in his arms. She missed him a lot, but denied herself acceptance of that reality. She accused him of disrespectfulness, but she could not establish any evidence to validate her accusation.

"Why is it that he is not calling?" she asked herself again, and again, and again.

The next day, which was on Thursday, she decided to call him and to find out why he had not called her. Then again, she hesitated. It became boring and very difficult for her to follow those daily office routines. Sometimes she sat in her chair and felt shattered and drained by her own thoughts until something woke her up.

She did not hear at first when the phone rang. Later, wanting to remain in that unbounded world of her thoughts, she tried to ignore the ringing phone.

It did not stop, and she became angry. She yanked it up and answered harshly.

"What is it?"

"I am so sorry for disturbing you..."

The voice coming from the other end was very polite and smooth. She reacted without thinking.

"Oh... how come that you call?"

"You mean I'm not allowed to call you?"

"I didn't say that..."

"Very good, then. Hmmm... are you busy tomorrow afternoon?"

"What?"

She was expecting him to talk around trying to straighten up her disappointment, but he was not doing that.

"How dare you...?" she wanted to shout at him, but he was giving her neither time nor an opening to do so.

"You know what? I was thinking about you, about us very thoroughly these last three, four days. I want to share with you my thoughts. If you say yes, I want that we go out on a bike tour here, on the northern part of our beautiful Senja Island, and have a picnic at the end of our tour. I have already started making a 'Sambusa'. I will stuff it with biff and hot chilli. I assure you, you will like it. And..."

"Please stop now. Hmm... you want me to come to you and have a picnic with you?"

"Yes... pretty much!"

"You didn't bother to call me for the last four days; you haven't even asked me how I got home last time we were together; and now you suddenly erupt my composure and want me to have a picnic with you. I didn't know that you are so selfish."

"Sorry, my dear; I thought it was me who is a foreigner here, and I had expected that it was you who would have the confidence to call me. You were so determined to avoid me last time I followed you to your car and I was trying to figure out what I did wrong. You seemed to be very angry and the way you left was not an encouraging invitation for me to call you. Otherwise, truly speaking, I was waiting for your call each passing minute. I was itching to hear your voice."

"You are so maddening."

"Now look, I have even chosen the place where we will have our picnic. I have two bikes here. I want you to drive to my place right after work, and we will take on our bike tour from here."

"What can I say?"

She tried to catch her breath.

"You became my Queen these days and I am offering myself to your service. The only thing I need from you is to grant me the honour to be with you one more time."

She felt lost. She felt powerless. Suddenly, her tongue jumped ahead of her mind. "Have you received some answers regarding your family?"

Is that the right question? Part of her confronted her. Part of her waited to hear a drop in his voice when he answered, without telling her why.

"Not yet... my dear!"

He remained warm and flamboyant. She felt disoriented.

"I will call you!"

Suddenly, she replaced the phone and went out of her office.

"Don't you think it is beautiful?" He smiled wide and big.

Indeed, it is beautiful. The green grass, the various colours of the wildflowers glowing by the impact of the late sunshine under the blue sky of the month of July, the dark green trees and bushes in the background, and the gorgeous tides of the ocean rolling against and washing over the shore full of small and big stones, had constituted such dreamland scenery.

She watched him silently. The way he prepared their picnic-place overwhelmed her with passion. She thought he was doing his best to please her. That by itself gave her back her confidence and calmness.

"Have you been here before?" She suppressed her smile.

"I was here the day before yesterday. I usually make a bike tour twice a week in this direction. This last Wednesday I suddenly stopped and climbed down here. I sat on that grey stone facing the green nature and listened to the waves of the ocean thundering behind me. Then I forgot everything and surrendered to thinking about you."

"Oh... you surrendered to thinking about me?" She purposely sounded ironic.

He ignored her sarcastic comment.

"Yes, I did. I thought about you very much. I thought how your presence in my life is getting powerful each passing day. I thought about how fast everything has happened. I thought about the way we felt so near to one another, and the way we made love. I thought about the way I remained turned on all along until you left me without any goodbyes. At the end I decided to call you and invite you to come here, to this place with me and to listen to my confession."

He looked at her and inhaled the fresh air deep into his lungs.

"Now, if you don't mind, I want you to sit by my side and allow me to confide in you."

He begged her with his eyes.

She felt the wetness of her tears in her eyes and tried to suppress them. She picked up a small stone from underneath her shoes and threw it into the ocean. Then she did as he asked her. He moved himself a little bit and settled himself right in front of her, facing her gaze.

"You and me, we became acquainted very intimately in such a short time. Since that adventurous day, every thought about you knocks me into confusion. On the one side, I cannot stop thinking of being with you every now and then. On the other side, my conscience tells me that what I did and want to do with you is wrong. I know I cannot make you mine, because I have an obligation that hinders me to be yours."

"Are you sure about that?" she asked him without looking at him. He stopped talking for a while.

She gazed at him while searching for words to tell him her feelings without hurting his.

"Please don't try to explain to me that you cannot make me yours by telling me that you love your family more than you love me. That is unfair."

"You say unfair? Hmm... isn't it true that nature itself is full of unfair events? We humans, too, regardless of our civilisation, have always had such bad records of fairness. However, we try, at the end of the day, to reflect upon the difficulties and fluctuations of human life and to establish a better future. Look, Ingrid!"

She smiled and interrupted him. "I love the way you pronounce my name."

He smiled back and continued talking. "As to me, love does not mean only about liking a person and having sex. It also is a responsibility that involves various emotions that are not so easy to harness. Unfortunately, most of us prefer to neglect this fact. Please, Ingrid, do not hate me when I say to you that

I love my family and I feel responsible for what is happening to them both emotionally and physically. There wasn't a single day that passed without me thinking about them; about the situation that I put them in; until the day I met you. Now, every time I ponder about them, the feeling you created in me blurs my vision. This scares me very much. It scares me because I have started feeling like taking a break from all the worries I have for my family and to be near you and enjoy life with you. I have never imagined that it would reach so far so quickly. I was not lying when I told you that I liked you the moment I saw you. But I was thinking that it was simply a fascination and an infatuation that might go over after a while. It did not happen that way, all right. I like you very much and I want to keep it forever. You will remain my precious Lady, but I want that you should know I am a family man. It was because of them that we two met. I want you to be rational in this regard. If you do that, if you are willing to understand my worries, I will do whatever you want me to do."

"Right now, I want you to stop arguing and start kissing me!" It seemed as if she was looking deep into his soul.

He leaned towards her and they kissed each other. She slowly separated her lips from his and looked into his eyes with such intensity that only a worried lover could generate.

"You don't believe yourself that I am going to buy this argument of yours and forget what happened between us."

He scratched his head.

She continued, "You have already opened the Pandora Box of a loving relationship, my dear friend. You erupted my entire feelings and awakened into life my sexuality. You made love to me and energised me to feel like a woman. And now you ask me to acknowledge that you are a family man and to respect the love you have for them?"

She smiled.

He hesitated for a while. "The truth...?"

"Yes, the only truth and the whole truth...!" She ran over him with her bulged eyes. "Yes, I do."

With all the power she had, she pulled him towards her and kissed him deep and then relaxed her grip.

"But you are not saying that you are not going to make love to me...?"

"Not after my family has arrived...."

"What about today...?"

"Hmm... you are not mad at me?"

"To be frank with you, I rather began to like you more. You seem to be a man of principle, and that must be a rare occasion from what I generally hear about the men coming from your continent."

In his turn, he pulled her towards him and kissed her gently.

"Ingrid, you should drop the last comment, because... hmm, it sounds a negative generalisation. There are men of principle on my continent, too. Regarding the first comment, I mean the fact that you began to like me more... don't you think that is dangerous?"

"My dear friend, you crossed the dangerous line the day you let me enjoy you."

She kissed him. She forced him to lie down on his back. She smiled and swallowed hard when she felt his hardness. While caressing him all over his body, she whispered into his ears, "You know what? I have been without my underwear all along..."

"Oh... Ingrid, we are getting crazy. I don't think it is wise to..."

Before he could finish his sentence, she opened his zipper and took his hardened jojo into her hands. When she was about to go down on it, he stopped her.

She looked at him.

"I don't want you to do that. I rather want you to kiss me deep and wet while I am doing it to you down there. I am hard enough to make you happy, and I prefer it must stay that way!"

She sighed.

He gently pulled her towards him and kissed her wet and deep. When he gradually pushed her to the ground, she gasped and fell on her back. She closed her eyes and opened herself to him.

3

"Wow... what is the special occasion today for all these to be served? It looks so cheerful."

He looked at the table for some time. It was a big breakfast. Toasted bread, honey, bacon, scrambled egg, milk, cheese; the sight of all those things made him hungry. Then he looked into her eyes. She was standing by the side of the dining table.

"You know what? I like this!" He smiled.

"I just wanted you and myself to start the day with full energy, that's all." She smiled back.

"Yes, Mum!"

He went to his chair.

"Yes..."

Suddenly, she stopped breathing.

She looked at him, letting her mouth hang open. "What...? You called me Mum...?"

He smiled big and wide.

"Yes, of course. Why not...? Are you surprised...?"

"No..., no, no. Just..., oh my God, let me sit down and catch my breath."

She pulled out her chair and cautiously brought herself down on it. She kept silent for a while.

He watched her seriously.

"What is wrong with you?"

He left his chair and approached her. He lifted her right hand from the table and sandwiched it between his two small palms.

"I didn't realise that you don't really know that you became more than that to me. Right now, you are the only thing and everything I have. You are my friend. You are my girlfriend. You are my sister. You are my brother. You take care of me. You talk to me as if I am your equal. I feel you in all directions. So what is wrong, you think, if I call you Mum? Maybe it took me unnecessarily too long to call you that."

He paused.

"I love you. I really do. I've thought about it for the last three months. In addition, I thought that it is like such a pure love a child would have for his mum. And it must be like the one I still feel for my mum."

"Oh...!"

She could not suppress and stop her tears from wetting her face. "You have become grown-up, my boy. You really have."

She hesitated to face him.

"I would have liked it more and better if you called me 'My Son!' instead of my boy."

"Hmmm..."

She looked into his eyes. She was sitting, and he was standing by her side, holding her hand. At first, she wiped her face unceremoniously. Then she pulled him to her and kissed him on his forehead.

"Okay, I will call you from now on 'my son', my precious son." She realised he, too, had tears in his eyes.

"Now, my son, let us calm down and eat our breakfast. Okay?"

They went to the bathroom, hand in hand, and washed themselves. After they came back and settled down for their breakfast, she tried to remind him of the day's occasion.

"You know for sure, today is the first meeting with your parents since you have been placed with me."

"Just imagine how fast the time has started running, especially for me. It was not like this before. It is unbelievable those three months are over now. You remember. It was my wish not to meet them for the last three months. I wanted to find myself, my real self, without interference. I wanted to know how I am feeling. I wanted to know whether I am capable or not of thinking positive. I really wanted to stop fighting and start communicating. That was why I wished not to see them for these last three months. I wanted to feel missing them. In a way, I did miss them. But... I did also find in you a person I love and trust."

He stopped talking, put a big bite into his mouth, and started chewing on it.

"That you called me Mum on this very day, it is huge..."

"You mean a huge surprise..."

He smiled and followed her with his eyes. She smiled back.

"Yes, it is a very huge surprise. By the way, to tell you the truth, I loved you, too. I loved you as my own son."

"I know. You have shown me that."

"Thank you."

She began sobbing, but stopped immediately. She turned her attention to the breakfast table. She took a bite of the piece she took from the French baguette served on her favourite service-plate and added to it a spoonful of scrambled egg. She chewed on it gracefully and sipped her coffee repeatedly. Slowly, she turned her attention back to him.

After he took three mouthfuls from what he had on his plate, he stopped eating. He drank his milk and wiped his mouth clean. He took her stare with a smile.

"I want to tell you something. At the same time, I want you to keep it as our secret. Would you mind promising me that?" he asked.

"Oh, my goodness, you sound very different today. You talk like a grown-up. Remember, you are only thirteen years old."

"I know that. I want you to know that I also know how much the institution has changed my life and turned me into what I have become today. Since

I was six, I had been exposed to the mercy of very different grown-up personalities, and to both their cunning behaviours and shortcomings. I had to cultivate a language that helped me to scare them away. I tried to resist the pressure of taming that they exerted upon me all along. Under the institutional circumstances of caring, your childhood is defined through non-family members. There are no such things as love or loyalty. These people, believe me, their priority is to satisfy the system that pays them a living. For them, the eagerness that the age of a child puts on display does not count. A normal behaviour of a child that seeks attention turns to be a reason for scolding. The pain such devastating ignorance has created in me forced me to rebel. I started reacting to it right from the very beginning. I needed to feel grown-up and act as one to resist the intimidation exercised by these people. Therefore, I learned their language. I learned to disentangle their sophistication by systematically deciphering what they were doing, and what they were saying. I also learned to understand them in my own way, and chill them out by ignoring them as they used to ignore my eagerness. So, for me, it was a logical outcome to be or to appear like a grown-up."

He paused and looked at her. She was speechless.
He smiled.
"Now, let me ask you again. Would you mind promising me?"

"Never at all, I don't mind."

"What...?"

"I mean, I do mind to promise. I promise..." She smiled big.

He took a deep breath before he started talking to her.

"The two people we are going to meet today, neither are they my parents, nor are their kids my siblings."

"What...? What are you talking about?"

"I am telling you the truth. The man is my uncle."

Her face turned red.

"That is the truth," he said.

"How come...?"

She forced herself to calm down.

He took a long time before he tried to answer her question.

"Right before I had been placed with you, there was this earth-shaking discussion between this uncle of mine and me."

He paused and looked into her eyes.

"Please do not think I am such a bad person when you listen to my confession here."

She smiled and moved restlessly in her chair. "Go ahead, I will not."

"My uncle, I knew that for sure, felt powerless and devastated because of what I made happen to myself. As to me, believe me, I was not sure why I did what I did to him and his family. I really do not know even why I behaved and kept behaving the way I did throughout all those years I spent alone, away from him and his family. There, too, was just something at the back of my head which forced me to rebel. The one thing I remember, however, was that I had missed something. At the end of the day, I wanted to know what that was. That day, I confronted him and begged him to tell me what I was missing. I cried and made him cry. He was not a bad man at all, you know. I knew how caring and compassionate he and his wife were towards me. When he saw me weeping, overwhelmed by grief, he suddenly took me into his arms, cried as a helpless child himself, and asked me for forgiveness. He confessed to me that what I was so terribly missing were my parents. Do not think I did not know that myself. But, although I knew and was so sure from that first day I travelled to this country together with them, that they are not my real parents, I became through time used to them and have totally accepted them as my real parents. Do not ask me why. As a child, I allowed myself to suppress and deny what my memory reminded me and kept displaying to me now and then. When I heard him telling me that what I was missing were my parents, I became very disappointed. It is true; I was having mixed feelings every time I thought of them, my uncle and his wife, as my parents. However, I expected that he would do his best to prove me wrong and to erase my suspicions once and for all. Therefore, I failed to stomach what he was trying to tell me. I looked into his eyes and loosened myself of his hold and ran back to my dormitory. While running, I shouted to him that I did not want to see him again. I collapsed into my bed and tried to reach out to my juvenile memory."

4

Ambo, called the land of life, is a well-known city in the central part of Oromia in Ethiopia. It is located about one hundred and twenty kilometres to the west of Finfinne/Addis Ababa. It is surrounded by the chain of mountains that are bequeathed by the evergreen natural forest to the south and southwest. It is also adequately supplied by natural and mineral water from the various rivers and springs in the area. The city has about six main entrance gates. The people from the countryside surrounding the city who come in large numbers to do business on market days, to attend the summoning of government officials, to go to court and pursue various legal matters, mainly use these gates. The city is also known for its beautiful and old-time swimming pool attached to the first modern hotel in the city named the 'Ras Hotel'. Another characteristic landmark of the city is the old building of the Elementary and Comprehensive Secondary School that in its long life went through various name-changes.

Arada, the name that is reminiscent of the city structures created during the short sojourn of the Italians after the occupation of Ethiopia in 1936, is the main business centre of the city where varieties of commodities and services are sold and bought. In Ambo, Saturday is the main market day, and Customs officers assigned to the entrance gates collect due and undue money from peasants pouring to the city with their products ranging from sacks of grain to chickens, eggs, dairy products, goats, and sheep. From early in the morning to late in the afternoon on this day, Ambo's Arada gets overcrowded and swarmed by hundreds and thousands of people from all walks of life, doing all kinds of business.

Characteristic for almost all the entrepreneurs of the city is that they are mostly engaged in buying cheap from the farmers and selling expensive to the consumers dwelling in the city. To that end, they wait for the farmers at the entrance gates from early in the morning until midday and apply all the talent and the tactics they must use to persuade the farmers to sell their products to them. One of their bargaining chips is that they cover the money the seller should pay to the Customs officials. Later, the products and various items they have bought from the farmers by labelling it a bad quality, they sell to the consumers by exaggerating its excellence and superiority at an unfair high price. This *modus operandi* lived for years without seeing any kind of innovation, reorganisation, or transformation.

Market days in Ambo are also feast days for beggars and pickpockets. Handicapped people, victims of leprosy with sores, disfigured skins and nerve damage in their various body parts, crawl around, display their mutilation and cry aloud to win the hearts and minds of those who can give them alms. While for the beggars the calm but crowded corners are preferred, every heated bartering corner in this open market hugely attracts idle bystanders and pickpockets. The amalgamation is colourful, the outcome is hilarious. Suddenly, somebody shouts "thief, thief!", and then waves of the marketeers' commotion follows.

Around five o'clock in the afternoon, the gathering loosens. The colourful exodus of people on their way back home, accompanied by their transport animals, horses, and donkeys, fills all the roads leaving Arada. The traditional beer-houses and mead-houses (mana farsoo, mana daadhii) located alongside these roads have, through the ages, thrived by selling their services to these exhausted market-day dwellers, coming from near and far. After visiting these last money-sucking stations, the peasants, with some or no money left in their pocket, flock back to their countryside-fortress, the life-sustaining surroundings still foreign to the modernity of city-life, that are bestowed by naturally rich grazing areas spreading alongside beautiful chains of mountains, magnificent hills covered by precious trees and bushes producing various kinds of sweet berries, shallow gorges upholding rainwater and flowing rivers all year long, and the black and reddish soil farmlands colourfully distributed among the possessions of individual farmers.

The main highway linking the capital city Finfinne/Addis Ababa to Naqamte in Wollagga and beyond, dissects Ambo in two, adding prominence to what the Hulluuqaa river did to the city. Hulluuqaa is the river that lives its life without being disturbed by the settlements of those peasants sparsely populating its embankment alongside the stretch that covers dozens of kilometres starting from its source at Lake Dandi up in the highland. Although peaceful and easily accessible to any kind of irrigation system, Hulluuqaa remained more the place for thanksgiving than the source of agricultural marvels. Because of its natural beauty, it's both wild and mild nature and the provisions that it grants the population as a source of drinking water, the river used to receive the attention of the local population going to its various 'melkas' (crossing points) to praise their Almighty God during the springtime that comes after the hot summer, and during the autumn, the time of transition from rainy season to the harvesting time. The praise is meant to thank God for his generous protection of his creatures both during the hardest time of the year, the dark and stormy winter, and in the sunny and dry summer.

About fifteen minutes to the south of the town, after crossing the Hulluuqaa River, is the heartland of the Oromoo clan, who recount their ancestors to the very senior name in that clan, Qooraa Jaarsoo. Accordingly, the place is called Qooraa, and most of the farmers and their families inhabiting the area are relatives and have inherited their farmland. One of the families settled at this area was the newly-wed couple, with a college education, named Daansoo Margaa and Miidhagaa Mijana. They had hugely surprised the local population by choosing a life in the countryside, defying its common description by the locals and the public at large as hardship-filled. They were so convinced that they could have a meaningful life in this area if they made use of their academic knowledge in addition to the experience they had acquired while dwelling in the countryside from their childhood on until they reached high school age. They hated the suffocating city life and wanted to be near the life itself. They made a case, both to their friends and families, that the countryside is the mother of all happiness, and the guarantor of a healthy life. Their dream came true when the husband, Mr Miidhagaa Mijana, inherited the twenty hectares of farmland from his mother after she died suddenly of a heart attack. Since he was the eldest son and none of his siblings were interested in taking care of the farmland, he decided to take over the responsibility. As he graduated from Ambo Agricultural College, his fiancé, Mrs Daansoo Margaa, who was also from Ambo and had graduated from Tikur Ambesssa Nursing College in Finfinnee a year and a half before him, agreed to his idea of moving to the countryside and resettle there.

It was not a decision made at once, at least for Daansoo. Before she gladly announced the quitting of her job at Paulo's Hospital in Addis Ababa to join her husband in his new engagement, she was silently fighting the insecurity and uncertainty she felt when it came to quitting her job. She knew it was the dream both had had for so long, to work and live in the countryside, but when she had to walk the talk, she hesitated. Many whom she knew preferred to work in the big cities, and she felt at times insecure about whether she was making the right decision. There was this lack of services she always registered when she sojourned in the countryside that kept encroaching on her mind, reminding her of the hardship out there, and the benefits of the city life she was used to.

At last, she decided to move on. She told herself that they were from the countryside and were very aware of the hard work waiting for them. Gradually, she expressed her full support of his intention. They married and moved to the countryside. They had their first child after three years of hard work reorganising their way of life, making friends, establishing alliances, and securing the means of living.

Beyond their private daily labour, Daansoo and Miidhagaa were more than willing to assist their neighbours and the farmer-families in the area. Their engagement included the work of giving basic protective health education to the women, enlightening the women and their husbands alike about the economies of their households, about using better means of production, about changing the old habits of sticking to unproductive methods, about administering income- enhancing measures. At first, their frankness, their deliberate attack against old habits and norms, made both men and women in their vicinity suspicious of them.

Daansoo especially, encountered enormous resentment from the women she wanted to educate about sex and sex-related issues. Her choice of words, her boldness in telling them that sex was not a bad thing but a good thing, brought to the fore unforeseen negative reaction. Unforeseen because she thought among the Oromoo people sexual life was freer and more liberated. Her disregard for the consideration of sex as taboo that some religious entities promoted made some of the well-to-do and admired individuals in the neighbourhood resentful. They told her to keep her profane wisdom away from their children. The message reached her through this special envoy, an elderly woman, a permanent church-goer who had, in her old age, vowed to dedicate her life to religious services and was known by the name of Dirribee Mooti.

"Our women are angry, you know."

It was one late Sunday morning, Dirribee came to Daansoo and confronted her right away by telling her what was on her mind.

"Why are they angry?" Daansoo wanted to know.

"We never heard a woman talking about sexual life so openly as you do. Our God doesn't allow such a blasphemy. One of the reasons we insist girls are circumcised is just to fend off such unbridled sexual feeling you want to inculcate in the minds of our women. You are against circumcision. You are against involuntary sex. You are saying that sex is a good thing that both men and women can enjoy equally. You want our women to tell their husbands whether they want to have that thing. You seem to know more than what we elderly people know about it. You defy the state of celibacy some of us are living in and force us to think of what we shouldn't think. That is a blasphemy, Daansoo."

Daansoo was overwhelmed by what she was hearing from this elderly woman. She was not angry but became very curious. She took the incident as a very good opportunity she might be able to capitalise on. If she won the heart of Dirribee, the rest would be easy.

She smiled and approached the elderly woman with open arms. Dirribee hesitated to let her, but Daansoo did it. She hugged her.

"I am so sorry, mother. But first things first. Let us go into the house. I was about to make coffee. I know you are just coming from the church, isn't it?"

Daansoo took Dirribee's arm and guided her to her house.

Not long after Daansoo encountered Dirribee, the waves of opposition against her teachings ebbed away. Gradually, Daansoo became popular and sought after more and more for advice on all fronts.

The breakthrough came after two years of engagement both in enhancing the health situation of the children and their families, and the productivity of the farmers. The practical result that came gradually contributed big in winning the trust of the community at large in such a short period. They had contributed a lot to the wellbeing of their small community by not being afraid to take a step.

Their popularity, however, brought them into conflict with local politicians. Their actions led to them being accused of some hidden agendas. The one good reason for them to be suspected was their refusal to be part of the government-run party-political work in the countryside. They refused to be members of the party that claimed to represent the entire Oromo people in the new coalition that had overthrown the military government. As a result, they ended up being accused of all types of transgression and concocted oppositions against the government. Under the shadows of the political logic that defined anyone who was not with the governing party as the enemy of that party, Daansoo and Miidhagaa happened to be easy prey.

When Miidhagaa was summoned to the police station in Ambo city for the first time to answer some questions, their son was only six months old. After this first meeting with the police, everything for him turned upside down. Miidhagaa missed his purchasing and selling rights, from buying fertilisers to that of selling his dairy products. The police accused him of being a member of the Oromo Liberation Front and arrested him. On his release on bail, his friends advised him to leave the country. His answer was negative. Then they convinced him to send his child out of the country to secure him a better future.

"How on earth can people advise you to send your only son away?" he consulted his wife.

She was everything to him. She was his wife, his friend, his counsellor.

They discussed the fate of those people who run away from their country because of political problems. They envisaged how it was going to be when one must adapt to a new way of life, a new way of making meaning, and suppressing their own cultural bearings. They argued and argued regarding things happening in their surroundings.

His younger brother was very much against the entire national order of things in that country, and the political and economic undertakings of the government. He criticised the government openly and worked against it clandestinely. When the day came where he could oppose the government no longer, he consulted Miidhagaa regarding his decision to leave the country. Miidhagaa opposed his younger brother by saying that it was impossible to bring about a change by running away. He wanted him to stay and to work for genuine change. Working for genuine change meant for him paying attention to the reality on the ground. Bad feeling from the past should not blind a person's sight and insight to see and analyse the thing that is in reach and that is not. However, he failed to convince his brother and he did run away.

One year after he ran away, he came back and offered Miidhagaa an opportunity to let him adopt his son and allow him to take his nephew with him so that the child could get a new chance in life, which he probably could not get in his country. He declared himself willing to take the son of his elder brother as his child to the country where he would be granted resettlement. At first, the idea was unacceptable for both the mother and father.

When Miidhagaa's son was three years old, they discussed the proposal very seriously. There was a lot to say, a lot to discuss, a lot to grasp, a lot to acknowledge. At last, Daansoo and Miidhagaa came to one conclusion. They convinced themselves that, if their child was to leave them, it was better for the child to think of those people whom he was going to be with as his parents. However, they agreed to take more time and rethink how they were going to make their son believe their story. They needed more than what they agreed upon to be able to inform their son about the new situation. They put themselves through a painful process.

Without knowing how it leaked out, the neighbours had started relaying the information back and forth, adding many details to it. They were saying that the child was born with a golden spoon in his mouth. They were chatting about his destiny ordained for the life in the country beyond the big ocean. They said he was lucky to be able to be there where people do not need to work hard, where the government took care of everything.

Daansoo and Miidhagaa had built up and established a very beautiful country home through these past few years. They made use of their own creativity and the natural resources around them. The green bush-tree known by the name of 'Miessaa' in that area became the well-done hedge, fencing their place of residence. The various bush-trees and green plants they had planted in their compound had given their homestead a majestic look.

One of the fields in which this energetic couple wanted to rally the people for a change was the housing field. They had discussed with one another many times very seriously that the reason why the people settling in the countryside were exposed to a very bad housing condition was sheer ignorance and a lack of knowledge of how to use the abundant material nature was providing. Daansoo and

Miidhagaa believed from the very beginning that they could make a difference if they practically showed and guided their neighbours as to how they could build a healthy house by properly using those materials easily accessible.

Without completely negating the ways in which traditional thatched hut housings in their neighbourhoods used to be built, they came up with a design that happened to give and assure the feeling and sense of a healthy and comfortable home. Miidhagaa's architect friend, Tullu, helped them with their new sketch. The first approach was to introduce the cemented floor that would have one big axis in the middle and other axes originating from the mid-section of the big axis and rested on the wall-pillars intended to support the semi-conical-shaped roof. The second, very gracious and genial touch was the spiral-formed stairs that went around the centre axis and to the upper floor, where two bedrooms would be built. They also introduced the sectioning of the various indoor rooms with windows big enough to assure natural ventilation. The very new thing they came up with in that area was the introduction of a kitchen room to the countryside home and the effort of building a cellar room that would serve mostly as a refrigerator to keep the shelf-life of various food productions for as long time as possible. In addition, they effectively used the stones lying idle in the fields, called 'kattaa' in their vicinity, to build attractive outdoor latrines, shower rooms and a comfortable shelter for their domestic animals.

After only two to three years of engagement, their vicinity became home to very many self-educated peasant architects and planners who shaped and built their own country homes and those of some of their neighbours. Hedge- fences, ground-plus-one floors, toilets, kitchens and refrigerating cellars became the vital parts of homes that had been built by both old and new generations of these countryside dwellers who happened to produce a little more extra income.

By managing to acquire a very comfortable home among those mostly single-roomed Tukuls of their neighbourhoods, Daansoo and Miidhagaa had given their only son a place to be fond of as a child and a playground where most of the times their domestic animals were involved. Feeding the mother hens and holding the newly hatched chickens in his small palms gave him huge excitement. Moreover, he used to chase around baby goats and calves of the few milk-cows his parents owned. He had names for them and scolded them seriously whenever they did not obey him. On the weekends, he played with his mother and father the popular hide-and-seek game of his, behind those beautifully treated garden bushes and flowering plants inside their hedge-fenced compound.

One Saturday afternoon he was chasing the three-week-old small baby goat all over the place because it happened to disobey his order to be with him.

Running out of energy, he at last called for his mother's help to catch that impossible creature. Both mother and child implemented their tactics and overwhelmed that baby goat at the end. They laughed and laughed afterwards. Both sat on the ground and tried to catch their breath.

He paused and looked up into her eyes. "Thanks, Mum, I will not let her go now."

Suddenly, he saw a change in her face and did let that baby goat run away again. He pulled together the contour of his child face. She knew him for this. His eyes caught so swiftly the slightest change of mood. She always wondered how he, being of such a minor age, detected her feelings and read her face.

"What is it? Are you hurt?"

He climbed upon her and tried to get a good look at her.

While holding him against her chest, she turned her face away from him. He moved himself and faced her again.

"What is it?"

She breathed deep.

"Stop nagging, please! There is nothing wrong with me." She tried to be serious.

He smiled.

"I know there is something. Maybe the kick of that baby goat hurts." His eyes went towards the baby goat jumping around.

He smiled and turned to her.

She, in turn, looked into his eyes.

"How for God's sake do you know whenever there is something?" She hesitated for a while.

He smiled.

"Don't you know? You are my Mum." He embraced her as strong as he could.

"No, I am not...," she whispered to herself without knowing that she was thinking aloud.

At first, he simply smiled and crawled down. Then he jumped to his feet and looked towards the baby goat. He managed to make two, three steps forward and suddenly he stopped. He turned back to her slowly.

"What was that you were saying?"

She worried more now and looked away from him.

"Mum..."

"I said nothing...," she whispered.

"I heard you. But do not say it again."

This time around, she could not stop her tears.

"You are my Mum, and I love you very much."

"I know that."

"Why are you saying that you are not my Mum, then?"

"That is because I am not going to remain your Mum for ever?"

"Why?"

"I don't know how to tell you. Maybe you are going to have a new mother and father soon."

"I don't want another mother and father. I love you and I love Papa."

"We are not your real mother and father."

He stopped talking to her.

First, he smiled softly. Then he went towards one of the bushes inside their compound. He sat under the shadow and started picking at the green grass.

She cried quietly. Her whole body started trembling.

Her conscience bombarded her about how she in the first place had been convinced to send her only son away from herself and away from such surroundings that he loved most. She threw her gaze towards him.

'He has already forgotten,' she thought, 'and started playing with that baby goat. I'm sure this time around it must be that baby goat that came to him.' She registered, however, that he was still sitting where he sat after he went from her.

She remembered the days and nights she spent alone with him when his father was sitting in prison. She remembered how she felt insecure and vulnerable during her interrogation at the police station. As stubborn as she used to be, it was her tactical choice when she showed complete obedience to the offensive and rude police demands in order not to exacerbate her son's situation. Fully determined neither to give in, nor to blow the trumpet of blaming the government, she smoothly protected her husband's human and political dimensions by denying any knowledge of what the police were accusing him of. She even agreed to report to the police in case she sensed some irregularities with her husband's daily activities.

After the release of her husband, they discussed the possibility of running away. He was very cautious not to make her feel bad by simply imposing on her the products of his own soul. He wanted to show her that it was meaningless to run away and start a new living. He argued about the essence of life. He reminded her about the adventurous path they had chosen when resettling in the countryside and the end result they rejoiced in after they had executed well what they had planned from the very beginning.

His indifference to the inevitable danger of being imprisoned whenever a powerful politician got suspicious irritated her. She was not missing his point, but she thought he was missing the whole picture of how those men of power in his country were thinking. To Daansoo, this country, from time immemorial, happened to be the land where men of power were there to be admired and to be absolutely obeyed. People never hesitated to pay their tribute to any authority they thought would help them win their case, falsely or righteously. Supporting righteousness for the sake of righteousness had never had market value in this country.

"Or does it?"

She hesitated for a while. Immediately, she continued arguing with herself. For most dwellers, the men of power were there to rule, and the commoners, to the contrary, to be ruled. They seemed to have lost the energy to stomach the perspective of fighting for their own rights through decades of brutal intimidation.

She experienced how this felt by herself after her husband was arrested and imprisoned. Most people in the neighbourhood wanted to know more about why they were suspected by the power-holders, rather than to understand that the power-holders were harassing them. It was very tiresome for her to explain her husband's innocence to the members of their own community that he served with all his guts and knowledge. They came to her home individually, showing her their concerned and worried faces, but left putting her constantly in a defensive position.

She looked back to her son. Suddenly, she felt very weak. She wanted to cry and to scream aloud. She was about to stand up and run to him and hold him tight in her arms, when she saw her husband entering through the big gate of their hedged outdoors. She heaved a sigh and leaned back.

Miidhagaa smiled and sent his greetings to both the mother and son loudly. His son reacted first. He stood up from the ground very fast and ran to him with all his energy. When Miidhagaa knelt and took him in his arms, the boy was trembling and trying to catch his breath while asking questions.

"Papa? Are you my father or not?"

Miidhagaa understood immediately what had happened. He looked towards his wife. She was on her way towards them. She seemed very tired. The boy wanted his attention.

"Papa, Papa! Mama told me that you are not my father, and that she is not my mother. Is that true? You are my father. I love you. She is my mother. I love her. Is it because you do not want to be my father? Why?"

"Please, stop."

He looked at his son. His small face was wet beyond recognition. His eyes turned red and tears flowed in all directions messily. That miserable sight sucked all the energy out of him, and his knees started jerking. He held his son tightly to his chest and slowly sat on the green ground. He fought hard not to cry.

She approached them breathlessly, crying silently.

"I messed it up!" she said in a voice hardly audible.

However, her husband heard her. He followed her with his eyes while she was trying to sit on his side. Her son gave her a quick look and turned away from her.

"That hurts, my son. Don't do that to me," she whispered.

Miidhagaa smiled at her and started singing to his son the familiar 'rudee, rudee' Oromo song he used to sing to him during bedtime. The boy fell asleep.

That was a blessing happening at the very right moment.

After they put him in bed, they took each other in their arms and comforted one another. Soundlessly, they went to the sitting room. She collapsed on the three-seat semi-sofa. He helped her to raise her head and to lie on his thigh after he dropped himself beside her on the sofa. He put his arm on her shoulder and kissed her on her forehead.

"Now that it is out in the air, we must try to convince him as smoothly as possible."

"I cannot, Miidhoo, I cannot."

She never called him his full name. He was always Miidhoo to her. She started weeping.

"You can, my love. I will help you. We must help each other."

"To get rid of our own child?" she whispered.

He gasped. "You know that is not true."

They kept silent for a moment. She raised herself up.

"Can't we forget the whole project? Cannot we simply tell him the truth why we want him to be with them and the future we are dreaming for him? What if my child suffers?"

He kept quiet.

"I know I am making it hard for you, Miidhoo, but this child, he is our flesh and blood. He loves us, and both he and we will get crushed when we insist and dare to tell him we are not his real parents."

"We have already discussed this matter and the reason why we wanted to do just that. Please, Daansoo, it does not help if we start fighting over it again. I will talk to him tomorrow. I will spend the whole day with him. And we will see what will happen." He looked into her eyes.

She stared back at him.

"You think you can convince him?" She paused. "You know what? Even if I can visualise that you can, my wish is that you fail, and he will remain with us."

She looked miserable. She wanted him to see that she needed comfort and love more than anything else right now. Through her gaze she invited him to take her into his arms and comfort her in any way he thought was proper. She felt that her only child had abandoned her because she was denying him his birthright. The only remedy she could think of was to collapse into the arms of the very person who fathered this child of hers.

He stood up first and helped her up. "Let us go to our bedroom."

She stared at him and searched him for clues. "What? It is daytime. If somebody comes...?" She hesitated.

"Shshsh! I was not thinking of anything of that kind. Besides, this is our home. You are my wife, and I am your husband. Don't ever forget that!" He smiled broadly.

She smiled, too, and led him to their bedroom.

They were sipping on their evening coffee when the boy came to the sitting room. "Why was I in bed? It is not yet dark outside."

As usual, he leaned to both, one after another, to get the usual hug he was accustomed to. Then he placed himself in between them and swung his stare from his father to his mother and back to his father again. He smiled. "Papa...!"

"Yes...?" He felt uneasy and unprepared to deal with anything coming from his son at this very moment.

"This baby goat I used to chase around; these cow calves we have; do they know their parents?"

Miidhagaa swallowed hard. Daansoo turned her face away and looked for something that could break into this painful conversation and change the subject. She did not get that chance.

"Mum, I really wonder sometimes how they find and identify their mum from among all those mother-goats and mother-cows."

Miidhagaa gave him a hug and laughed aloud. He desperately wanted to ease the tension.

"You are very smart, my boy. Those who are mothers are the ones that identify and pick up their babies. They identify them by their scent. The baby goats and the calves cannot differentiate who their mothers are, and who are not, but the mothers do. Besides, those mothers do not want to breastfeed those calves who are not theirs. It is a long story, my son. I am sure you will learn with time."

"Ha, you say my son!"

The child smiled.

Miidhagaa looked into his eyes and then turned his gaze towards Daansoo.

"You know what? You are just like your mother; always to the point and always doing it very carefully. You scare me sometimes. Hmmmm, now come on! Sit properly and relax! We must talk."

Miidhagaa tried to compose himself. Daansoo stood up and wanted to go.

"Mum, I want you to be here. I want to hear, too, what you have to tell me."

Mechanically, she turned around and threw herself onto her seat.

Miidhagaa started very slowly. "You know what? We are very proud of you. Not only us, but also everybody in our community likes you very much. You know that you get whatever you want, even if we are not around. The neighbours adore you because you are such a lovely child. In our human world, mothers do not chase away children who are not theirs. It is our custom and tradition to give children comfort and love. That is if we can, of course. However, mothers are mothers and fathers are fathers only to their own children. Even if the community cheers up and adores all children equally, their parents are always responsible for them. Sometimes, people who are not biological fathers and mothers can take the responsibility of parenting. They may have either adopted them or have been given the trust by their relatives to take care of those children as parents."

"Now, what are biological fathers and mothers?"

"That means..."

He hesitated for a while. He looked towards Daansoo. She stared back at him.

"Look, Daansoo and I, we are married. We share the same bed, and we do things that grown-ups do in bed."

"I know what you mean."

"What...?"

Miidhagaa smiled widely.

Daansoo, wide-eyed, tried to catch her breath.

"I say I know... I saw my nanny and that man who is helping you in the field doing it on the floor. They thought I was asleep."

"Hmmmm, when was that?"

"Long ago..."

"Why didn't you tell us?"

"She begged me not to."

Everybody became silent for a while. Miidhagaa started again.

"Well, after such things happened, women get pregnant, and they get child. Those parents we call biological parents."

"Does that mean that my nanny is going to be a biological parent?"

"I think so."

"And you are saying that you and Mum did get me without..."

"Please stop! He is only four, not even four."

Daansoo started crying.

Miidhagaa stood up and went to her. He took her hand and helped her to stand up. He followed her to their bedroom, closed the door behind her, and came back.

He knelt in front of his son and kissed him on his forehead.

"What you are saying is right."

"And you want me to believe that...?"

"I don't want you to believe anything. I want you to know I am always willing to remain your father if you allow me to be one. Daansoo, too, is always there as a mother to you if you let her. I want you also to know that there are some people out there who want to show you that they are your real parents."

"I don't want other real parents. I have real parents here and I want to be with them. I think you have another reason why you want me to be with others. I saw Mum crying many times. When I asked her, she only denied it and said she was okay. Tell me the truth."

He looked serious.

"That is the truth, my son!" Miidhagaa whispered and tried to hold him in his arms. The boy pulled himself free and ran to his bedroom.

It was in the middle of the night, two weeks after they had that sudden conversation with their son. Miidhagaa and Daansoo were having harsh discussions.

"He is not a baby anymore. Can you not see that? He knows everything."

He heard his mother yelling. He woke up and went to his door. He stopped and listened.

"I know he is smart, but we cannot tell him the real reason behind all this," Miidhagaa insisted.

'Okay, they are in their bedroom,' the boy thought.

He opened his door. Cautiously, he crossed the sitting room and came near to his parents' bedroom.

"Look, Miidhagaa. Through all these times, we talked to him without getting his slightest understanding. He even started laughing at us. My heart bleeds each day when I am thinking that he is going to leave me."

"Me, too, Daansoo. I do cry inside, on my own. He is my only son, Daansoo. He is our only son. But I am sure that he will be better off with my brother abroad, rather than in this godforsaken country."

"What happened to you, Miidhagaa? This was not your principle."

"Daansoo, I told you many times. These people are very cruel. When they know they cannot break you, they harm you by harming your family, your children. They are inhuman. I do not want him to grow up in these surroundings. Public lawlessness and hatred are very devastating for children's psychology. That is why I want him to go. My brother is a decent person."

"To let him go with your brother is not really the problem. But why should we say he is not our son?"

"You know perfectly well that we do that for his own benefit. He will be more comfortable to be with them if we convince him that they are his real parents. Do not forget he is not yet four."

'Ahaa, thank God,' thought the boy. ' I was about to give up and to start believing what they were telling me. There is some danger they want to protect me from. That means they love me. They do love me, and that is why they are so concerned. If it is so, it should not be difficult. Okay, I will do what they want me to do, but I keep it to myself, as they tried so hard to keep everything to themselves.'

He smiled and went back to his bedroom. Back in his bed, he started crying silently. He thought he loved them more now than before. He tried to grasp how powerless they appeared to be against the thing they were talking about and that made him very sad.

'Who are these cruel people my Dad and Mum are afraid of?' he asked himself. 'Is something going to happen to them? That is why they want me to go – before I see it happening?'

He cried and cried. Before his little brain managed to provide him with any kind of interesting answer, he had fallen asleep.

In the morning, when he finally came into the sitting room, the breakfast table was full of slices of fresh-baked bread, scrambled egg, milk, and honey. He was about to take his usual place when he heard his mother coming from the kitchen on the right corner of the sitting room.

"Good morning! You already woke up. Come on, cheer up! Your father is outside feeding the chickens. He will be here at any moment. Sit down, sit down."

She smiled broadly and tried to suppress the bad feeling that kept churning in her insides.

He yawned and smiled back.

"Shall I go outside and feed the chickens with him? You know I like doing that."

"He will be here at any moment. I think you are too late today."

Just then, the door opened and Miidhagaa came in.

"Hello, you two; I hope you are not talking about me behind my back. Let me guess, Latiinsaa, you are asking to come out and feed the chickens? Is that right?"

He put down the small basket that was half-filled with the chickens' food, and turned to his son with a wide smile on his face.

"Good morning, my son, you are too late today. Didn't you sleep the whole night?"

For a moment he thought his father suspected that he was eavesdropping and listening to what they were talking about last night. But he immediately recovered and overwhelmed his parents with his lovely smile.

"Of course I did. It is just that I felt tired after all we went through... you know what I am saying?"

He giggled.

Miidhagaa became more cautious and gave his son a strong good-morning hug and accompanied him to their breakfast table.

"Well, well, soon you will get back your energy. Look what is waiting for us. Today must be the day of large breakfast. Daansoo, come on, let us eat. We cannot let such a beautiful and tasty meal wait for so long."

He tried to cheer up all of them, including himself. But the smile on his face vanished immediately when his son started talking.

"Dad, Mum! I want to tell you something before we start eating. I was thinking about those things you told me yesterday. After all, it is not a bad idea to travel abroad. If, as you told me yesterday, these parents of mine do miss me, it must be very hard and painful for them to hear that I refused to accept their proposal. Therefore, I say I will accept. But you must promise me..."

He stared at both for a moment and his eyes filled with tears. He rubbed them dry and swallowed hard.

"But you must promise me to remain forever my mother and father, and not to forget me after I leave you. I do not think this is too much to ask."

He let his tears flow freely.

Miidhagaa and Daansoo stood up simultaneously and went to him. They were sobbing silently.

"You will always remain our son," Miidhagaa whispered.

"Of course, my darling, you will always remain our child!" Daansoo supplemented, shivering through her cries.

"Please, why do you cry, then? Crying is not good. If you keep crying, I think we are not going to meet again. Please do not cry."

They both bent down to his chair and hugged him at the same time.

That day became the longest day in his life. Failing to grasp whether they were happy or devastated by his decision, he felt enormous sadness and remained out of touch the whole day.

Norway became his new country, hosting his new parents. The first few months he tried to be truthful to those two people he loved most in his life. He wanted to do exactly what they wanted him to do. He wanted to be the child of these new parents of his. As the time went by slowly, he couldn't stand the longing for his real parents. He became desperate and wanted to do something about it. He listened eagerly to what his teacher was telling his classroom , day after day, regarding the rights of children in this new country that had become his home. He loved to hear that the government was doing everything to fulfil the best interests of the children. He followed seriously the child protection talks, and the preferred way of child-upbringing. At the end, he decided to do whatever he could to be able to depart from his new parents.

He remembered very well that very day of his first rebellion against his new parents. He completely rejected the demand his father raised to put on his winter shoes. He said no and preferred a simple shoe, although the outside world was covered by the white powder snow of the winter in the northern hemisphere. His parents insisted, and gradually he seemed to give in and did as he had been told. When he saw that his parents were occupied accompanying the other two children to the car, he swiftly replaced his winter shoes with the simplest ones and took the back seat in the car without being noticed.

After they arrived downtown, his father was shocked seeing him coming out of the car with the simple shoes he shouldn't wear in such hard weather conditions. He didn't receive any kind of reprimand and scolding right there. But after they came home, his father accompanied him to his room and shouted at him. He took away all the toys he had in his room. He punished him by forcing him to stand still, facing the wall of his bedroom and stretching out his arms for almost half an hour. After that, his father left him with a warning that he should not behave like that again.

Sitting on his tiny bed, Latiinsaa smiled.

"This is perfect. I got him there where I wanted him to be. Now I have a reason to do what I've wanted to do for so long. I will leave him."

Immediately, he felt sorry and bombarded his conscience by asking why he was doing this to such good people who had taken on the burden of giving him a new future.

"But that is... the future I never asked for; the life I never needed."

He started weeping silently. The more he wept, the more he came nearer to deciphering the real reason that kept churning his inside. No word could explain how much he missed them. No material gadgets, no toys, no cleaner bedroom could replace the love of his childhood, his parents.

"I am not a material boy. I am not able to choose anything, to adore anything, to appreciate anything, none, when they are not around. I love them, and I cannot live without them. Whatever will happen, I must be with them, and on their side."

With that, he enforced once again his commitment to protest his new bearing, his new attitude, his new surroundings, his new parents, and his new country. He wanted to stage his protest until he convinced everybody that these people were not his real parents.

He wanted to bring to light the truth why his real parents had to abandon him, and why these two people wanted to take the burden of offering him paternal care and protection.

Convinced as he was, and with a big smile on his face, he climbed into his bed.

Randi Pederson was a veteran elementary school teacher. She was known for her non-stop chatter and child-friendly attitude. It had been said many times throughout the school year, both by her fellow teachers and by parents, that she could read the faces of her pupils like a piece of writing addressed to her. Without any effort, she picked up the signals her pupils sent out knowingly or unknowingly. She followed and registered their wellbeing and security inside and outside the school compound. In her world, children were to be trusted above everything. The charge against children as manipulators was something that Randi, an old-timer, showed zero-tolerance to and campaigned against it very strongly. That was why, maybe, she happened to be the most referred-to teacher when it came to childcare cases. There were numbers of families of schoolchildren who had been contacted by the office of child welfare service because she alerted child welfare officers whenever she suspected child abuse. Few hated her for her action. Many parents appreciated her for her effort. Very few accused her of exaggerating things.

It was after the second break that she noticed something was wrong with him. Instead of running out of the classroom right after the break was announced, as he usually did, she saw him remaining in his chair, looking out the window, very vague and far away. She approached him with a full smile. He looked at her, stood up, and went to the window. She hesitated for a while.

"Latiinsaa!" she called him softly.

He didn't turn toward her. "Yes!" he answered.

"Is there something you want to tell me?"

"What do you want me to tell you?"

He slowly turned to her and faced her.

She saw a very different, very angry, troubled boy standing in front of her.

"I don't know really. But I think you want to tell me something."

He appeared to be hesitant at first.

"We can go to my office if you want to talk privately." She smiled.

He looked into her eyes and shook his head in agreement.

The words came out of him as if he had rehearsed his storytelling for so long. The description he made of the violent actions he had been exposed to made her shiver. When he concluded his accusation by telling her that he was not willing to spend a single night with these parents of his, she swore to herself that she would do everything in her power to prevent that.

That afternoon, Latiinsaa didn't go back home. He remained at school until the child welfare officers found an emergency home where he could remain until his case was scrutinised. While his placement underwent processing, his parents were informed by the police about the accusation raised against them and that they would soon be summoned for interrogation.

The Norwegian couple, who were willing to give him shelter for the first time as an emergency solution, took him with open arms. They were very polite and seemed to understand both his situation and feelings. They were accompanying him the first time he was interrogated at the police station. After his case had been finalised by the 'fylkesnemnda', the county board, he remained for some months with them, and he had to move out because of the inconveniences caused by the children of his foster family.

The various families he lived with thereafter all took him with open arms at first. They all promised to give him what he needed. Until, at the end, he figured out, or thought to have figured out, that what they were weighing up was their own comfort, not the natural responsibility that followed his placement. 'That is the way it is,' his child-brain concluded for him. He felt cornered and pressed, and ended up revolting against everything and everybody. He lived with complete distrust until the day he had been introduced to this woman, Ingrid Gulestad.

Ingrid Gulestad listened to her son's story with such a deep curiosity that she failed to respond immediately when Latiinsaa concluded his account with such a big smile on his face.

As she woke up in the morning, she was sober, and her mind was occupied with all kinds of things she could do to bridge the gap and create a truce between her boy and the parents he had run away from. She was thinking how important it was for her boy to revive his relationship with them. She thought about the possibility that he would really miss them, although he never said it openly. She was thinking about the strong family bond typical of people with a strong collective identity in places like where he came from, and how much the absence of that bond had devastated her boy psychologically.

But now, she felt completely lost. She became emotional.

"All these years? Alone? How can I even imagine his fight against the habits of all sorts of people surrounding him? It must be so painful to stand up against his own feeling, to permanently cry inside without any end in sight?"

She tried hard to block her tears.

"Why in heaven's name has such things happened to such a bright and lovely kid?" She stared at him for so long that he felt uncomfortable.

"What?" he asked her, and tried to smile.

She repeated his word. "What?"

Then she smiled back, realising how absent-mindedly she had acted.

"Sorry, I was overwhelmed. My goodness, Latiinsaa, all that has happened to you is not fair. It is too much for such a little boy like you to live with. All these years!"

She stood up, went to the back of his chair, took him into her arms and started sobbing.

"OH, I swear to you, I cannot even imagine what a pain you went through."

He started sobbing, too.

It took them a long time to stop crying and compose themselves.

"Now, we shouldn't spoil this good breakfast, Mum…" He smiled wide and looked up into her eyes.

She looked at him with such motherly love and stroked his hair.

"You are right!"

She went back to her seat.

Just there and then, she felt a powerful urge to go as far as it took to help him find his parents, his real parents.

She looked at him again and smiled.

He smiled back and stared at her for a while. "Something is on your mind?"

She looked at him, worried.

"Look, Mum, whatever happened, nobody did it to hurt me. In a way, they were all thinking to grant me a secure life. I have sometimes tried to imagine how devastating it was for my real parents to separate themselves from me. I remember those nights I just told you about as clearly as if it is happening now. They – I mean my real parents – were so terrified of things that could happen to me, the things I could not figure out as a child. After I left them, my new parents who were willing to take me with them here to Norway were very good to me. They never stopped trying to inculcate in me the idea that they were my real parents through their love for me. But…"

"Please don't look for excuses to justify your suffering. Nothing in this world could make me see the point of putting you in such trying conditions."

"You are right; it is not easy to see that very point, even for me. That is why I want to find my real parents and experience the truth."

"That is a very, very long plan. But right now, how do you think we should behave at our appointment today?"

"That is exactly what I wanted to talk to you about. I beg you not to give the slightest signal that I have revealed to you my real story. Now I realise more than any time that what happened to me did hurt them very badly. They promised to my parents that they would always be there for me, and the realisation that they failed to keep their word made them very depressed. I was registering this very feeling from the day I ran away from them. I do want neither to soothe them nor to confront them right now. I would like to try to normalise my relationship with them while you and I look for a way to get in touch with my real parents."

She hesitated at first.

For her, everything that he told her was an unforgivable act of misdeed, if not a crime. How wouldn't a child be allowed to grow up with people it loved most? Why are parents so desperate to send their child away into the unknown? Why?

She remained silent.

Just then, the other part of her confronted her with another question.

How much do you really know the ugly reality out there when it comes to having a right to live or not to live?

She did not like this kind of confrontation. It disempowered her and challenged her philosophy of life. Poor or rich, north or south, children are children, and they deserve the best.

Her conscience stopped her by begging her to see the point her son had raised.

She looked into his eyes, herself shining with a motherly love she had never experienced.

"Okay, my boy, I give you my word on that."

She smiled.

"You mean 'my son'!" he laughed.

"I am sorry, my son!" she laughed back.

Two months after her son Latiinsaa disclosed to her the secrets of his parents, Ingrid felt good and confident to leave him with his so-called parents and take a week-long vacation in Rome together with her long-time friend from Sørreisa, Solveig Gunderson. They used to fly together to the south for short breaks now and then. This time around, they chose the eastern Mediterranean culture, Italia, and its capital city, Rome. The main purpose of their trip was to have fun and go shopping. They ordered their flight, hotel, and their rental car through a travel agency.

Their flight route took them from Trondheim to Amsterdam, from Amsterdam to Turin and from there to the Italian capital city, the city that hosts the Roman Empire history, and harbours; among other things, the arena of Flavian Amphitheatre built in the first century and given the name Colosseum that was once used to host gladiators fighting.

Arriving at Fiumicino airport at midday, they realised their choice of Rome in the middle of July was a mistake. They felt helpless when they saw the temperature scale standing at thirty-seven degrees centigrade. Cheering one another up, they went to the airport shuttle stand and took the shuttle towards Via Po 8, the address of Maggiore Rent spa, the rental car company, where they were supposed to collect their rented car.

At the Maggiore office, their intensively studied Italian language could not take them far. Their "Exscuza, signore, non parlo Italian..." bubble was met by an American-accented, fluent English-speaking woman...

"How can I help you, madam?"

"Thanks, we have rented a car from you online."

"Do you have the voucher number?"

Ingrid looked at her friend, a little confused.

"I mean the reference number for your order."

"Oh, here it is!"

Ingrid gave it to the woman.

She read it quickly and asked her for a driving licence and passport.

"I need your credit card, too."

Ingrid produced a Visa card.

After a quarter of an hour, everything was settled.

"I have charged your Visa card four hundred euros as a guarantee. When you deliver the car back to us without any damage, you get the money released. There is an additional payment for GPS, which you will pay when you close this agreement at the end of your rental car contract. I want you to sign here. And I wish you a good stay in Rome."

"Thank you. And... where is our car?"

"You will find it at the garage."

The woman pointed to the garage across the street in front of the Maggiore office.

"You know what, Ingrid; I hate to depend on such inanimate, lifeless guidance," said Solveig.

Ingrid smiled and said, "Do we have another solution right now, my dear?"

Solveig took a deep breath.

"Are you sure that this GPS thing and this talkative satellite lady alone will get us to our hotel, in a city where we are both complete strangers?" she asked, trying to be as calm as she could manage to be.

"That is the idea. Look, my friend, those nerds who stood behind these kinds of discoveries, they want us to trust them. Therefore, they invested everything in their capacity to make sure what they promise us is going to be a hundred percent reliable. Therefore, my friend, please do not forget that we are in the era of information technology. I beg you to relax and learn to trust the information and our nerds."

Ponte Bianco Hotel and Residence was located at the area which had the postal code of 00152 in Rome. The street address was Via Francesco Cornaro 19. Ingrid seemed to be very knowledgeable regarding the use of GPS. Solveig watched her in complete astonishment when she fed the GPS gadget their destination and then started driving with the confidence of a grown-up woman. Although the GPS indicated that the hotel was about 5.9km away from

Maggiore's rental car office, Ingrid and her friend could not easily find the hotel with the help of the GPS. It was just then that Solveig started feeling insecure. Three times they drove away from their destination without understanding the message of the satellite woman saying, "Arrive at your destination on the left" and without recognising the destination flag they were looking at on the screen of the GPS gadget. At last, Ingrid parked the car on the side of the street where the GPS destination flag was shown on the screen, and she got out of the car and asked one of the pedestrians where to find Ponte Bianco Hotel.

The man smiled and pointed at the side road that would take ~~took~~ her to the hotel, which was about fifty metres away. She smiled and thanked the man and went back to her car.

She looked into her eyes and smiled.

Right after they checked in, they drove out to find this restaurant half a kilometre away from their hotel. They were lucky to find an open parking area right in front of the restaurant. Equally lucky were they to be received by a smiling and English-speaking waitress. It was not so hard to feel at home and order the refreshments they needed. First, two big glasses of cold beer, then the pizza, the thin vegetarian Italian pizza.

"What? The pizza doesn't taste the way you expected it?" Solveig scrutinised her.

"No, I was thinking…"

"Stop your wild thoughts and get used to the hot weather here and now."

"Imagine if we meet him here?"

"Meet who?"

"Remember… fifteen years ago!"

"What? No… impossible. How could you dare to think about it…?" Solveig looked at her with surprise.

"You never stopped thinking about him, ha?"

"Especially after Latiinsaa came into my life, I thought a lot about him."

"Get old, my friend! That kind of world was over for us long ago."

"Actually, age is what makes the wine taste good."

Solveig smiled reluctantly.

"Seriously, Solveig, I was thinking how he could help me to solve Latiinsaa's problem, if I in any way manage to get in touch with him."

"Please, Ingrid, let us have this afternoon for ourselves and relax. Then we will settle down on the problem that forced us to take this crash vacation. Okay?"

"Okay!"

5

Seven hundred and twenty-three kilometres away from Rome, at Turin International Airport, a man holding a Norwegian passport was about to make a transit flight by boarding Alitalia Airlines AZ 2438 that was destined to Rome. He started his flight from Norway in the early hours of the morning. He arrived at Flesland international airport in the city of Bergen at five thirty a.m. When he at last boarded KLM Airlines flight number KL 2248 that would take him to Amsterdam, he started all over again contemplating about his five days' vacation in Rome.

'Is this trip really necessary?' he asked himself repeatedly.

"Necessary or not, I am on my way!"

He reminded himself that he could not undo his decision right now. Before he made up his mind, he indeed went through various evaluations and reflections. At first, he tried to convince himself that his choice of destination was just a matter of convenience. He wanted to see Rome and to be part of the human exodus roaming the historical sites of Rome. As such, three days were going to be enough, he told himself. Then, at the end of his visit, he would call her and talk to her, he argued with himself.

'Is that enough to find out why I still have such a strong feeling for this woman?' his conscience confronted him. Reluctantly, he ended up booking his vacation for five days.

She was not his first, although he knew he was hers. She was not his last, either. However, she happened to be constantly there, somewhere at the corner of his mind, where she often knocked on his composition and blended herself into his imagination. Why?

He always wondered.

There was no doubt in his mind that he loved his wife and his children. He had established a very good life with them. He dedicated his time and mind to building up a very good family life. He was not on shaky ground whatsoever, either economically or socially. Yet this woman, the woman he was so madly in love with more than two decades ago, haunted him permanently.

Why?

He kept wondering.

One thing was sure: his love for her was special. Her personality, her stubborn character, her independence, he admired all those parts of her. Her jealousy often threw him out of balance. He loved her for that, too. As to him, she was such a natural puzzle, with a very difficult manner to understand. He was convinced then that she truly thrived on negations. He registered all the occasions he spent with her that she delightedly started her conversation with a 'no' answer and, after going through well-disguised manoeuvres, she slowly transitioned to a 'yes'. In some cases, he remembered, the transitioning she was making traversed back and forth. Mostly, she did this to him when she wanted to boost the suspense and the uncertainty thereof.

Causing someone to feel confused about her thoughts and about what she was going to do seemed to him to be her primary objective. But then, she used to implore him to admire her without uttering a word. She smiled and whispered in such a way that it impacted his memory to be short-lived and making him forget what she caused. He had also registered that the connection between her smile and the sparkling look in her eyes fluctuated according to what she wanted to accomplish. And, when she was sending out the signal of love and admiration, the connection was so powerful that it could soften the heart of a beast.

Things he did with her, they remained unique and special all these years. However, after he had lived for so long away from her, this kind of feeling was supposed to be dead, buried and forgotten. It was supposed to be part of his past life, not a life to be felt and lived. Now, he was about to witness the culmination of such an undying feeling by willingly following its pressure and push.

But why?

'There is no special reason!' he told himself. 'The only reason is that one is tempted and desirous of the hidden love one feels.'

'Isn't that a special reason?' he doubted.

He remembered how she came into his life, and how she walked out of it. 'Did she walk out?'

This was the painful part of the truth, he admitted. He often conceded that he separated himself from her suddenly and radically. He never explained his disappointment and his reasons to her. He never gave her a chance to tell him why she did what she did.

'That was not fair,' he thought.

Some years ago, he accidentally saw her picture posted on the timeline of a friend of his on Facebook. Her gorgeous smile and the radiation from her eyes spellbounded him anew. He felt her just the way he did the first time he saw her in person.

He was in a private taxi, driving towards Piaza, the centre of Finfinnee, Addis Ababa. She was standing together with a girl from his neighbourhood, in front of the then Commercial School. He suddenly asked the driver to stop, then paid him and got out. He greeted the two girls and from that moment on, she planted her love inside him that refused to dry out, even after so many years of separation.

She looked unchanged in the picture, beautiful and very young. At first, he did not see any reason to look for her. Subsequently, after he read the two books entitled *Aleph* and *Adultery*, authored by his favourite author, the famous Brazilian writer Paulo Coelho, he decided to look for her, find her and talk to her.

'Sorting out the past cannot be judged or seen as adultery,' he told himself.

It took him more than two months to locate her. When he first received her confirmation of his friendship request on Facebook, he was terrified. He did not want to wake up a beast after all these years of tranquil and serene family life. For him, the love he had for her was a beast, the beast that never let him breathe properly, argue calmly and convincingly, be himself and act. It was a kind of war experience, of which the cherished ceasefire moment, the break from fighting, not the fatiguing survival engagement for hours or days, is willingly remembered. He remembered their intense lovemaking, although the days were many when she chose to deny him that very privilege after she turned him on made him hot and hard. He remembered the kind words they had exchanged, although these were fewer compared to the days they spent fighting.

He speculated, often, that her sense of independence blocked her from showing the true love she had for him. Rather, she preferred to throw words that could inflict some pain upon him and get confirmation from his reaction about how much he loved her.

This was how he felt then. These days, he had challenged himself whether he was stubborn, too.

Had he done the right thing to behold her and protect the love he had for her? No, he had not.

Was there some external pressure on him to let her go?

Maybe.

Or else, was it because he loved her that he did let her go?

That was what he told himself at the beginning. Rather than hurting, by failing to understand her, it was better to let her go.

Why was it then that he wanted to go back now and find out the truth about the love he abandoned for so many years?

For one thing, he thought that he was mature enough now to handle the issue properly. 'There is nothing that I want from her!' he tried to convince himself.

Therefore, it would not do any harm if he tried to find out why he still valued this woman so much. Moreover, he wanted to know more about her because he never had enough time to know her then. He wanted to know what a person she became through time. In a very bizarre way, he wanted to know whether she felt the same as he did about their relationship, the historic relationship.

He sent her a request to send him her number so that he could call her and talk to her. She made him wait for her answer for more than a month. In the end, she sent him her number. He lastly found out that she lived in Rome, Italy, was married and had children. The day he called her, they immediately started talking as if there had been no years of separation between them. They started with a lovely conversation at first and ended up with a very coarse discussion and fight at the end.

"It seems nothing has changed with us!" he told her.

"You are right!" she seconded him.

There was a long pause before she said it. "I love you, Michael!"

She used the nickname she used to call him by during those days. He became out of his equilibrium, and was breathless. He could not utter a word.

"Are you there?" she asked.

"Yes, yes... I am here," he answered.

"Thank you for looking for me and finding me, Michael. I'll look for you later today online. Maybe we can chat. Have a nice day."

"Have a nice day then."

"Look, I am at my workplace now. I cannot talk more."

"Okay, have a nice day. And..."

"And what, Michael?"

"I truly love you."

"That is very good. I love you, too. Now, if you don't mind, I must hang up."

"Okay, bye!"

"Bye!"

She hung up.

'I don't believe this is happening to us right now. Am I dreaming?'

He kept thinking for a while. 'Michael!'

He smiled. He remembered very well the day he got that nickname from her. She invited him to come to her graduation ceremony held at her parents' home. When he arrived, her father was receiving guests at the entrance of their compound. Instead of welcoming him, her father summoned her and told her, "Your guest."

She smiled and gave him a kiss on his cheeks in front of her father.

"This is our beloved teacher. His name is Mr Michael." She introduced him to her father and followed him into the house.

He breathed deep and smiled.

'It is good!' he said to himself.

"It feels really good to talk to you again."

With this one telephone conversation, they opened the way to their years-long, online chatting afterwards. They shared sweet comments back and forth. Their chat, however, could not escape emotional eruptions now and then. As sweet as they would converse in one moment, they turned on one another and quarrelled in the next moment. There happened to be months of shutting one another off because of their intense quarrel.

He thought most of the time she misinterpreted his words. There was a moment when he told himself that he could never be able to revive a workable relationship with her. As a result, he stopped communicating with her for months. One Wednesday morning, he received a message sent from her on his phone.

"Michael, please give me a call. I miss you so much!"

"Miss me?"

He felt lost.

'Why is it that she misses me? Why is it that I miss her? We are both in a relationship. We both have commitments. Besides, there was this decades-long separation between us. One sure thing is that we do not belong to each other. So, why do we even bother about each other?'

He hesitated the whole day to call her. Reluctantly, he dialled her number after work. She answered immediately. Her voice was so soft and calm, her language very articulate. She asked him, as independent as she was, not to disappear.

"I missed you so much. Please do not make me wait for your messages for so long. Do not forget that you make me feel like a woman. You are the love of my life, Michael."

He could not say much.

"I miss you, too, Bliss. I love you so much."

After he hung up, he argued with himself as to what this feeling of love meant to him, and especially to her.

'I don't know why, but I do love her,' he tried to conclude.

Then he got stormed by various questions.

Was he really after reviving their love relationship that he himself had abandoned so many years ago? Was he not happily married and became the father of such wonderful sons? Was he betraying the trust of his family by looking for an old, broken relationship?

He inhaled and exhaled, a lot.

What about her? How, for God's sake, does she talk to him like this after all these years? Do we really miss each other, or do we miss something else?

So many questions again and again, but no answer was in sight. He sighed.

'Having such a platonic, nonsexual love with somebody cannot be a betrayal. It must only be a good thing,' he concluded.

'However, a platonic love cannot describe a love a man can feel for another woman while having a good and permanent relationship. It must be a kind of camouflaging to hide selfishness.'

Then he paused.

'Where was that I read about something like this?'

He remembered it. It was in *Aleph*, written by Paulo Coelho.

The author was writing somewhere in the book about a love with no name and explanation, a love that is simply there without asking for nothing and giving nothing in return. It was an amazing wording of a love received and given without making a person belong to that very person.

Three years and eight months after he talked to her on the phone for the first time after their separation many years ago, they agreed upon meeting each other in person. Now he was less than two hours away from her. She told him that she was waiting for him at the Fiumicino international airport in Rome.

Waiting to board the Alitalia flight number AZ 2438, he sent her a message that he was about to board his last plane bringing him to her. His phone burst into life. He saw her number.

"Yes…" He nearly choked.

"Michael, you son of a gun; you are at last going to meet me in person. You made it ha…"

"*We* made it, Bliss. Your support was a key to this."

"I am terrified, though. I do not think I can make it to come to the airport. I am rather waiting for you at the rental car office you are going to collect your car from."

"Okay, my dear, no problem at all. I am terrified, too. I hope everything will be okay."

"I hope so, too. I love you, Michael."

"I love you, too, Bliss."

"See you soon…"

"See you soon."

He waited until she hung up. Then he hung up.

The Fiumicino international airport in Rome was not as confusing as those big airports in European big cities. He easily found his way to baggage claim. After he stepped out of the compound, it took him a little while to figure out which type of transport he should take to come to the place where he was to collect his rental car. It was a relief to him when one of the service men outside the entrance to Fiumicino airport asked him whether he needed help.

"Yes, I need help. Can you please find me a shuttle transport?"

"Ahm, you want a shuttle transport? Where do you want to go?" The man's English was like a melody.

The accent brought a smile to his face.

He produced the address of the rental car office and showed it to him.

The man smiled big. "Okay, follow me."

The service man stopped a minibus and asked its driver whether he had a seat for one passenger. Without knowing what was happening, he found himself and his luggage deposited in the minibus full of young Danish tourists, who greeted him loudly and cheerfully.

"Welcome!"

"Thanks!"

He smiled and looked around. A driver in his forties, Danish-speaking young boys and girls, and then he looked out of the side window. The traffic was moderate. They were moving at an acceptable speed. The sun was blazing. Then he turned towards the driver.

"Sorry, sir. You didn't tell me how long the trip would take, and how much you charge me for that?"

"About forty-five minutes, and you pay fifty."

"Fifty what?"

"Fifty euros!"

"Okay!"

He silently calculated the price in Norwegian Krone, and he felt it was not bad at all. He turned to the girl sitting next to him.

"Is this your first time in Rome?"

"Yes, it is."

"Everyone in this car is a first-time visitor to Rome, then?"

"Yes!"

All those young people in the car answered as if in a choir.

After a while, he relaxed and opened his Samsung Galaxy Note 3 mobile. He fed the address of the rental car office into the Google Map on his mobile and checked the time the trip would take from their current position. It indicated thirty-nine minutes. Then he sent her a message.

"I am thirty-nine minutes away from the rental car office."

Her answer was swift. "I will be there in about five minutes."

His heartbeat increased. "My goodness, I am acting like a man meeting his first date," he told himself, and smiled. He tried to imagine her and her reaction when they would at last meet. He looked at his watch. There remained twenty very slowly-moving minutes.

He tried to rest. He tried hard not to think about her. He was about to close his eyes and follow his thoughts, when those young tourists cheered, and the driver stopped the minibus.

He looked out and he read the name of the hotel. Hotel Romanico Palace.

"Where are we?"

"We have reached our hotel!" the girl sitting next to him answered.

"Your destination is on the corner, too. It is just three to five minutes' drive from here," the driver assured him.

"Can you give me the street address of this hotel?"

"Via Boncompagni 37…"

He first hesitated.

Then he gave the address to his Google Map and tried to find his destination. Indeed, it was about three- or four-minutes' drive. First, they drove straight forward, then they turned to the left, then to the left again and at last they turned to the right and then they arrived on Via Po 8.

He was alone with the driver. He looked out of the side window as they turned into Via Po 8. At first, he saw the 'Maggiore' sign, written in white on a blue background. Then he saw her. Dressed in a perfectly fitting summer sundress, a sleeveless V-neck semi-maxi dress with bright patterns, and zebra high-heel shoes. She looked gorgeous and flattering. He asked the driver to stop the car. He opened the door, cleared his throat, and called her name while stepping out of the car.

"Bliss!"

She turned around with a full smile on her face. He suspected she saw him before he saw her. He responded with a broad smile. He carefully approached her and bent down a little and took her hand and pressed it gently.

"OMG, Bliss, you look nice."

Without thinking about it, he hugged her and kissed her on her cheeks. She responded by kissing him on his lips. Then she looked into his eyes.

He carefully rubbed his hand on her protruding boobs.

"Michael, don't worry. They are still yours!"

He blushed. She smiled.

She hugged him, raised herself up and kissed him powerfully.

"Wait!" he said.

He turned to the driver and paid him fifty euros. He took his baggage from the driver and turned to her.

"You are not even slightly changed."

He caressed her on the nape of her neck.

He kissed her gently by holding her so tight against his body. She responded the way she used to.

He looked deep into her eyes.

"I know now, I love you," he whispered.

"I love you, too, Michael! I always did."

She raised herself up again and plastered her lips upon his. Then she retreated. He took her hand and watched her eyes.

"Thanks for allowing me to meet you."

She smiled. "You are welcome."

They acted like teenagers.

"Let us collect our car!"

He slowly managed to control himself. She smiled.

"Where is the rental car office?" He looked around.

"There, across the street!" She pointed at the building.

Together with the needed documents, he gave to the receptionist his voucher number. She looked at his passport and spoke with a low voice.

"Pardon me?" he said.

"No, no, nothing. I was just talking to myself. I had another Norwegian customer hours ago."

"How funny. A woman, or a man, or a family?"

"Two grown-up ladies, in fact."

"Good for the business." He smiled.

Bliss leaned her body towards him and wanted to kiss him. He gently stopped her.

After driving about five hundred metres, Bliss asked him to stop the car in front of the grocery store she was pointing at on the right side of the street.

"Wait for me here without killing the motor."

She hurried towards the grocery store. After nearly fifteen minutes, she came out with two plastic bags filled with various groceries. She opened the car's back door and placed them inside. Then she took her place and gave him her gorgeous smile.

"I thought we might need some cold drinks and snacks since it is so hot here in Rome."

"You think about everything."

"That is me!"

She kissed him.

"You were afraid to kiss me in front of that woman, ha?"

He smiled.

"Not afraid. Rather, I felt like I was dreaming. It all seemed to look as if nothing happened to us all these years."

"Is that good, or bad?"

"We will find out."

He settled himself and allowed the car to move again.

While driving on the streets of Rome, he rested his right hand on her thigh.

"What a wonderful world it is, Bliss."

He looked at her.

"I never expected that we would receive one another the way we just did. I thought it might take us a long time to trust one another again. But look at us… I believe we are in love still."

She stretched herself, leaned towards him and kissed him on his cheek.

"Believe me, Michael. I never stopped loving you. I never stopped trusting you. The things we shared were very special. The beauty of the language you used while conversing with me, I could not forget. The respect you granted me and the pure love you gave me remained affecting my relationship with other men. I always remember the way you treated me and the way you used to touch me and make love to me, and I somehow failed to adjust to the worlds of other men. You planted inside me the strong commitment to despise the vulgarity of men whose only desire is to impose their superiority on women. Even your maturity, the calmness you bear, that happened to be something in terms of which I tried to measure the qualities of other people. There are so many other special things with you, Michael, of which I was not lucky enough to get from other men, men who came into my life after you. You were the right man for me, and I learned that after I lost you."

She touched him.

He looked at her, tears in his eyes.

She turned around and balanced herself in her seat. She looked in the distance through the front window of the car.

"As foolish as I was, I was all ears listening to the rumours those people told me, those who did not want you and I to be together. I kept exhausting myself by trying to envision what you were doing to those girls I was told you were dating behind my back. Besides, I was not smart and mature enough to trace and jump over the lasso your wife placed for me in her attempt to win you back."

He looked at her again. He turned his attention to the traffic and sighed.

"What do you mean, Bliss? Do not confuse me before I even start believing that your presence here and now is real. We agreed that we wouldn't involve our partners in this."

"Do not worry, Michael. We won't involve them. Regarding me, I waited for you with my heart wide open. Telling you what happened will not hinder you from having a good life with your partner. Or it will not stop you from cherishing me non-stop if you really want me."

Still she was looking into the distance.

"Okay, then, what do you mean by the lasso my wife placed for you? You really mean there was conspiracy?"

"Yes. I have learned from our chat and conversation that you did not know about it. That is why I decided to tell you after you came here. I want to tell you this so that you really understand how helpless I was in confronting the fight that you left me alone to face."

She turned around and looked at him.

"If you try to remember, you told that person you shared your office with that you did not want to talk to me in case I called you at your workplace after you abandoned me."

"That I remember. I did that because of what you did to me on our last appointment. I tried to explain it to you on the phone, and during our chatting session. For me, that was the reason for our separation. At that time, I swear to God you were my dream girl. You made me love you with all my heart and soul. I had no appetite for other women there and then."

He looked at her seriously.

"That day, you did not only come too late to the place of our appointment, but you came with another guy, hand in hand. After you greeted me, you ignored me and proceeded flirting with him. I told myself to be patient and I agreed when you asked me to take a taxi. We took a taxi together and you sat beside me and continued flirting with this guy who took the seat in front of us. Your friend from your workplace, who took the taxi with us, she tried to introduce me to this guy by telling him that I was your boyfriend. He seemed to be confused, and you seemed to be enjoying the moment. That was the last thing I remember that had driven me mad. I was convinced that I could not stand such behaviour from the girl I love. If I remained with you to witness such a wild act of yours one more time, I thought that I would end up committing a crime. That was when I decided to distance myself from you. Before I lost my mind and did something that hurt you and other people, I wanted to run away from you."

He faced her, with scary seriousness.

She smiled.

"But this part, Michael, what you are telling me now, I really don't remember. Nevertheless, I did call at your workplace and I asked your friend to get you for me. He told me that you did not want to talk to me and that you meant it."

He stopped the car.

She looked at him with a little bit of suspicion on her face.

"The GPS is telling me that we have arrived at our destination."

"You mean your hotel is around here?"

"I think it is on the left side. So, do you mind if we stop our conversation for a while and continue after I check in?"

"Not at all, I do not mind. I hope we have enough time for everything."

She stretched herself towards him and kissed his lower lip passionately. He responded.

He started the car again, they turned to the left and he drove carefully past so many parked cars and arrived at Ponte Bianco Hotel and Residence after about fifty metres. It was cloudy and the sun was hiding itself behind them. She helped him with his luggage, and he checked in. She accompanied him to his room. She closed the door behind her, and she took his hand in hers.

"Michael...," she whispered.

"Bliss..."

Suddenly, she was all over him. She kissed him. She touched him.

He kissed her. He touched her. He had never seen her or experienced her so lustful, so hot. "Oh, my Bliss," he groaned.

He lifted her up and placed her on the single bed in his room. He kissed her passionately and sat by her side. She took her turn to hold him tight and show him what she wanted. He slowly found the courage to calm her down after he fearfully registered that she would give her body to him so that he could do whatever he wanted to do to her. He admired her for that.

She looked into his eyes.

She whispered, "Michael, you are my true love. Michael, I give you my life, if you need it. Michael, I truly love you."

She touched him, and he was not as hard and pulsating as she expected him to be. She pressed him a little bit away and looked at him.

"You are not ready to enjoy me?"

He sighed. For a moment he felt a kind of guilt.

"A family man forsaking his relationship?"

"How come I can do this?"

He sighed again.

He looked deep into her eyes.

She looked so gorgeous and so ready to be loved. There was the fire of true feeling in her eyes. Her lips parted and he took them with his. Then he kissed her behind her ears, on the nape of her neck, and cautiously he took on her boobs. He proceeded downwards slowly and kissed her on her belly button. The vibration he created inside her overwhelmed her and she moaned uncontrollably. Then he took her hands. Slowly, he raised her up and pulled her towards him. She tightened her arms around his neck and hid herself under his jawline. She trembled. He tried to control the way he breathed.

She moved herself and looked into his eyes.

"Oh my God, Michael, you make me so happy." She kissed him hysterically.

"You make me happy, too."

He kissed her and gently made her come to see his point.

"Bliss, my love. Let us take our time."

She disengaged herself from him and settled on the bed.

"You don't want to make love to me?"

She watched him seriously.

"Of course, I want it, very much. We have all the time we need to do just that. But I want first to be with you a little longer, although I do have a desire to do it to you. I didn't come here just to jump into bed and have fun. Truly speaking that was not what I planned for. I want more, Bliss. I want to know you. I want to know why I am still in love with you. You were the love of my life and I lost you without stopping loving you. Now I want to discover you again. Help me to do that."

"Wasn't it just that what I did, opening myself to you so that you discover me anew?"

She took his ears into her hands and pulled him towards her and kissed him hungrily. Then she jumped to the floor and went to the bathroom. When she came out, she was all smiles.

"Okay then, my dear Michael. One of the reasons I kept loving you is this gentleness, this quality, this self-control. I love you for that."

He ran his eyes all over her.

She came to him and sat on his lap. She kissed him and smiled.

"Welcome to Rome. Let us get out of here and find some refreshments. And then we will see how much of me you have discovered."

Before he made it to kiss her, she jumped out of his embrace.

The restaurant was beautiful. Sandwiched between the classic residential buildings to the left and right, it offered cool and quiet refuge from the suffocating and noisy summer evening in Rome. It was located a thirty-five minute walk to the south from his hotel, in the middle of the place called Piazzale Enrico Dunant. The moment they entered through the gate of the outside compound, the waitress welcomed them with a big friendly smile. They chose to sit outside, under the big, cream-coloured sunshade, with candlelight on the table. The waitress gave them the menu and asked them if they wanted to order a drink. They ordered the local beer, one big and one small. Bliss took the responsibility of going through the menu.

Right after the waitress left with their order, he stretched his hand over the table and touched her wrist. She looked at him with her soulful eyes and gave him her smile that he loved so much.

"To tell you the truth, being with you like this, again, after all these years, it makes me so happy!" he Smiled.

She put his hand between her palms and rubbed it, and then kissed it. She looked into his eyes and smiled, full of life and joy.

"You make me happy, too, more than you can imagine."

There had never been a shortage of compliments between them. From the first day they met so many years ago, they always had good words for one another, even when they were not together at the same place. When he could not reach her on the telephone, he used to write down in his notebook what and how he felt about her whenever he felt it, jotting down the day, the hour, and the place. She, on her side, did the same. Later, when they met, they used to read to one another the things they had jotted down in one another's absence. There were occasions when they wrote almost similar flows of feelings about one another, on nearly the same day and hour, while sojourning at different places. This was amazing then, both for them and for their friends who heard about it, at a time when there was no such thing as Short Message Services, Facebook, Twitter or Chatroom.

He looked into her eyes and smiled big.

"Now would you mind finishing the story you started telling me earlier?"

"Okay, if you ask. In fact, I, too, was thinking to find a way to take you back to it."

6

It was the coldest of the months in the rainy season for this place, the month of August. The car traffic on the mostly dilapidated infrastructure of the city was brought to a standstill by the overwhelming floods created by the enormous amount of rain. The city of millions named Finfinnee/Addis Ababa had a unique privilege of stretching unrestrictedly in every direction since its foundation. No one ever tried to demarcate the boundary of the city. As such, its enlargement resulted in the coarse eviction and termination of innocent peasant families who had lived and worked on their farms in the surrounding area for generations.

One of the vices of Finfinnee/Addis Ababa as a capital city was the fact that the government technocrats and the engineers who stood behind the constructions of the city never cared or thought seriously about the construction of an underground sewage system that could serve the draining and disposal of waste and rainwater far beyond the centre of the city. The lack of co-ordination in the work of those ministries responsible for infrastructure, pipeline and network development resulted in unforeseen digging here and there that contributed to the chaotic traffic in the city. The lack of well-built pavements for pedestrians was another burden.

She spent most of the previous night crying. It was right after work that she went to his place, together with her friend. The trip that usually took about twenty-five minutes by car to her friend's home, took her almost two hours because of the chaos created by the rain. From her friend's house it was a five-minute walk to get to his place. It was late in the evening when she knocked on the door of his house. He didn't open it immediately. When he saw her standing there with her friend, he sighed and told her that he did not want her visit any more.

"At least let me come in and talk to you!"

"There is nothing we can talk about."

He was about to close the door when she suddenly threw him out of his balance and went in. Her friend followed her and started looking around the house with bulging eyes. He stood by the door and begged them to leave.

She placed her handbag on the dining table in the middle of the sitting room and turned to him.

"Okay, she can go, but I want to talk to you."

She followed her friend out of the house, and then out of the compound.

When she came back, he waited for her at the outer entrance of the compound, holding her handbag.

"You have trashed and belittled the love I have for you. By doing so, you destroyed the respect I had for you. As far as I am concerned, without love and respect for one another, there is nothing left for us to talk about."

"Please, Michael, let us go in and be together for a while."

"No, Bliss, that is not going to happen. You have no idea how much pain you caused me. I am convinced that I must let you go because I love you. I do not want to hurt you. I want to keep to myself, as precious as it is, the love I have for you. That is why I want you to go and forget me."

She felt something churning inside her stomach.

She did not want to cry in front of him.

She snatched her handbag from him and left.

He followed her and asked her, "Can I follow you to the taxi?"

"Are you joking? Why?"

She walked as fast as she could. She blocked her tears until she reached the house in the far neighbourhood where her friend lived.

Then, when her friend opened the door for her, she collapsed into her arms. "Oh, Liz, I know now that I have lost him."

Leizan was a very cool, reserved girl, two years older than Bliss. Her beauty lay in her quietness, in holding her mouth shut. If she opened her mouth, the stained enamel of her teeth switched off the radiation of her femininity. She was the opposite of what Bliss really was. She neither radiated nor overwhelmed when she talked or smiled.

Leizan helped Bliss to take a seat on the sofa and then she started moving around restlessly.

"Forget him. I told you he is a Casanova. He never loved you. That is why he treated you like this. You know he is arrogant."

Bliss looked at her in a very sad way.

The one thing she wanted right now was anything but an accusation of him.

Just a few weeks back, she felt so secure in his arms and so grateful for having him as her lover. She was so sure that, whatever she might do to anger him, he would never let her down.

She wiped her eyes dry.

"I don't know, Liz. I've never seen him so serious and so hurt before. You know me. I sometimes act like a child. This time around, I do believe my childishness has cost me the person who loved me truly and whom I loved so much."

Leizan frowned. She expected that Bliss would start condemning him clear and loud, accusing him for what he did to her. She thought Bliss would get mad about the disrespect and arrogance he displayed towards her in front of her friend. Looking at her being distressed by thinking that she was going to lose him, she felt sorry for her. Leizan could not find a word of sympathy for her friend.

Bliss imagined what her friend was thinking.

"I am sorry, Liz. I know what happened. I know what I did. That is why I have no energy and willingness to accuse him for that. Now I know how delicate it is to play with feelings, especially when the feeling is plain and genuine."

"You know what, I'll ask Dad to drive you home, okay?"

"No, Liz. I'll take a taxi. Thank you for your support."

"Are you sure?"

"Yes, I am."

"Please try to forget him."

Bliss smiled.

"It is easy for you to say that, Liz. This, however, is not going to be my last fight. I will try my best to win back my love."

Arriving home, she greeted her mum with a big smile. Right after that, she excused herself and went to her room. All that her mind and soul were occupied with was the sense of losing the only right person in her life. She had never seen him boasting, although he had all the reason to do that. He was not a material man. She did learn that part when she showed him bundles of money she was carrying in her bag and told him that she was planning to enable him to buy a house before they got married. But then she felt ashamed for just doing that when he told her that he didn't fall in love with her for her money, and he had no plan of marrying her some other place than the one he had if that was going to happen. Next day, she read a writing hanging on his wall in the sitting room: 'A shack is a paradise with the one you love'. She never saw him trying to impress her or any other person. He always tried to be himself. His compliments were genuine, and his comments were to the point.

It took her a couple of hours to exhaust her bitter feeling by magnifying his strong side. Then she fell asleep. She woke up early in the morning and took a long shower. She planned to go to work early so that she could figure out her last move before she gave up on him. After a lot of quarrels with herself, she called his office. As she expected, his friend answered the phone. She remembered that the first time she called and asked for Michael, the man was very polite and sympathetic. He told her that Michael had seriously warned him not to relay any message from her to him. However, he promised her to try to do his best. That was a week ago. This time around, he sounded very indifferent. After some Ah's and Oh's, he asked her to have a cup of coffee with him after lunch so that they could discuss the matter face to face. She agreed.

"Look, my sister. I want to be frank with you and tell you this. You fell in love with the wrong person. You were at the wrong place at the wrong time. At the time you met him, he was hurt and broken. He had just had a conflict with the woman he loved very much.

Trying to dress his wound, he immediately responded to your charm and young blood. He thought he had fallen for you. He had not."

"Bullshit. Don't pretend as if you know him. None of you know my Michael. I wonder how he really tolerates sitting with you all day, time after time. It must be the worst thing that happened to him to call you a colleague. You sit here in front of me and dare to judge Michael and the feeling he has for me? This is what makes my Michael special. He does not judge. He never meddles in other people's matters. If he was in your place, he would never tell me that I have fallen in love with the wrong person. He respects people's choices and perceptions. But you, sorry for my word, you are one of those arrogant people who seems to know how we feel about each other and even how we are."

She insulted and cursed him inwardly.

He paused and continued, "Look, you are emotional right now. You cannot, or you do not, want to see my point. My take still is that his wounded heart betrayed him. He has fallen for you without taking into consideration the consequences. He is at least seven or eight years older than you are. Now, the moment he ended up in conflict with you, this woman tried to reason with him. All that he has been told about her, his ex-fiancée, happened to be a mere fabrication. At first, he tried to avoid her and to keep cultivating the relationship he started with you at any cost. It was at that very moment that some of our colleagues approached you, do you remember?"

"I remember that, and I was too late to understand that it was a conspiracy. Or to use your word, that it was a fabrication."

"What?"

"Listen. I have a story to tell you, too. I know now what you people did to me, or to us, or to our love relationship. Now I know that you people are not capable of loving. You are used to looking out for benefits, not for love. You calculate consequences of the relationship you want to establish. For you to love and to commit yourself, there must be something beneficiary. That is why you don't understand what is going on between Michael and me. We love each other, and that means a lot more than what you can understand."

She looked all over him with her fiery eyes.

"Yes, this colleague of yours, that short and stout man by the name of Tezha, not long ago he waited for me in front of my office, and he introduced himself as a man of a very high position. He told me that he and his friends did not want me to destroy a very strong relationship between two very decent people. He lectured me not to be selfish. Then he invited me to witness myself the things he was trying to tell me. By that, he provoked my curiosity. Besides, I was so foolish and inexperienced and agreed to follow him. He took me to an office that was parallel to yours and Michael's office, and he opened the curtain. He asked me to sit and watch what was going to happen, as if he was a shaman or magician of a certain kind. Right after that, a woman came to Michael and asked him about something. I assume she was telling him that somebody wanted to talk to him. Then I saw her, Michael's ex-girlfriend, coming and entering the office. You were not there. I did not know what she said to Michael, but I watched her standing by the door, and smiling and looking towards me. Your colleague Tezha told me that she couldn't see me because of the mirror-type reflection of the window. Then Michael came to the door, and it seemed to me as if he was asking her to go. She kept looking towards me and smiling, and suddenly, he was standing there, not responding to her smile, but looking towards me. At first, I thought she was deliberately directing his attention towards me. I could not breathe. I thought he saw me, too. Slowly, I left that office and ran to my office without looking back at Tezha."

She fought to hold back her tears.

"That evening, I called Michael to be able to trace a change in his behaviour. I wanted to know whether he knew that I was watching him that day when he met her. Surprisingly, he was only mad at me because I was not answering his call. He begged me to meet him the next day after work and he promised that he had many surprises he wanted to share with me. I was suspicious, but I said okay. The picture in my mind

– him standing with her – wouldn't let me rationalise. I felt angry and irritated. So, I started thinking and planning how I was going to irritate him, too. Next day, I made him wait for me for so long. When I at last came to the place where he was waiting for me, I was with a young man whom I knew from my high school days, pretending as if he was a man I had an affair with. Michael ignored the boy and gave me a hug and a kiss on my cheek. I greeted him superficially, then went back to this boy and kept flirting. Whether what I did was right or wrong, I was mad at Michael at that time and I wanted him to get angry and fight me back. Instead, my action made him hate me silently. When he at last concluded that I was disrespecting him and betraying his love, he became quiet. He did not utter any bad word. When I reluctantly followed him to his house, he told me that he was having a headache and begged me to excuse him so that he could take a nap. I waited for about two hours. He woke up as serious as he was when he went to his bedroom. I asked him if he might accompany me home. He reluctantly followed me to the taxi station a few hundred metres from his place. Since that very day, he either stopped or suspended everything he had with me. He chose to run away from me. Now I realise that I made a big mistake. That is why I am trying to get in touch with him."

The man smiled.

"You are very innocent. You do not know what his ex-woman is capable of. You are very intelligent and young, but I do not know why you repeatedly fail to see the point here. I advise you to forget him the way he has forgotten you."

"Thank you for trying to scare me. For your information, I do not believe that Michael can easily forget me. He cannot do that. We will never forget each other. I do know that much. We are not like you."

He smiled and scratched his head for a while.

"I am telling you, try to find people of your kind and age. Forget Michael."

Without saying goodbye, he went to the cashier, paid for the coffee, and left the coffee bar.

Coming back to her workplace, she thought deeply about what that man had told her. What was the implication of "try to find people of your kind"?

She laughed while listening to her inside. Her conscience and integrity told her that in love there is no boundary. You cannot choose the educational background, the profession, the ethnicity, the age of a person you fall in love with.

She paused in the tormenting flow of ideas inside her. 'Maybe I am missing something.'

She tried to concentrate.

'Is he telling me that the ex-girlfriend is Michael's kind more than I am?'

Slowly, the adrenaline started pumping through her system and her mind reacted by working very fast.

'Oh my God, is this what is going to be the destiny of our society in the future? People must first check the bloodline before they fall in love with anyone. That is terrifying.'

She tried to calm herself down. For her, Michael was a person, a human being who conquered her loving heart. Ethnic background had never been a discussion point through all the time they spent together. She loved him for the person he was and is. The only obstacle she knew about was girls who wanted to take him away from her, or to steal him. There were times she believed he was a womaniser, a Casanova, but never an extreme nationalist who would abandon her by choosing 'his kind', whatever the meaning of the word was.

'Oh my God! Maybe that is the case. Maybe he is involved in something that he values more than what I am for him. Oh God, no, that would be unfair!'

She pulled herself out of the distressing abstract thinking and reasoning. She rather wanted to remain on the ground and look at things as they are now. Michael was the person she really loved. She was so certain that he loved her, too. She chose to keep it as that. Whether she had the capacity to win him back or not, she wanted to behold the true feeling he created in her. She told him many times that he made her feel like a woman, and that was true. He himself told her many times that she made him feel the happiest and luckiest man in this world, and she thought that was true, too. Time would cure the wound, and they might give one another a chance, she concluded.

That chance came after four and a half years. She was mourning the passing away of her father. Wearing black from top to bottom, she was coming out of the building of Addis Ababa's city administration. He was entering the compound from the opposite direction. He saw her first. When she was just passing by, he called her name. She turned around and she saw him. First, she smiled and then she wanted to go her way without further ado. From the corner of her eye, she watched him coming towards her. She breathed deep and waited for him. He appeared to be the same old Michael. He greeted her with a big smile and a strong hug. She was in a way reluctant to hug him, but she responded at last.

"Oh, Bliss, it seems ages since we met last. How are you doing?"

"I am fine. How are you?"

Then he looked at her with a thoughtful face.

"What happened? Why do you wear black and why is your hair…?"

She turned her face from him and stood there with bent head. He turned her towards him.

"What happened?"

She looked at him. With saddened and wet eyes, she told him that her father had died three months ago. He instinctively took her into his arms. He could not say anything to share her grief and to extend his condolences. Instead, he asked her whether she wanted or not to ignore him and go if he had not managed to call her name.

"No!" she said.

Right then, he came to his senses.

"Bliss, I am sorry for what happened. I did not know. If I did, I would have come home to you to extend my condolences. I am sorry."

She looked at him with a soulful smile. "I understand. Thank you."

He felt inside a turbulent passion. She was about to bid him goodbye, when he asked her for her telephone number. Without hesitation, she gave it to him. The next afternoon, he called her. They agreed to meet. Their meeting place was one of the old and best restaurants in the city. The atmosphere inside the restaurant was very cosy and there were few customers. They ordered mixed grills for their dinner, the red Gudar wine for their drink, and they dined under dim lights.

Suddenly, she asked him a question. "Now you are married to her, aren't you?"

He hesitated at first and looked down. He recovered immediately and faced her with longing eyes.

"Yes, I am married to her. She was the only person there when I needed someone on my side."

"She is just wise and smart. She happened to be available for you at the right time."

She smiled and looked deep into his eyes.

He understood the sting she wanted to inflict.

"Did you have a child?"

"Yes, two boys."

"You are lucky, but that is not good," she said, thinking that it was not going to be simple to win him back.

"What?"

"I am kidding."

She smiled and changed the topic. Then they started talking about what truly happened between them. Without condemning one another for their failings, they came to the conclusion that they were not wise enough to handle properly their passion and love. When they at last came out of the restaurant and went to the taxi station where she could catch a taxi home, she invited him to ride with her. He was more than happy that she asked him. Halfway to her home, he kissed her tenderly but voraciously. She responded well. The taxi dropped both at her destination. He walked her some fifty metres towards her house.

"Thank you very much, Bliss, for spending your time with me. Believe me, I do want to keep you as my memorable friend. I do not dream of winning you back, but I do want to love you forever."

She leaned towards him and kissed him. Then she quickly went to her house.

The night was long. She could not sleep. His memory was so fresh. His tender voice, with all his love talk, kept vibrating in her ears.

'One thing is sure. I cannot force him to leave his wife and children. But I can enjoy him. I can spend time with him, sharing my love with him. If it was not for my mistake, he could be mine. They say everything is right in love and war. Who said, then, it is wrong to keep true love alive? See you, Michael!'

She smiled and felt good. She fell asleep immediately.

He took up his glass and looked at her with such strong feelings of love and passion that anyone could easily read from his face.

"Bliss, you are amazing. I think my trip to Rome had indeed been the best decision I have ever made in my life. If not for this trip, I would never know about things I heard from you today. I would never know that I have foolishly abandoned you by not suspecting any kind of conspiracy. I would never know that I exposed you to so many confrontations and pains. Most of all, I would never know that you swore to yourself to love me forever. Regarding the thing that happened between you and me when we met last, I wrote it in my diary by saying that it might herald a comeback between you and me. Of course, without knowing your decision not to try to win me back. Now I know a lot more about us than I did before I came to you. Now I know a lot more about the smart role my wife played by employing a hard gun to scare you away and secure a husband for herself. Now I know why my heart, all these years, kept bleeding for your love. Bliss, you are a special woman in my life. Thank you for creating in me such a passion."

He leaned towards her and kissed her. She responded passionately.

When he followed her to the tram station at the square of Piazzale Enrico Dunant, it was fifteen minutes past midnight. His thoughts on his flight to Rome were about the possibility he might be going to wake up in the morning with her beside him. However, this first day he spent with her, scores of things happened. First, she received him with such a passion that he decided to respond cautiously. Later, as they arrived at his hotel, he turned down her gleeful and open approach to have sex with him by talking about the need for them to take time and for him to get a chance to discover her anew. They took their time, and he did indeed discover her anew. He listened to her story and became aware of what really happened to them many years back. And then the desire started running through his veins. He wanted her to go back with him to his hotel so that they could start from where they had stopped earlier. She smiled, kissed him, and told him to wait until tomorrow. Regardless of how much she wanted it, she told him that she didn't plan to stay away from home this very night. He agreed. The tram she should take home came immediately. She promised to meet him tomorrow afternoon. She kissed him and jumped into the tram.

He did not remember how, but he found himself at the gate of his hotel in less than twenty minutes. He rang the bell, and the receptionist pressed the button under his desk that opened the outside door. He came in and greeted the receptionist fleetingly and went to the lift that would take him to the sixth floor. To the right from the lift, at the corner, inside the well-lit room, he saw this white woman, wearing a sleeveless white dress showing her seemingly strong arms, standing with her back towards him, working on the beverage and snack dispenser machine. He watched her inattentively while pressing the button on the lift door. As he turned his attention to the arriving lift, the woman took the bottle of water she just bought from the dispenser machine and turned towards him. For a fraction of a second, she felt as if a thunderbolt had hit her. She blinked and blinked. When she saw him entering the lift, she shouted, "Wait!"

He slowly stepped out and looked towards the direction of the dispenser machine. The woman was hurrying towards him. At first, he thought she was hurrying not to miss the lift. When he clearly saw her and grasped who the woman was, he felt like he was dreaming. He blinked and blinked.

"I don't believe this."

He rolled his eyes. He called her name. "Ingrid?"

"It is me. And you are Me'naan!"

She herself was having difficulty breathing.

They stood there and looked at each other without saying or doing anything. He looked around and looked back at her.

"It feels strange, doesn't it?"

She smiled at last and stretched her hand towards him in greeting. He took her hand hesitantly. He looked into her eyes without letting her hand go. He saw some sort of glimmer in her eyes, and he quickly let go of her hand.

"I really don't know what to say!"

He turned his back to her.

"Me'naan, do not tell me you are not happy at all by seeing me here and now?" she chuckled.

"Happy? That is not the word I am thinking about right now. I am confused. How in heaven is this happening to me?"

She sighed.

"Are you alone here or with your family?"

He was not listening.

His mind was busy analysing things.

He came to Rome to meet the woman he loved so much but had been separated from so many years ago. By doing so, he had already signed a case for betrayal regarding his current family. He met that woman hours ago and had a good time with her. Then he sent her home and came back to his hotel thinking about what was going to happen between them. Before he even got the chance to work out the things his hippocampus had registered about that coming together, he met the adorable woman that once knocked him down with the kind of love he never expected to cherish in the foreign country he emigrated to.

That part of his life was meant to be forgotten.

It happened at a time when he was lonely, desperate and with less hope about his future.

Right from the beginning, he told Ingrid that he had a family, a wife, and kids he loved so much. The adventure was meant to be temporary.

'Was it not?' he asked himself.

He knew he was not a gigolo whose job it is to give a service to a woman without being attracted to her. For him to be intimate and to cherish a woman, there must be a true feeling. If that feeling is true, then it obviously cannot be doomed to be temporary. "No…?"

He shook his head and told himself that he did not want to think about it. He tried to completely shut off his thoughts.

And then he looked at her with undivided attention.

She smiled. "I asked you a question."

"What?"

"I asked you whether you are alone or with your family."

"I am alone… No, I am not, I mean…"

She laughed.

"Relax, man. I am here together with my friend Solveig. We will stay here for the next six days. Our room is on the fifth floor, number 510. That is for your information in case you want to talk with me afterwards."

She entered the lift and pressed the button to the fifth floor.

He did not try to take the lift together with her. He just stood there and followed the indicator light showing the floor the lift had reached. When it stopped at the fifth floor, he turned around and took the stairs up to the sixth floor. Entering his room, he felt ashamed of the way he had treated Ingrid.

'That is not the way to greet a person who shares a special past memory with you,' he told himself.

What was he afraid of?

She could not be a threat to his expedition to Rome. He could proceed with his exploration uninterrupted. She didn't even need to know about his rediscovery of a lost relationship.

So now, why was it that he was so confused and unwilling to start a meaningful conversation with Ingrid, remembering the things that happened between them?

Did it spoil in one way or another the encounter he had just started to engage himself with?

He hesitated.

He sat on the edge of his bed. 'Of course it does!' his conscience told him.

'So, I have to abandon her by any means!' He chose confrontation.

'Yes, you have to!'

"That is unfair," he sighed.

He shouldn't abandon that bygone history of such a rough infatuation and wild lovemaking at any cost. Or should he? It used to be his life's principle that running away from such a kind of passionate experience was an act of cowardice. Besides, between Ingrid and him, there was no bad feeling or broken hearts when they terminated their relationship. They agreed from the start to do just that. So, for him, there was no reason at all to be afraid of that special relationship.

He opened the mini-refrigerator and took out the six-pack brown beer Bliss had bought earlier for him to cool down his body temperature.

'I hope they don't mind,' he told himself.

He went out of his room and took the stairs down to the fifth floor. He knocked on the door of room 510. Someone approached the door from inside and asked, "Who is it?"

"It is me, Me'naan. I am sorry for knocking on your door so late."

She opened the door and stared at him. "Well, I was telling Solveig about you."

"Please, would you mind if I come in? I am so sorry for behaving the way I did down there."

She turned towards Solveig. Solveig nodded her approval. "Okay, come in!"

Ingrid opened the door wide.

Before entering the room, he presented to her the six-pack beer he held behind his back. "Wow, cold beer after midnight!"

She chuckled and took the package from him.

She turned towards Solveig. "I don't think you people have met before."

Solveig rose from her chair and came towards him.

"I heard a lot about you. My name is Solveig. You won't believe me if I tell you that she was wondering about the possibility of meeting you here right after our arrival."

"Really?"

He looked at Ingrid. She nodded.

He smiled.

"My name is Me'naan. Well, I did not hear about you so much"

"Well, whose mistake would that be ... » She turned to Ingrid.

Ingrid smiled.

"That would be my mistake, of course."

He smiled and approached Solveig and gave her a strong and good handshake.

Ingrid made a place for the beer pack on the table that was already filled with other beer bottles.

"This is our first night in Rome and we wanted to stay longer. That is why!"

Ingrid smiled and opened for him the bottle of beer that was already on the table.

"Besides, Rome is so hot, and we needed to chill down."

"Rome is hot indeed."

He smiled, too.

After the three of them said cheers and sipped their beer, Ingrid sat on the edge of her bed, leaving the two of them to sit in the two chairs in the room.

It was Me'naan who was first out with his question. "You came to Rome today?"

"No, it was yesterday. It is past midnight right now," Ingrid chuckled.

"Yes, I meant yesterday."

"Yes."

"Were you those Norwegians who collected their rental car from Maggiore?"

"How do you know that?"

They both looked at him with bulging eyes.

"I was there to collect my car, too. And the lady at the counter told me that I was another Norwegian, and that there were two grown-up Norwegian ladies who collected their car a few hours ahead of me."

The two women looked at each other.

"What a coincidence."

Solveig smiled.

"It is your first night for you, too, here in Rome. Let us cheers for that, then!"

The three of them rose and brought their bottles together.

Ingrid's question made him sit on his chair quickly.

"Earlier, when I met you downstairs, I asked you whether you are alone or not. And it was very difficult for you to answer. Why is that?"

"I don't know really."

He fixed his eyes for a while on the beer bottle he was holding in his hand. Then he looked at both ladies.

He deeply inhaled the hot air in the room and turned towards Ingrid.

"Sure, I came to Rome alone and that is why I have ordered a single room at this hotel."

He smiled.

The two women smiled back.

"But I am looking forward to spending some time with a person I abandoned so many years ago. When I met you downstairs, I was just coming back after having dinner with this person at a restaurant not far away from here. The reason I couldn't answer your question by saying yes or no, I think, was just that."

He tried to smile.

"Is this a pre-planned reunion or something that happened accidentally like between you and me a few minutes ago?"

He sighed. "It is a long story, Ingrid."

Solveig took up her bottle and said, "The night is long, and we have enough beer!" She smiled. "I'd love to hear about it, too!"

Ingrid scrutinised him, looking deep into his eyes.

7

The day was Thursday, the month was October, just around lunch-time, before noon. Me'naan came out of his employer's office and waved a taxi to a stop and asked the driver to take him to the city centre, Piazza. He had come back to Addis five days ago, on Sunday, after he had spent almost five and a half years in East Europe. His scholarship didn't end the way he wanted it to end. His plan was to proceed with his PhD after he received his integrated Master's degree in political science. Unexpectedly, he received a letter from his employer to return home before he started working on his PhD. As a government employee, he couldn't proceed with his scholarship without due permission, and therefore he couldn't say no. He was suspicious at first.

'What did I do?' he tried to figure out, to no avail. Most of the time he failed to clearly understand the rules of the game he was supposed to follow, strictly or otherwise, as a government employee under the military regime. As naïve as he was, he always thought that he could have his say as a technocrat in the field of his expertise. But he failed to see time and again the open charlatanic and kleptomaniac behaviour of assigned office holders from top to bottom who for that very reason couldn't feel safe and let technocrats do their job. They were suspicious of even their own shadow, he remembered how the saying went. To overcome their fear, they used various kinds of ruling techniques. They made you invisible by ignoring your ideas and suggestions and denying you opportunities of any sort. They built up their confidence by making those they suspected to be the enemy of the State and as such subject to imprisonment or to death. Those kinds of uncontrolled ruling techniques caused the disappearance and death of many young and old, educated and uneducated, women and men.

In his case, although most of the time he spoke his mind, he had been very careful not to engage or to provoke the people of power. The general understanding of the elites and the mass alike was that power is the source of wealth and respect. You have power, so everybody is supposed to respect you. You have power, so those under you are subject to your wishes and interests. The governance formula in this country, from time immemorial, did not consider the power of the people. It rather underlined that the people are the subjects of the rulers of the country. So, he convinced himself that this trend was not going to change in his lifetime. Therefore, it was better to avoid confrontation. That was what he told himself.

He at last decided to return home. Returning home, he found out that the government had suspected him of involvement in one of those opposition political movements abroad, which had its biggest base in Germany. Because of the lack of evidence, or just because somebody was kind enough to put in good words for him, they didn't throw him in jail on his arrival. Rather, they wanted to scrutinise his behaviour from close range. On top of this, his fiancée had decided not to come to Addis to meet him as he expected it to be. She created various excuses not to come. He visited her at the place where she lived with her relatives, about forty-eight kilometres to the east of the capital city. He took a bus, and the bus ride took him almost an hour. When he finally met her, her cold reception and lack of affection for him was a big disappointment. More saddened was he when she told him candidly that she was not allowed to spend time with him. He returned to Addis the same day and felt abandoned and devastated.

As his taxi was about to drive past the Commercial School in Addis Ababa, he saw through the window two girls standing in front of the main gate. The one girl he did recognise. She was from his neighbourhood. The other one, he just got a glimpse of her shiny eyes. He felt as if he had been hit by something with sharp edges. Suddenly, the adrenaline entered his system and his heartbeat increased immediately. Without knowing it, he asked the driver to stop, paid him the full tariff to Piazza and jumped out of the car.

He calmed himself while walking towards them. First, he greeted the girl from his neighbourhood, who took him with such a big smile and open arms. He hugged her and turned his attention to the girl who had given him the shock of his life minutes earlier. To his surprise, she didn't wait until her friend introduced him to her. She reached for his hand and told him her name was Bliss, and he immediately found in her a serene joy. The liveliness of her smile, the delightful look in her eyes, and he was totally mesmerised. When he came back to himself after a few seconds, he told her his name was Me'naan and he invited both girls for a cup of coffee.

As they came out of the coffee bar hours later, she asked him where he was going to. He told her, and she took the taxi with him to Piazza. In Piazza, they spent the whole afternoon together. He told her that he believed he had a fiancée when he returned home from his studies abroad, and that he found out two days ago that she did not want him anymore.

Bliss did not comment. She spoke very little. She quietly listened to what Me'naan was telling her. In between, she touched his hand and let him know that she was there for him, listening. At last, when she walked him to the taxi station, she gave him her number and a surprising kiss on his lips.

Arriving home, he went directly to his bed. Lying there, he couldn't stop thinking about Bliss. He thought about his fiancée, too. That she was abandoning him might be a blessing in disguise, he thought. But the solution came so fast, he wondered. If his friends saw him going out with Bliss, they might suspect that he had had this relationship for a long time, and that he had been dumped by his fiancée because of this, he told himself.

'Who cares?' he concluded.

The next day, Bliss was more than willing to meet him. They ate dinner together at the restaurant and talked and talked and talked until late in the evening. Their love affair established itself. Gradually, it became obvious to everybody, and even his ex-fiancée got wind that Me'naan and Bliss were taking their love-relationship seriously. Bliss started visiting him at his workplace more often, and he did the same. They mostly spent their leisure time together, at his house or outside in the city, visiting restaurants. However, she made him wait until the day of her graduation to cross the barrier she had erected and to touch her intimately.

That day was Friday. She called him early in the morning and told him that she had a plan to stay with him in his house until midnight. He was both surprised and happy.

"What time are you coming?"

She felt the eagerness in his voice.

"Around, let us say, 1800, the way you say it."

"That is wonderful."

"I want us to be alone, undisturbed."

"Wow, Bliss. Okay, there will be no breathing life around when you arrive here."

"What about your maid?"

"Don't you know? She is here only during the daytime. I thought I told you that she doesn't live with me."

"Just curious. I wanted to be sure."

Sharp on time, she knocked on his door. He opened it for her with a big smile on his face. She entered the house quietly and then directly went to his bedroom. He locked the entrance door and followed her. She turned to him and closed her eyes. He hugged her and kissed her on her closed eyes. She pulled him down and kissed him eagerly. They ended up falling on the bed. He touched her where he had never touched her before. She did not protest, and he felt excitement. He undressed her while kissing her all over her body. She unbuttoned his shirt and slowly touched his bulging erection. While helping him to get undressed, she whispered in his ears, "Do not hurt me, please!"

He felt as if he was choking. He tried hard to whisper back,

"I will not, my love. I certainly will not."

He begged her to trust him and to let him do it to her. He told her that he would not force himself, but that he would do it gently. Indeed, he was more than gentle at first.

He took time cushioning her, and suddenly penetrated her tight body, entered her hard and touched her deep down. She screamed, trembled a little bit, and sucked on his tongue, before she slowly started moving her body. He followed her rhythm.

"Me'naan, I love you. Please do not let me down."

"No, Bliss, I will never let you down. I love you. I am so lucky that I met you. I could have made a mistake in my life if it was not for that day on which I met you."

She stopped moving. She trembled again. She squeezed him. Slowly, she started whispering, "Oh my God, this is it. I am coming. But, Michael, I don't want you to come inside me. Please do not do that."

She quickly forced him to disengage. He was fully hard. He was not even near to finishing. He raised himself up and looked down. He saw a blood stain on the bed sheet under her. She looked up into his eyes.

"Oh, my Bliss, does this mean that you gave it to me?" He kissed her voraciously.

She closed her eyes and whispered, "Yes, my love. Sorry I made you wait for so long." She opened her eyes and smiled.

He smiled back and kissed her very passionately.

They lay there and kissed one another. After a short while, she engaged him again. This time she sat upon him.

"Be careful!" he whispered.

"I will," she answered.

Their move was so gentle and energetic while he felt the glow in her body deep down. He started doing it to her harder and harder. When her inside started chewing on his joj o, he shifted his position and lay on top of her. Now he entered her deep. She did not scream. She came repeatedly. At last, he disengaged himself and exploded outside. She gasped and took him into her arms. Immediately, she pushed him away and ran to the bathroom.

That evening, they made love several times. At the end, they took a shower together and sat down to eat the food his housemaid had prepared earlier for the two of them. While eating, she told him that she was supposed to be with her friends at the graduation party. Her father drove her there and told her that he would collect her after midnight. She had asked her friends to cover up for her and came to him.

"I love you, Bliss. And I will be yours forever if that is what you wish."

"I love you, too, and I ask you to help me to find out what my wish is."

"What do you mean by that?"

He hesitated.

"That means that you would be nice to me and don't let me down. I gave you myself. I ask for your patience while I try to get matured in the process of loving you."

His eyes became wet. He could not say anything. She stood up and kissed him.

"Now follow me to the place where our graduation party is. If my old man does not find me there, there will be big trouble."

He kissed her gently and passionately.

"Okay, my love, let us go. By the way, do not make me feel old. I do need to get matured, too, in the process of loving you."

She smiled and stepped out.

A few months later, Bliss suddenly changed her behaviour. She suspended the daily telephone conversation she used to have with him. Whenever he called her, she refused to answer. She broke off their ritual of meeting after work. Friday arrived quickly and Me'naan could not stand the idea of spending the weekend without her. He decided to visit her at her office.

The door was open, and she was busy sorting through various papers spread over her mahogany office desk. He cleared his throat, trying to get her attention.

"Oh my God, Michael…!"

Her first reaction was genuine.

Quickly, she changed her tone, and also the look on her face.

"What are you doing here?"

"What am I doing here? Are you serious?"

"Look, I am busy now. I must find the letter my boss asked me for. I cannot talk to you now."

"Well, I can wait until you are done, if you allow me to sit here and wait."

"Are you kidding? I cannot concentrate on my work while you are sitting here."

"Bliss, I, too, was having problems of concentration all these four days. Why are you doing this to me? Abandoning me without telling me the reason is unfair. I want to know what happened."

The phone on her table rang.

She hushed him and answered the phone. "Yes?"

She listened and nodded.

"If you give me ten minutes, please!"

She waited for some time, holding the receiver to her ear before replacing it. "Michael, let us meet at lunch-time. As you see, I am very busy now." She pointed to the papers on her desk.

"Okay, Bliss. I was out of my mind and very sad these past four days."

"Why? Have you done something wrong?"

She gave him that disingenuous smile of hers he knew all about. She did this to him whenever she suspected something.

"Bliss, do not do that to me, please. If there is something bothering you, tell me and we can solve it together. I love you."

"Okay, go now. Meet me at lunch-time."

He wanted to give her a kiss.

"I said go."

Her fury was powerful.

He retreated, shook his head, and left her office.

They met at lunch-time and went to the coffee bar they regularly visited. He tried to find out why she so suddenly changed and abandoned him without any kind of warning. He told her how desperate he had become when he could not talk to her.

"Bliss, I do believe you know how much I love you. I do believe, too, that you know how much it hurts when you leave me without warning. I thought we had found love, harmony, and strength in one another. What did I do wrong that made you just shut me out for all these days?"

He thought he saw a glimpse of tears in her eyes. However, she immediately cleared them without even blinking.

"Michael, you might be over-reacting. One thing you should know about me is that when I am angry, I simply detach myself from everything, drop everything and close myself inside my own world until I work things out."

"That is unfair. How can you tell me you love me if you cannot trust me and share with me the thing that angers you? Remember, we are here for each other."

She smiled. This time genuinely.

"That is the problem, Michael. I really don't know who to trust."

For the first time he seemed to be disturbed. He looked deep into her eyes. She winked.

"You are telling me that you do not trust me?"

"I see and hear those things are happening around us. I do love you, Michael. You are an adorable man and I do not know whether it is my destiny or not to keep you for myself."

He was confused.

"I do not understand. Have I done something that did hurt you, Bliss?" He looked at her. He begged her with his eyes.

"No. I don't think so."

He became furious.

She looked at her watch.

"We'll talk about it some other day. I must go back to my office now."

He took her hand and held it between his big palms.

"Look, Bliss, today is Friday. You know what Friday means to us."

She smiled and suddenly she let her tears fall.

He hugged her and kissed her.

"Let me go now, Michael."

"Okay, but can we meet after work?"

"I will be late because there are so many office-works to attend to."

"I'll wait for you as long as it takes."

She looked at him.

"Okay, if that is what you want."

Without saying goodbye, she left him and hurried to her office.

Post Office Rendezvous is the main road-side coffee bar in Addis Ababa, serving varieties of cakes, pastries, hot and cold drinks. He arrived there earlier than the time of their appointment and he wanted to stay outside and wait for her. In front of the coffee bar, he found an empty corner and summoned one of the shoe-shiners lounging around and asked him to give him his service. While the boy worked on his shoes, he allowed his mind to ramble. He tried to find out what he had done that made Bliss angry.

He did not see anyone these past days. Yes, his ex-fiancée had tried to talk to him at his office. She first sent a woman messenger who told him that someone wanted to talk to him. When he told the woman from the office next door to let that someone come in, it was she, his ex-fiancée. He reluctantly greeted her and talked to her. To his surprise, he realised that he still had feelings for her.

It was true that he was head over heels in love with his ex-fiancée. He liked the way she was: shy, unsophisticated, innocently beautiful, light skinned, taller than the average women, bearing voluminous hair at shoulder length, smooth and simple talking, easy to converse with, and always smiling. He understood her quiet behaviour as the result of her upbringing in a cultural context where everything but an independent and opinionated girl is appreciated. In her world, an open love affair before marriage was immoral and he liked her for that, too. He convinced himself that she was a girl to choose as a life-partner. All the years he spent abroad, he was planning how he would get married to her and how many children they would have. He wrote her love letters for which he never received an answer from her. She never told him how much she loved him. He never learned what kind of impression his writing gave her. Nevertheless, these things never disturbed him because he knew, or he thought he knew, that she loved him from the way she looked at him, the way she held his hand, and the way she said 'yes' whenever he asked her for some favours. When he was asked by his employer to return home for a short sojourn before he proceeded with his PhD study, she was the main reason behind his decision to accept the request to return home.

But these days, he felt that she for him was a very different person. Compared to the level of intimacy and understanding he developed with Bliss in such a short period of time, he strongly reasoned out that their relationship from the very beginning was phony. They did not build up any kind of intimacy between them. He did not know her, both as a person and as a woman. When she gradually tried to contact him, both in person and on the phone, several months after she told him that she was not allowed to spend time with him, he frankly told her that he was in a serious relationship and that he did not want her in his life again. He told her that he had no itching memories or bad conscience because of the break-up between them. Now, when last Monday the woman from the office next door told him that somebody was looking for him, he did not expect at first that very somebody was his ex-fiancée.

Yes, he greeted her reluctantly but politely and asked her to take a seat. As she sat down and the woman from the office next door left, he begged her, lowering his voice but seriously, not to try to come back into his life. While talking to her, he realised that his feelings for her had become more rational. He registered that he was calm and no more emotional. However, he couldn't abandon the feeling of the need to know and to understand why she abandoned him. Caught up with a bit of jealousy, he started thinking about the person who did conquer her heart in his absence. He even thought about making love to her and finding out how good she was in bed.

She suddenly stood up, moved towards the door, and looked outside.

"I am not trying to push you to change your mind and let me come back into your life. I do know that I treated you wrongly. I apologise for that. But I swear to God that I did not do that because I had a relationship with another person. It was rather a family issue. If you give me a chance, I will explain it to you."

She turned towards him for a moment and turned back again to where she was looking. He felt as if she was talking to some other person than to him. He slowly brought himself out of his chair, left his desk and came towards her. He looked outside, passed her, searching for people. He saw his own reflection in the windows of the office building in front of his office. Without saying a word, he went back to his seat.

She smiled and looked at him.

He wondered why he was not feeling any anger towards her. He looked at her and was amazed by the whiteness of her teeth and the dark, sexy, voluminous smooth hair covering her shoulder.

He turned his eyes towards his desk and stared at the various papers.

"You know what, I have things to do right now. Thanks for your visit. Okay?" He looked at her.

She looked at him.

Without saying a word, she stretched out her hand for a goodbye.

He took her tiny hand and subconsciously squeezed it a little bit. She rolled her eyes and she let her under-lip hang.

"You hurt me!"

He saw her beauty and he smiled. She smiled back and left his office.

After she left, he thought about her for a while.

Then he shook off his nostalgia and tried to come back to reality. Then he thought about Bliss, about his love for her.

"How dare I allow her to come back so easily into my life? Especially now, when I truly have found my true love; this shouldn't happen."

He took the phone and called Bliss at her office, thinking to share with her this very news. She did not answer. He tried many times. After work, he called her home. She did not answer. He failed to get in touch with her on Tuesday, on Wednesday, and on Thursday. On Friday morning, he went to her office.

He looked at his watch.

Forty-five minutes had passed over the usual time. They used to be punctual when they met after work.

He became restless.

'Could it be possible that my ex-fiancée has something to do with this?' he asked himself.

'No, no way, impossible!'

He tried to block the idea. It took him not very long to remember his conversation with Bliss at lunchtime.

"That is the problem, Michael. I really don't know whom to trust."

"Oh my God, it could be possible. Maybe somebody is conspiring." Then he saw her.

He started feeling relaxed. It was good that she came. He would talk to her and try to settle the problem once and for all. Then he realised that she was not alone. A woman he knew, her colleague from her workplace, and another man were accompanying her. She was striding towards him, hand in hand with this man, but talking and smiling to both. When she saw Me'naan, she didn't let go of the man's hand immediately. Me'naan registered that. A few yards away from him they all stopped. She looked around and turned to him. Leaving the two behind her, she went to him slowly. "I didn't expect you would wait for me for so long."

"No? I thought you told me that you would be late at work and that I could wait for you if I wanted to."

She didn't pay attention to his sarcastic opinion. "I was with my friends!"

Without waiting for his response, she went back to her friends.

"What does that mean...?" he whispered to himself.

"It means nothing!"

She looked back to him, and she smiled.

"You heard me?"

He hesitated. "Yes, I heard you."

As if the incident had cheered her up, she went back to those friends of hers, laughing.

He paid the shoe-shiner and followed her. He greeted her friends. He did not know the man. He looked very young. When the greetings died out, Bliss turned to the man and started flirting.

"What?"

Me'naan said to himself, 'I don't believe this!'

He felt both confused and embarrassed.

He was not alone in this. The woman that accompanied Bliss knew about the relationship between Me'naan and Bliss and seemed not to understand why Bliss was behaving like that.

She approached Me'naan, smiling.

"My name is Dezidi. We have met before."

"Yes, sure, but you never told me your name."

"You never asked. You were very much occupied by only one person."

She smiled and turned her eyes to the young man. She seriously gave the young man the shock of his life.

"Meet Bliss's boyfriend."

The young man couldn't hide his confusion. He seemed to be dumbfounded. He slowly stretched his hand out to Me'naan without uttering a word.

Me'naan took his hand, squeezed it hard and looked into his eyes. Then, he introduced himself in an authoritative voice, "I am Me'naan."

Then he released the young man's hand. The young man couldn't utter a word. Bliss couldn't help him, either. She stood there and smiled to all of them. Dezidi interfered and seized their attention.

"Shall we have a cup of coffee since we are here at Post Rendezvous?"

"I am sorry, Dezidi, I just lost my appetite for it. But thank you." Me'naan turned to Bliss, then to the young man, then to Bliss.

"Have a nice time, Bliss. Thank you for everything. I would like to take a taxi home now."

Without waiting for any response, he walked towards the nearest taxi station. Me'naan had a habit of being quiet, very quiet, when he was angry. He was not the kind of person who could shout out his anger. From his childhood, he was against everyone, big or small, who humiliated others by insulting or by being rude to them. As to him, rudeness and discourtesy was for those who lacked merit. He, therefore, usually kept things for himself and was hurt by that. He loved Bliss and he could not be rude to her. It was better that he chose to run away from her, rather than being forced by her to subconsciously hurt her. This was the intention on his mind when he jumped into the minibus taxi that was waiting for passengers.

Following him, Bliss entered the minibus and took a seat by his side. He wondered what she was doing.

"We have a date, if I am not mistaken," she smiled.

He did not say anything.

"Where are you planning to go while leaving me back there?" she scrutinised him.

"I want to go home."

"Me, too. I want to go home with you."

"I beg you not to do that."

"Why?"

"Because I want to be alone."

"You are selfish. You only think about what you want. You never care about what I think and what I want."

He looked at her.

"Do not, please, Bliss, do not force me to do things I've never done, and never want to do to you."

She saw rage on his face. She had never experienced him in such a temper before.

She tried to cajole him with her eyes. She would prefer hearing him say something, even bad things to her, rather than succumbing to such graveyard quietness. She lost her wit when it was so quiet with him. She looked at him one more time.

"You cannot stop me from coming home with you," she smiled.

He looked at her for a while, and then resigned into his dull quietness.

The forty-five-minute taxi ride to his home became an eternity for her. After they arrived at his place, the two hours she had to wait until he woke up from his nap were more challenging.

She knew after all that she had made a wrong move by trying to make him jealous by flirting with someone she hardly knew.

What was the other choice she had?

She was mad at him because of the things she heard and saw. She never tried to think whether all these were a conspiracy or not. For her, even if she hadn't a shred of evidence, it was not necessary to disprove what others had described for her about his personality, a womaniser. She had seen a lot of other girls trying to get his attention while she was with him on a date. Although she liked the way he ignored them, she never stopped speculating what he would do if he met them alone. Then, after she saw what she saw, she convinced herself that he was never in love with her. He was simply waiting for his ex-fiancée to knock on his door, she argued.

'I was so foolish to fall for him!' she cursed herself.

It was that same day he tried to contact her by phone, and she decided not to answer.

She was sure about one thing and that was that he was not a quitter. Somewhere inside her she hoped that he wouldn't give up on her. When he came to her office, she felt a kind of relief. She was grateful for that. But she wanted to keep testing his love for her in her own way. She wanted to see him and hear him fighting for her. Unfortunately, her action backfired.

Now, at his home, he ignored her presence and excused himself to take a nap.

'He must be in love with me, and that is why he became mad.' That thought brought a smile to her face.

But that smile disappeared the moment she saw him coming out of his bedroom. He was still upset.

"My goodness, Michael, you made me wait for you for almost two hours."

He looked confused. He yawned and scratched his head. "What are you doing here anyway?"

She felt real anger.

"What is your problem? Remember, it was you who wanted to talk to me. If you are looking for excuses to get rid of me, I don't think you need one."

She collected her handbag from the chair in the sitting room and went to the door. She was expecting that he would say 'stop', and she was happy he said it.

"Wait, please."

She turned around and looked at him with fiery eyes.

"Can we sit and talk a little bit?" he begged her.

She raised her shoulders and eyebrows and went to the chair. He sat in front of her at the dining table.

Facing his gaze, she looked deep into his eyes and was scared. She saw the loving eyes no more. What she saw was mere sadness.

He stopped staring at her and opened his mouth. "I love you, Bliss."

The way he said it churned her emotions. It sucked the air out of her. She felt that something wrong was truly happening between them. He stared at her again.

"I'll always love you. There is no one who can take over the place you have conquered inside me. Wherever you go and whenever you can, just remember this. That is the only thing I wanted to tell you."

He stood up and went to his bedroom. He put on his overcoat and came back to the sitting room.

"Let us go."

He opened the door and she followed him silently.

The next day at lunch-time she met the courier, a handsome but shy boy, that Me'naan had sent to her office. The boy had with him a bag full of fiction books that she once loaned to Michael, and a note.

"*My Dear Bliss!*

Please do not try to vindicate your wild behaviour by accusing me of dishonesty. In case somebody has told you some wild stories, which I do suspect, you could have come to me, and we could have talked about it. My love for you was unconditional and I gave you my soul and heart. No one could be dishonest to the person one loves unconditionally. What you showed me yesterday was far beyond what I could imagine you would do to me, the person who adores you and respects you. My conclusion is that if we proceed with our relationship now as if nothing has happened, it will end up hurting one of us, or both of us. My decision is to leave you alone now, but love you until my last day in this world. I wish you all the best.

I do not want you to look for me.

This is my last message to you. Michael."

She looked at the boy and smiled. She couldn't stop her tears from falling.

"I am sorry. Would you mind coming back tomorrow? I want to talk to you."

The boy nodded and left her office immediately. He never came back to her.

Me'naan, while nursing his love-wound, had registered, with such a saddened heart, the falling apart of the world of the socialist system, which once was alleged to bring a fundamental change to his country and the world in general. Exposed to the fundamental change spearheaded by the communist liberal from the then Soviet Union, or the Union of Soviet Socialist Republics, Mr Mikhail Gorbachev, the Eastern Europe that once granted him a scholarship went through tremendous opposition uprisings. The uprisings were so intense that they at last brought both the emergence of several independent countries out of the former Soviet Republics, and the complete demise of the German Democratic Republic, the very country that had emerged after the Second World War, more as a puppet than an independent ally of the winning party from the East, the Soviet Union. As a result, Germany and the German people fully reunified and the Iron Curtain that divided Europe into two under the Cold War was removed.

He witnessed also first-hand that his home city Addis Ababa, the capital city, was falling into the hands of the rebels from the north. The demise of the military dictatorship seemed at first to have heralded a new era of peace, reconciliation, and prosperity by ending the civil war that had ravaged the country through many decades. However, it didn't bring peace, reconciliation, development, and equality for all people in the country as was predicted. Shortly after the newcomers usurped the ruling position, fully supported by the Western powers, they took the first harsh step under the pretext of dismantling the military institutions condemned for being responsible for perpetrating and engineering the civil war that devastated the natural, human, and material resources of the country.

After the swift abolition of the Ethiopian marine force in line with the liberation of Eritrea and the disappearance of Ethiopia's access to the sea, the rebellious transitional government of Ethiopia dislodged the military institutions of the country from the top down, stubbornly erasing both the 'national' record and any kind of history attached to it.

The hundreds of thousands of Ethiopian soldiers who lost their lives during the civil war under the banner of keeping the unity of Ethiopia had been desecrated, their families and relatives, numbering in the hundreds of thousands, randomly ostracised, when the country's military institutions were condemned as hosts of criminals. The psychological and physical devastations of those families that resulted from these brutal actions were celebrated as one of the supreme achievements of the new ruling elites.

The military academy and air force academy graduates, the bureaucrats, and the technocrats with many years of work experiences gave way to the combat-hardened, Kalashnikov-guided, revenge-oriented, resolute and stubborn 'winners' from the northern mountains. Emboldened by their victorious achievements, the winner-cadres totally disregarded the feeling they hurt among ordinary citizens who used to see all the fighting factions under the military regime of Colonel Mengistu Hailemariam as hoodwinked Ethiopians. Furthermore, the new rulers replaced the workforces of such multi-faceted and giant military institutions by the rebellious loyal fighting force that was trained and formed in the jungle.

The prestigious and prominent Ethiopian Air Force, with its more than half a century experience and expensive aeronautical knowledge-bank, recklessly stripped off all its components, and the pilots and the ground crews were sent to the various detention and rehabilitation centres. The new men in power opted for the smaller Air Force and put the whole organisational structure of the Ethiopian Air Force under the auspices of ailing and ageing new recruits from the jungle that by no standard could have fulfilled the old criteria of recruitment to being able to join the Air Force. Even those experienced personnel who had served under the ousted military regime and who had been reassigned to facilitate both the functioning of the institution and the transfer of knowledge to the newcomers deserted their positions because of the friction and mistrust that evolved between them and the new jungle-born generals and military commanders.

Other civic organisations in the country, the likes of the Ethiopian peasant association, the Ethiopian labour union, the Ethiopian teachers' association and others who were condemned for being pillars of the military regime, were forced to be replaced by those designed to serve the interests of the newcomers. Parallel to the giant dislodging process of every political and national order of things in the country, the newcomers appealed to their enablers from the West to train them how to exercise power; to teach them the ruling businesses and the statesmanship they truly lacked. While the civil servants of the ousted military regime and the whole resources of State institutions were stranded and made subject to mass arrest, the rebellious transitional government assembled its ageing cadres, from top to bottom, to be trained for the new job of ruling Ethiopia.

Me'naan became one of these victims. First, he was taken from his workplace to one of the rehabilitation centres opened at the outskirts of the capital city, Addis Ababa. He had been told the aim was to indoctrinate the old guard and to introduce the new philosophy that the newcomers had in store for the people. Next day, around lunch-time, he heard his name called through the speakers hanging at various places inside the compound and heard the order for him to come to the entrance gate.

Me'naan was surprised when he saw her waiting for him. As he arrived at the gate, the sentry told him he had a visitor. He smiled and reluctantly went to the reception room. There she was. His ex-fiancée, smiling, a huge traditional food-bag hanging over her shoulder. He felt good and admired her for being there at this moment. He admired her for daring to come to the rehabilitation centre when it was not so clear what his future would be.

And then he approached her with a big smile. He hugged her, and he kissed her on her cheeks as she turned them to him. That was her speciality. Kissing one another on the lips belonged in the bedroom. Then she looked into his eyes and started sobbing.

He smiled and tried to calm her down. "I am okay. Why are you crying?"

It amazed him how she found the right time to reach out for him.

Three days after he dissolved his relationship with Bliss, she asked him to meet her after work. His first response was a 'no'. He told her he could not. She insisted, and she convinced him at last. They met, and they spent a joyful time together and she told him that she regretted putting their relationship in jeopardy. She asked him seriously to give her another chance.

With all her soft talk and shyness, she brought back his memory of the love he had for her. Slowly, he promised to himself that he would give her another chance. But he waited for some days before he asked her to come to his place. That day, they prepared dinner together, ate together, and he made love to her for the first time, in his bed. They conversed as if the break-up had never happened between them. They laughed together over every small story they shared with one another.

He was about to kiss her when he heard a knock on his door. He looked at her. He saw how scared she looked. He tried to calm her down and went out of his bedroom. He slowly opened the door and there she was, Bliss, together with her friend from the neighbourhood.

He felt very angry. He immediately suspected she knew he was with his ex-fiancée. And he thought that was an attack on his privacy.

He sighed and told her that he did not want her to visit him anymore.

"At least let me come in and talk to you!"

"There is nothing we can talk about."

He was about to close the door, when she suddenly threw him out of his balance and went in. Her friend followed her and started searching around in the house with her bulging eyes. He stood by the door and begged them to leave.

She placed her handbag on the dining table in the middle of the sitting room and turned to him.

"Okay, she can go, but I want to talk to you."

She followed her friend out of the house, and then out of the compound.

When she came back, he waited for her at the outer entrance of the compound, holding her handbag.

"You have trashed and belittled the love I have for you. By doing so, you destroyed the respect I had for you. As far as I am concerned, without love and respect for one another, there is nothing left for us to talk about."

"Please, Michael, let us go in and be together for a while."

"No, Bliss, that is not going to happen. You have no idea how much pain you caused me. I am convinced that I must let you go because I love you. I do not want to hurt you. I want to keep to myself the love I have for you as precious as it is. That is why I want you to go and forget me."

She felt something churning inside her stomach. She did not want to cry in front of him.

She snatched her handbag from him and left.

He followed her and asked her, "Can I follow you to the taxi?"

"Are you joking? Why?" She walked as fast as she could.

He closed and locked the door and went to the dining table. He sat there supporting his chin with his palms, resting his elbows on the table. He felt bitter sadness.

"Why is it that all these things happen to me?" he asked himself. He did not go further.

She came out of the bedroom and whispered, "Are they gone?"

"Yes."

He looked at her and smiled without knowing it. "Did her friend see you?"

He smiled.

"No, I hid myself behind the side of the closet."

He smiled, but he could not get rid of the sadness that engulfed him. He looked at her and thought about Bliss.

"If it was not for you, I would have allowed her to come in and talk to me." Slowly, he raised himself from the chair and followed her to the bedroom.

And here she was again, at the right time, at the right place. She looked at him for a while and sighed.

"I am crying because this is happening to you. You did not come back to your home country to face this kind of suffering. I am so sorry."

He took her into his arms and pleaded with her to stop crying.

He asked her about his residence, and whether she had talked to his housekeeper.

"Yes, I talked to her before I took the bus to come here. I told her that there was no need for her to come to your place daily. Then she asked me how she would be paid her wage. I asked her how much you owed her and paid her the amount."

"Well, that is nice of you. But how can I behold the house not knowing when I am getting out of here? It is a State-owned rental house. They will confiscate it if they come to know that I am in detention."

"You are not in detention. You are in the rehabilitation centre. There is a rumour out there that you people will be released soon after you get some crash courses about the new system."

She smiled.

"About your house, I will discuss the matter with my friends at my workplace and I will try to do my best so that you don't lose your house."

She smiled again.

"If you allow me, I will reside there until you come out," she laughed.

He always wondered about the beauty of her teeth in contrast with the dark gums insulating them.

He smiled widely.

"Do your parents permit that?" He watched her eyes.

"They will not find out unless I tell them."

"Are you going to tell them?"

"NO."

They stopped talking. He breathed deep.

"You know what? That is an incredibly good idea. I thank you for being ready to take this risk. The day I get released from this detention…"

He saw her stretching her lips in disagreement.

"Okay, okay, from this rehabilitation, I will propose to you, of course, if you want me to be your…"

She smiled and raised her eyebrows. "What?"

He expected some sort of happy approval.

Then the guard came into the guest room and told them their time was up.

She gave him the heavy traditional food-bag she had brought with her and kissed him goodbye on his cheeks. She promised to come back and visit him.

Her determination to stand by his side in those challenging and trying days became her ticket to fully win back his trust, and six months after Me'naan was released from detention, they were married. Three years into their married life, after their two boys were born, Me'naan ended up in trouble with the government. This time, his extensively critical journalistic work infuriated some people in power, and he became a wanted person. Since the day his friends and he had established a privately-owned shareholders' publication agency and started with the publication of weekly newspapers and magazines, he, as editor-in-chief, had been summoned by the police dozens of times, kept in police custody for days or weeks, and then released on bail. Given the pressure on publishers to make noisy headlines from those street vendors of the tabloid newspapers that had mushroomed excessively in the aftermath of the government takeover by the rebels from the north, Me'naan was not, at the beginning, so fearful of the shoves and harassments the journalists were facing. Gradually, when he often became a witness to the persecution of journalists critical of the government that had been intensified everywhere in the country, and to the growing determination of the regime to silence the voice of dissent by every possible means, Me'naan realised that he had no other choice left than abandoning his family and leaving the country. Escape became the only vocabulary circulating in his mind. Then again, he decided to wait longer when he knew his wife was pregnant their third child. The day the ultrasound check-up confirmed that she was pregnant with twins, after they came back home, he cried his guts out.

How can he leave her alone with four kids?

How can he simply allow himself to perish under the political pressure exerted by the incumbent regime that is bent to extrajudicially persecute its critics?

He knew staying with his family would not help them at all. Neither would his running away guarantee any success that would salvage them.

But his wife's appeal to his conscience to not let her suffer by allowing himself to be taken by the government, cleared the way to make his last decision to run away.

It was a dangerous decision to take a non-official route out of his country to the neighbouring country without acquiring any legal travel documents. It took him three days to reach the city where he could cross over the border and enter Kenya.

Before he headed to this city, Moyale, the collective name for the city divided between two sovereign countries, he somehow researched about the real situation regarding the over eight hundred and fifty kilometre-long and very porous border Ethiopia has with Kenya. The border traverses the Marsabit, Turkana and Mandera counties on the Kenyan side. On the Ethiopian side, it criss-crosses Borana and Dawa zones. Characteristic to the peoples leaving along these border areas is that they are largely mobile pastoralist people, transcending as they wish these international boundaries. These are Boran, Gabbra, Orma and Sakure, who are part of the Oromo-speaking people, the one thing he wanted to feel at home with.

In the city of Moyale itself, on both sides, there were people coming from various places to do business of different sorts. The Kenyan Moyale, besides the thriving livestock market, serves as a contraband hub for electronics and various consumer products flowing in from the western world. Even though Moyale's border is open to free-crossing movement, most of the merchants choose back doors for their luggage to avoid Custom duties. For a person without luggage, crossing is very easy. There is no visa control or ID-card check. This he found out the first day he came to Moyale. He checked into his hotel that was in the Ethiopian part of Moyale, a few hundred metres away from the free border crossing to Moyale Kenya, and after he took a shower and changed to a neatly ironed overshirt and jeans, he went directly to the crossing and entered Moyale Kenya. He felt both fear and excitement. The fear because he still suspected someone was tailing him, and the excitement because of his anticipation that this might be his first step into freedom. He had no idea where to go, but walked along the main road of the city for almost half an hour. As he passed the Ramata Health Centre to his right and climbed up the elevated sidewalk, he got a better view of his surroundings. Then he decided to go to the cafeteria he saw on the other side, to the left of the main road. The billboard sign with the name 'Galgaloo Cafeteria' stood tall and happened to be attractive.

Inside the cafeteria, the light was dim. It took him an unbelievably long time to find a seat, and then the waitress gave him her attention immediately. He ordered a double espresso with one jam-filled scone he had seen in the displayer as he entered the cafeteria. As the waitress left him, he studied all the other seats inside that relatively clean and well-kept room. Again, it took him an unbelievably long time to find out that he was rudely staring at a young woman sitting at the corner a few metres away to his right. He shook his head and yanked himself out of his absent-mindedness. "She must be a Kenyan," he whispered to himself.

"So what?"

"I might need to practice my few words in Swahili."

"Really?"

His conscience stung him and angered him.

He was about to hit his table when the waitress arrived, full of smile.

"Here is your double espresso and jam-filled scone. Enjoy it!"

She gave him a skewed look and hurried away.

The first sip was hot and bitter. The second sip was in a way acclimatised. After the third sip, he put the espresso cup on the table and took the scone. He took a mouthful and shook his head in agreement. It tasted good. He took his time to finish it and looked at his watch. It was late in the afternoon. He thought about going back to his hotel in Moyale Ethiopia before it got dark and find himself a good dinner.

For now, he must try to relax and to feel his surroundings as safe.

Slowly, he threw a look to his right and found that very young woman was watching him. Their eyes met and she blinked first and turned away.

He smiled. She was sitting alone, an espresso cup in front of her on the table.

He looked at the price-chart on his table denoted in Ethiopian Birr and Kenyan Shillings. He looked around and spotted the waitress and gave her a signal to collect her money, smiled at her, stood up, took his wallet out, then placed a 5-Birr note under the plate on the table. Then he took his espresso cup and went to the young lady in the corner.

"Tafadhali, kiti hiki kiko wazi?"

He smiled and begged her with his eyes, asking her whether the seat was free or not. She looked up and smiled.

"Siyo," she said.

He seemed to be confused with her negative answer. "Unasema Kiswahili, hapana?"

She wondered whether he spoke Swahili or not.

"No, not so much. I have just tried to learn a few words that could help me to start a conversation. I cannot speak Swahili."

He was about to turn around when she spoke to him in such accent-free English.

"Indeed, it has helped you to start a conversation all right. I said no to your question, but I didn't mean it. You can take the seat."

"Thank you, I am new in this city, and I needed somebody to talk to."

She smiled widely and pushed the chair for him.

"Yes, of course; sit down, please. I am a stranger myself in the city."

"Thank you," he smiled. "My name is Me'naan and this is my first time in this city."

She raised her eyebrows. "Where are you from?" She was not blinking this time.

"I am from Ethiopia, the capital city, Addis Ababa."

"Wow, I thought you were one of those Bangladeshi businessmen from Nairobi, looking for business opportunities out here in the northern periphery."

"Sorry for disappointing you. I am neither a Bangladeshi, nor a rich businessman."

"I didn't say I was disappointed."

He smiled. He stared at her unknowingly. "No, you did not."

He smiled again.

"Where are you from? Nairobi, I guess."

"You are right, I am from Nairobi originally. I came here five months ago, on a nursing internship at Moyale General Hospital, located some seven hundred metres from here to the west. I will be done with my internship in a month's time and will travel back to Nairobi. Have you ever been to Nairobi?"

"No, never."

Then he looked at the floor under his foot and disappeared into his thoughts for a few seconds.

She pulled him out of his thoughts.

"By the way, I know so many people from Ethiopia, well-educated ones for that matter, but I've never met someone so perfectly conversant in English like you."

She smiled.

He looked at her. He saw her eyes glowing, giving her sweet smile a very special effect.

"I could say something like that about you, too. It must be your profession that enabled you to easily communicate with strangers like me. But thank you for your compliment, if that is what you really mean."

"I meant that, all right." Her eyes ran all over him.

She smiled, registering a hint of shyness on his look. "What are you doing here in our Moyale city?"

"Oh, nothing. I came to Moyale Ethiopia today, a couple of hours ago, and I just wanted to experience being in a neighbouring country." He smiled. "But I never thought I would end up so quickly conversing with a Kenyan woman on a nursing internship minutes after my crossing the border." He laughed.

It was her turn this time around to disappear into her thoughts.

"You yourself speak a different English than your landsmen," he said.

She raised her eyebrows in surprise.

"How come you know that? You said you've never been to Kenya."

"I met a few journalists from Kenya in Addis Ababa, who came to participate in one of these investigative journalism workshops hosted by the US Embassy."

"Okay..."

She looked into his eyes.

He felt good and safe talking to her. He smiled.

"Yes, you have this American English accent, not the slightest hint of African accent in your pronunciation."

"You are quick to observe. Before I came back to Kenya on this nursing internship, I lived and studied in the USA for almost ten years. I studied nursing at the California State University in Sacramento and the university sent me on this internship."

"That is very interesting," he said.

"Why is that?"

She smiled and at the same time scrutinised him. He smiled back.

"Just it is interesting. Hmm, when will you travel back to the USA then?"

"I will not. I'll stay in Kenya. I have decided to live and work here. I have already signed an employment contract with the largest hospital in Nairobi."

"You are amazing!" He looked deep into her eyes.

"What?"

She looked like she was not comfortable with his sweet-talker compliments.

"I mean, choosing to live and work in your own country than in the USA, when you have the chance, that is amazing. There are many who have a big problem to just do that."

She kept quiet.

He smiled and took a deep breath.

"By the way, what was your name you said?"

"I didn't say my name. You did tell me yours and didn't ask for mine. Me'naan, correct."

He smiled again. "Yes, correct. May I ask for your name now?"

"Mary – easy to remember."

She looked at her watch.

"My shift starts at 1800, and I have to go home and be prepared for the night." She looked for the waitress and gave her a sign that she wanted to pay.

He hesitated for a while.

He couldn't raise the courage at once to tell her what he had on his mind. After she paid the waitress, she turned her attention to him.

"It was nice talking to you, Me'naan."

She stood up and stretched out her hand to him.

He stood up and took her hand and whispered without realising it.

"What are you saying?"

She wrinkled her forehead.

He shook his head.

"Can you give me five more minutes? I have something to tell you."

At first, she hesitated. Then she took a deep breath. "Sure!" She sat down before he did.

"I need your help to get in touch with this Kenyan journalist in Nairobi. I have only his name and his working address. I don't have his telephone number."

"Tell me that!"

He took out a piece of paper from his wallet and gave it to her.

"Mr David Ochieng, associate editor, *Daily Nation*, Nairobi, Kenya. What do you want me to do?"

"I want you to find his number for me. I want to get in touch with him as soon as possible."

"Are you in trouble, or what?"

He felt a sudden pang of fear. "Can you do that for me, please?"

"Yes, I can."

She looked into his eyes, and she sensed his fear.

"Is there something more you want to tell me? I am all ears."

He hesitated.

"You must make a choice, man. It is already unusual the way you contacted me. It was also such a remarkable thing to ask a woman you just met for such a favour of finding a journalist's telephone number. Now what is it that you are having such a problem telling me about?"

He sighed.

"Mary. Let us meet tomorrow here at this same time. I will tell you everything then."

"Okay."

She stood up.

"You'd better be very careful then."

She left him without saying goodbye.

Me'naan came out of the cafeteria half an hour later. At the beginning, he started moving faster towards the other side of the city in the Ethiopian territory. Thinking about the shadowy life he had started a couple of weeks ago, navigating between openness and concealment, he asked himself why he couldn't learn not to trust. That very question slowed him down.

"I might have made a blunder," he said, thinking loudly.

He checked his surroundings. No one was there.

"I am on the run. I must do something to get in touch with Ochieng. He happened to be the only person I could think of when I decided to run away to Kenya. Something tells me he could help me. So, I must get in touch with him. That is the only reason why I dared to talk to this lady. And now I am suspecting her?"

The other question that crossed his mind made him feel more troubled. "Really? Is that the only reason for you to talk to her?"

He shook his head. He had no time for such nonsense now.

He became angry about the feeling that had started churning his insides.

"She wouldn't have told me to be careful if her intention was to hurt me," he reasoned with himself.

The commotion ahead of him, on the vast, dusty open space to the left of the main road, near the roundabout in Moyale Kenya, brought him back to his senses. He saw a few dust-covered lorries lined up, and some old men guiding the livestock to the makeshift boarding bridge on to the lorries.

He had heard about these livestock transporting lorries in Moyale Kenya before he left Addis Ababa. For those commuters who could not afford to pay for the mini- planes from Moyale to Nairobi, these lorries were the only alternatives to travel by. People travelling sitting on top of a lorry, with animals standing underneath them, was a common exercise, he learned. And the ride would take three days at the minimum to cover the eight-hundred-kilometre distance between Moyale and Nairobi, with two night-long stopovers at Marsabit and Isiolo. Of this eight-hundred-kilometre-long road, about three hundred and seventy kilometres of it was gravel-surfaced road that used to easily be washed away during the rainy season.

Very much hesitating and not sure of what he was doing, Me'naan approached the commotion. He tried to figure out what language those people shouting at each other were using. At first, he was confused, listening to different languages and slangs. Slowly, he located one of the elders, who was speaking Oromo to a young man holding a bull by its horns.

He bent his head and tried to attract the attention of the old man. "Good evening, sir!"

The old man grinned in a very funny way. "Godivinin'."

He turned his eyes to the young man holding the bull's horn and said, "Gurbaa kootu namti kun mal barbaada?" – Boy, come here, what does this man want?

The young man shouted back, "Sangaa woo?" – What about the bull?

Me'naan interfered.

"Dhifama, ani Macicha, Afaan Oromoo nandubadha" – Sorry, I am Macha, I can speak Oromo.

The old man smiled wide.

"You can speak Boran?"

"If Boran means Oromo, yes," he laughed.

He stretched out his hand and greeted him. "Where are you from?"

"I am from Finfinne, Addis Ababa, Ethiopia."

"For us, Ethiopia and Kenya are our homes." He measured Me'naan with a serious look.

"As you see, we are very busy. What do you want?"

Me'naan hesitated a little bit. "Do these lorries travel to Nairobi?"

"No, these are to Marsabit. Those to Nairobi are here on Thursdays. The day after tomorrow."

"Do they take passengers?"

"Of course, if you pay good money."

"What is good money?"

The old man approached Me'naan. "You travel alone, or there are other people with you?"

"No, I am alone."

"Seven thousand shillings."

"In Ethiopian Birr?"

"I think it is 3500 Birr."

Me'naan kept quiet. Too much money, he thought. He silently calculated how much money he might have left after paying for the trip. Not so much. How could he survive both the trip and his stay in Nairobi with such little money?

"The payment also covers your two overnight stays at the hotel in Marsabit and Isiolo. But no food."

Me'naan wanted to leave the old man and run away as fast as he could. The fear inside him overwhelmed him. But he remained standing where he was.

"That is good," he said at last. "I will come back tomorrow, and we might be able to have a deal."

"You think the price is too much?"

Me'naan kept quiet. The old man smiled.

"Okay, since you are speaking my language, I will make it for you 3000 Ethiopian Birr."

"That is much better. I will be here tomorrow with the money."

"We have a deal, then?"

"Yes, we have a deal. Thank you. Bye!"

"Bye!"

The next day, he arrived at Galgaloo Cafeteria half an hour earlier than his appointment time. He wanted to be alone and think through what he would tell her and would not. When he saw her as he entered the cafeteria, he felt waves of emotion rocking his insides.

"Why is she here so early?... Is she alone?... What if she...?"

He stopped thinking as he saw her smiling at him. He smiled back and went to her. He was thinking of giving her a formal greeting. But she stood up, gave him a quick hug and shoved the chair towards him.

"Relax, man, you look frightened," she whispered to him.

"You should know, I am here because you asked me to be here."

He breathed in and out. He looked into her eyes. He stretched out his hand to her and took her right hand into his big palms.

"Thank you, Mary. I am a fugitive and very suspicious of my surroundings, you know. That is what I wanted to tell you when I asked you to meet me today. When I saw you here so early ahead of me, I was terrified."

She pulled her hand out of his soft grip.

"Early? We didn't say to meet at a definite time. You asked me to be here the same time as yesterday."

He turned his eyes to the waitress coming in their direction. Mary was first to talk to her.

"Can you make for the two of us omelettes with green chilli and tomato, please?"

"Yes, and... something to drink, too?"

"Coke for me."

And she turned to Me'naan with inviting look. "Coke for me, too."

The waitress thanked them and went back with their order.

"Sorry for not asking you what you would like to eat. I haven't eaten lunch yet, so I wanted you to eat lunch with me. That is why I took the liberty to order for two of us."

She smiled.

He smiled back.

Suddenly, the voice of the reggae king, the Jamaican Bob Marley came on the cafeteria's sound system.

"I shot the sheriff
But I didn't shoot the deputy.
I shot the sheriff
But I didn't shoot the deputy.
Oh, oh, oh. Yeh.
All over my hometown
They're trying to track me down,
They say they want to bring me in guilty
For the killing of a deputy;
For the life of a deputy. But I say
Oh no, no, no,

I shot the sheriff, But I say it was in self-defence...."

Mary moved in her seat following the beat, and smiled. "Fugitive, ha? What a coincidence."

She repeated the verse after the singer, still smiling: *"All over my hometown*

They're trying to track me down..."

"Please stop, Mary!"

She saw his fury. She stopped.

"You think it is a joke?" he whispered.

She moved her head repeatedly to the right and left. "No, I don't think so."

The waitress came with their food. The randomly broken loaf of bread and the puffy omelette on the big plate made him swallow hard. They devoured their food in silence.

It was he who started talking. She listened to his story without interfering. She felt sorry for him, for his family he left behind, for all that he was attempting to go through.

"If it was not for the passport issue, I could have helped you to travel by plane."

He looked at her.

He wanted to tell her about everything. But he changed his mind.

"You did your part, Mary. I was lucky to meet you. It didn't surprise me, but I was amazed that you could find David Ochieng in such a short period of time. Now I can call him and tell him I am on my way to Nairobi. About the trip on the cattle- transporting lorries, don't worry, my dear. I am going to make it. The old man told me there are others to travel with us, too. If they make it, I will make it."

"Then let me be with you when you go to the old man. What time are you going to meet him?"

"Wow, we only have forty-five minutes. Let me pay the bill." He looked for the waitress.

"That is not your problem."

She went to the waitress and gave her Kenyan shilling notes. The waitress thanked her enormously.

'There must be a juicy tip there,' he told himself.

As they came out of the cafeteria, she asked him, "Are you going back to collect your luggage?"

"No, I am not. I have no luggage. The one I left in the hotel was just to make them think – those who might be tailing me – that I am still around. I paid for four days. I am going to ask the old man if it is possible to stay with them tonight, for he said we are leaving early in the morning."

"Don't you need extra clothes? What if something happens on your trip?" She was serious.

He smiled.

"Do you have enough money?"

He smiled again. "Yes, I think so," he said.

He could not ask her for money. It was too much, he thought. They walked side by side silently.

As they arrived, Me'naan didn't get a chance to talk to the old man.

"Habari za jioni? U hali gani?" – Good evening, how are you? asked Mary.

The old man smiled.

"Asante, nzuri sana" – Thank you, I am doing well, he greeted her boisterously. "Na we we, hijambo?" – And you?

"Sijambo" – Fine.

Mary started the conversation in Swahili and after a long, very friendly-looking conversation, she smiled at the old man, took his hand, and pulled him to the side. Standing with her back to Me'naan, she opened her purse.

"Please help him to get to Nairobi and to make a phone call to his contact there after he arrives."

The old man embraced her gently. "For you, I can do whatever it takes. Mary, we in my family will never forget what you did for us."

"That has nothing to do with this. I was only doing my job then. I want you to do your job, too. Drive him safely to Nairobi, please."

She took the old man's big hand with her two small hands and smiled at him, asking for his assurance.

The old man smiled back and gave her his assurance without uttering a word.

Me'naan opened the door immediately as he heard the knock on the door to his room. She seemed as if she was ready to travel with him. He saw a backpack in her hand. "What is it, Mary?"

"You have only an hour. Come to the main house and have breakfast." And then she held the backpack up and gave it to him.

"I found trousers and a shirt that belonged to my brother in my wardrobe. I think it is your size. I packed bottles of water, a small bottle of marmalade, and a loaf of white sliced bread. You might need it. Hurry up."

She closed the door and went. He sat on the bed.

He searched for his wallet.

He took out the pictures of his wife and his two sons.

"The luck is on my side until now," he told them.

He wanted to cry aloud.

He missed them extremely.

Slowly, he wiped his tears, kissed the photo, and placed it inside his wallet.

To have Mary with him to the appointment he had yesterday with the old man was the best thing that had happened to him in all those experiences he was having. Not only was she softening the old man to trust Me'naan by whatever sweet-talking she had with him in Swahili, she even told the people there that Me'naan was staying overnight with her and that she would accompany him to them early in the morning. Everyone there seemed to be happy with Mary.

Me'naan was overwhelmed. Although he didn't want to be a burden to a woman he met just a day ago, he found himself in a very difficult situation to say 'no' to her offer.

'It is priceless that she trusted me to allow me to stay the night in her house knowing that I am a fugitive,' he thought.

As they moved a few yards away from those people, she smiled and patted him on the shoulder and asked him to relax. She told him that she was living in a big, rented house with two doctors and one nurse, and that they also had an extra service house in the compound intended for house workers. That is where he could sleep overnight, she told him.

When they arrived at the house, there was no one at home. First, she invited him to take a seat in the living room, and she went to the kitchen for a cold Kenyan Tusker lager beer and a glass, opened it and placed it in front of him on the sofa table.

"Bia yangu, Nchi yangu! It means my beer, my country," she smiled. "Come on, man, feel at home." She looked at her watch.

"My friends are coming home soon. I don't want to hold you here for so long."

He smiled.

She raised her eyebrows.

"No, don't take it wrongly. That is just to spare you from explaining yourself to them."

She gave him a serious look.

"Now, try to relax. Let the Tusker lager do its job. And later, you should have a very good sleep. And you need that because it is a bumpy road waiting for you for the most part of the three-day travel to Nairobi. I mean it."

"Thank you, Mary. I don't know what to say more than that."

He looked into her eyes. Then he took up the Tusker. "Cheers!"

He gulped down half of the glass without taking a breath. She smiled, passionately this time.

He finished his beer, followed her to the service house, and she showed him his bed, beautifully done.

He entered the main house carefully.

"Hello…"

He waited for an answer.

"Come to the kitchen, everybody has left. It is me alone. I have a day shift today."

He liked what he saw.

It seemed to be a big breakfast. But he was not sure what it was. She read his mind.

"Sit down, Me'naan. I'll tell you what it is."

She took one fluffy delicious pancake from the oval service plate and took a bite.

"Oh, this is sweet, and we call it in Swahili vibibi, a pancake made from rice and coconut."

She put one on his plate. She took another pasty. She placed it on his plate.

"This one is called manadazi, a deep-fried dough, similar to doughnuts." She looked at him. "This one you know. It is common over there in Ethiopia, too. We call it chapati, a flatbread fried in a pan."

She put it on his plate, too.

Then she offered him the plate holding scrambled eggs.

"This one you can serve yourself. Now, what do you prefer, tea with milk or without?"

"Without."

"Okay."

She gave him his tea.

"Here is sugar if you want."

Then she prepared her own plate and took a seat.

"Now eat your breakfast. We are running out of time. I'll drive you to your lorry." She smiled.

He smiled back.

"Is there any way I can keep contact with you, Mary?" he asked her.

She hesitated, then said, "I have plans about telephoning Ochieng in a week's time to find out how it went with you. So, if you want, I can track you through him."

"That would be nice. You are a very good person, Mary. I truly owe you a big one."

"Stop talking, eat; you don't have time."

She paused.

"Oh, for your information, you don't need to pay the old man."

"Mary... what?"

She didn't try to explain, or to give him a chance to comment on it.

After fifteen minutes, they arrived at their destination. He got out of the car first. She followed him to the lorry. He was about to take from his hidden pocket the envelope containing the money he had planned to pay with. Then he remembered. He turned to Mary and found her standing with the old man.

'How can I pay her back? Why did she take all these responsibilities? She doesn't know me.'

He sighed and looked at the old man.

His mum used to refer to such kinds of selfless persons as angels living in human bodies.

Mary must be one of those persons.

The old man grinned when he caught Me'naan's eye, and told him that he was assigned to the seat next to the driver in the cab of the blue lorry.

"Inside with the driver?" He wanted to be sure.

"Yes!" the old man smiled.

Me'naan approached Mary. She gave him a very strong hug and a goodbye kiss on his cheeks and left him before he could utter a word. He followed her with his eyes a little longer and turned around and jumped into the lorry he had been assigned to. He found a proper place at the back of his seat for the haversack Mary had given him. Then he rolled down the lorry's side window and inhaled the early-morning cold air and thanked Mary passionately while breathing out through his nose. He closed his eyes, uttered goodbye to her and made himself comfortable in his seat.

"I hope our paths might cross again, Mary!" he smiled, and leaned back.

Travelling miles on the trying road trip, the extremely jubilant lorry driver introduced all the villages and small cities they passed through: Butiye, Funanyaate, Sololo, Turbi, Bubisa, and the complementary explanation of the meaning of the names in Boran (Oromoo) languages.

After a couple of rest breaks for lunch and coffee, Me'naan registered at last that the sunset was approaching, and the energetic lorry driver was slowing down. Then he heard him saying that they were shortly arriving at Marsabit, the city where they were going to stop overnight.

Next day, they started their trip early in the morning and arrived at Isiolo after sunset. On this trip, the driver was less jubilant, but briefer and concise. On the third day, he was back again. An hour and a half into their trip from Isiolo, they arrived in Nanyuki and took a short break. Me'naan was about to fall into his own thoughts when the driver started roaring with excitement and happiness. Me'naan wanted to know what was going on. He gazed at the driver.

The driver smiled widely.

He pointed to his right through the side window and Me'naan saw it.

"That is Mount Kenya, my brother. The resting place for the Muwene Nyaga [God] of the Kikuyu people. Hereafter, he is supposed to accompany me so that I arrive safely in Nairobi."

He breathed deep and turned his eyes to Me'naan for a moment and back to the asphalted highway.

"How much do you know about the Kikuyu people?"

Me'naan raised his shoulder, saying not much.

But the driver felt very much relaxed and demonstrated to Me'naan the way he was changing gear.

Then he smiled.

"We Kenyans owe the Kikuyus a lot. They were the ones who fought against the British occupation that started at the end of the 1880s and against the waves of white emigrants that started right after the turn of 1900. Kikuyus were evicted out of their fertile highlands and were targeted by both the colonial forces and the Maasai tribes' warriors recruited by the colonial British East African Company. Though Kikuyus were brave fighters, they lost the war against the European settlers because of their substandard armaments. The ruler of southern Kikuyu land, the one who governed over the Dagoretti surroundings – the area's name is given to the marketplace we are heading to – was buried alive after he had inflicted a lot of damage on the settlers."

"I didn't know a lorry driver could be such an outstanding history teacher," Me'naan smiled.

"I have a first degree in history from Mount Kenya University and I am one of the owners of this business, too," he smiled back.

Me'naan raised his eyebrows and appreciated him.

"I thought you were Boran or Gabbra, from the old man's conversation with you."

"I am Boran, all right. But if one listens to the folklore of the Kikuyu, one can easily conclude that we are from the same ancestry. Kikuyu, the right name is Agikuuyuu, and it means 'children of the big sycamore'. We, the Borans and the Gabbras, have a big respect for the Oda tree, which in Afaan Oromoo means also Big Sycamore Tree. So, my brother, you yourself are related to Kikuyus, believe me."

Me'naan yawned and closed his eyes.

Arriving at Thika, the busy city about forty kilometres to the northeast of Nairobi, the driver wanted to have a fifteen-minute rest. Me'naan chose to remain in his seat in the lorry's cab. Twenty minutes later, as they drove through the last exit gate of the city, Me'naan observed the driver was very quiet and concentrated, maybe thinking of arriving in Nairobi before the sunset.

Me'naan took a deep breath.

He thought he would at last get the opportunity and the solitude he truly desired to sort out his thoughts.

When the driver turned to him and told him that their last destination, Dagoretti cattle market at the outskirts of Nairobi was only thirty kilometres away, Me'naan asked the driver if it was okay to take a siesta.

"I know it is not right to doze sitting beside a driver, but I just wanted to close my eyes and do some thinking."

"No problem, my brother. I am not the kind of driver to be distracted so easily. Unless, of course, you are snoring." He gazed at Me'naan and laughed aloud.

Me'naan smiled. "I don't do that."

Me'naan closed his eyes and sighed.

"Yes, I am a fugitive. Arrest is what I am running away from. But I didn't commit any crime except for openly criticising the government's abuse of power."

He thought of Mary moving in her seat following the rhythm of Bob Marley's song 'I Shot the Sheriff' in that Galgalo cafeteria in Moyale.

He smiled and went back to his thoughts.

Me'naan had resisted for so long not to flee his country and become a refugee, because that was homelessness acknowledged internationally. He hated to be treated as homeless and a nobody. A nobody was easy to victimise, as well as to mistrust. The word of a nobody against anyone serving any kind of a system was doomed to be doubted. No matter how truthful and innocent a person was, becoming a refugee robbed him/her of the right and the ability to be trusted.

Me'naan's decision to remain in his country for so long was not only because he hated to be a refugee. He was at his prime age, and he wanted to play a role in bringing progress. He thought his exposure to the better way of thinking and life-standards of other developed countries would arm him to smoothly bring forward ideas about the need to learn to accommodate opposing views in a country that happened to be a place where a constantly changing definition of internal enemy by the abusive elites had exposed hundreds of thousands of people to torture and extrajudicial killing. He wanted to play his part in bridging the gap that was widening each passing day among the various constituencies, eroding the sense of solidarity needed for good and constructive thinking to flourish, without being part of the pattern of the abusive power constellation. He thought the lack of equal and meaningful conversation could be addressed, if at least basic information was accessible to the uninformed majority. He wanted, using his pen and the resources he had, to fight and subdue the urge among elite politicians to become a ruling class by willingly climbing the bloodiest ladder to the podium of executioners, not to that of leaders.

'How foolish I was…'

Me'naan moved in his seat without opening his eyes.

He remembered how isolated he had become in his position as a government office-holder because of his political stand. His refusal to gratify nonsensical egoistical wishes by the decree of organisational discipline, to be a mouthpiece of any organisation, any group, or the government whose instruments were usurped by elites who defined their own landsmen as an internal enemy and worked hard to inflict damage on them, had almost cost him his life. After he was fired from his job, he clearly saw the hostility fomenting between those in power and the ordinary people. There was no common ground that could help ease the tension. Everyone seemed to be engaged in opposition. As much as he loved and appreciated independence, he hated those independent thoughts promoting a cancel culture, one of which he believed he was witnessing since he became able to understand the political dispensations in his country. When Me'naan himself became a victim to this cancel culture, he gave up. It was too much to cope with when he at last learned that he, in his own country, had been taken for somebody else than who and what he truly was. He was defined and painted in such a way with the goal to facilitate his condemnation. His dream to be able to see the leaders of his country give humanity, solidarity, and fraternity a chance, was wrongly interpreted.

It was Me'naan's engagement in such a titanic project to bring change in people's way of thinking as a journalist in the private sector that enabled him to face the ugly reality on the ground. The animosity that was fomenting everywhere was beyond his understanding. He uncovered the fact that the abuse of power against innocent citizens, especially by prosecuting authorities, amounted to horror staged by a maniacal transgressor. He registered how these brutalities shattered the lives of tens of thousands and the universe that embraced that very life. Everywhere he found sorrow and revulsion.

Me'naan had published the stories of victims who gave up on living, and by doing so how they conquered their own body and stopped feeling pain. He reported how the brave actions of victims to not feel pain exhausted their tormentors to the level that they were compelled to ask for a helping hand to continue the beatings of those tortured bodies that couldn't react to the savagery in the interrogation cells.

Me'naan always wondered: What was the real reason for these endless barbaric interrogations, and the willingness of the interrogators to perform such an evil act to flourish? What could be the justification for inflicting such unbearable pain on a human body by a human being?

It could not be the mere dedication to uphold the law, since the one thing the law clearly protected was and is the life and wellbeing of a person until proven guilty. Rather, it must be something devilish, maybe the ruling ideology that paints and defines the so-called internal enemies in such a bad image, or the constant misinformation, on State-owned media or elsewhere, that hardens the hearts of these people.

'And all these abuses start with a simple arrest,' he thought.

In an instant, people were made lawbreakers, and as such were subject to unlawful treatments, of which even the very law they were saying they were protecting wouldn't approve.

'One must run away from such barbaric incidents if it is possible,' he said to himself.

Me'naan's experience of an arrest was mild in relation to the experiences of the people he made news about. But at the time he was confronted with the inevitable: those stories he published triggered the flight alarm in him, and he decided to run away.

It was the police officer on duty that day who randomly asked him whether he had had his lunch.

At first, Me'naan thought it was a joke.

"Did you hear me?" the police officer asked him again.

Me'naan was alarmed.

"Yes…" He hesitated.

The officer became serious.

"The officer who summoned you here is out of the office right now. You can come back after you have had your lunch."

Me'naan got the message. But he still needed confirmation as to whether he understood him right.

"What time should I have to come back?"

"That one, you should decide yourself."

Then the police officer pushed him towards the outer gate and closed it behind him.

Me'naan hurried to his office. On his way, he thought about every possible scenario that was going to happen to him.

Did he need to inform everybody about what he had just experienced at the police station? His answer came quickly, no!

As he arrived at his office, he chose to tell his co-workers that he had received an emergency call from his mother and that he was travelling to her, and that he would be away for some days.

Then he asked his deputy editor-in-chief to have a private chat with him. In his office, he told him that he didn't meet the officer who had summoned him to the police station.

"I am sure he will come back to look for me. In that case, you just tell him where I am headed to, and that I will be back next week."

On his way back home, he thought about the police officer who had ushered him out of the compound of that police station.

"It must have been his life's decision to let a wanted man go free," he sighed.

"Indeed, it is one quaver from evil to good, as it is from good to evil," he concluded with a sentence from which he couldn't remember the source.

Coming home, he told his wife that he was going underground. He begged her to tell anyone who enquired after him on the phone that he had travelled to his mother because she had gotten sick and that he would come back after a week.

The news created insecurity and fear, both to him and his wife. Leaving her alone, pregnant with twins, and two small boys to be taken care of, it was a topic he knowingly avoided for he has no energy to discuss. Deep inside they both are terrified. But no one of them admitted it. Next morning, the officer called Me'naan's home. Me'naan's wife answered and told him as she was told.

There was no preparation for Me'naan's departure. He didn't bother with travel documents either. He realised that it would be impossible to get the necessary documents without being exposed. He decided to take his chance without travel documents.

Now, two weeks later, he was sitting inside the cab of a lorry for cattle transportation, heading towards Nairobi, a few kilometres away from his last destination.

He opened his eyes and closed them immediately. Mary came to his mind.

'What a kind and generous person she is.'

The hospitality Mary had shown him boosted his hopes of getting the help he so badly needed from David Ochieng. He sensed also that she might well get in touch with Ochieng as she promised.

'I am so lucky. Thank you, Almighty. What more should I ask for?'

It was late in the afternoon when the lorry reached the Dagoretti livestock market located on the outskirts of Nairobi city and Kiambu county in Kenya. The market was also known as Ndonyo, meaning 'marketplace' in the Kikuyu language, and served the residents of Nairobi, Kiambo and Kajido cities.

After watching for a while the driver getting into what looked like business commotion with those people surrounding him, shouting and arguing with him immediately after he had killed the motor of the lorry, Me'naan found a corner not far from where they parked the lorry with a tree shed and a stone pile to sit on. Just as he was about to rest on the bigger stone, lowering his backpack to the ground, the lorry driver called his name.

"Me'naan!"

Me'naan turned around.

"You have not arrived at your destination yet. We are on the outskirts of Nairobi. The old man told me strictly that I must look to it that you come to the Kilimani area in Nairobi. Do you know where the Yaya Centre is?"

Three people were following the driver.

He stopped them by telling them to wait for a minute.

Me'naan smiled and whispered, "You know this is my first time in Nairobi!" Me'naan grinned.

"Sorry. Mary wanted you to spend the night at her relatives' house at Tigoni Road, not far from the Yaya Centre. Wait..."

He took a piece of paper with a note on it from his coat's inside pocket.

"Twin Oaks Apartments is the name. Here is the number we should call. Mary said she would inform them beforehand, so they are expecting you. I will find a taxi, then I'll call the person and tell them which taxi is driving you to this address. Okay?"

Me'naan couldn't utter a word.

'Oh, Mary...," he sighed to himself.

Eleven months after he arrived in Nairobi, Me'naan boarded a bus together with other refugees destined for resettlement abroad that would take them to the Jomo Kenyatta International Airport, forty kilometres away from Kangemy Refugee Centre. All of them were packed with IOM (International Organization of Migration) paraphernalia.

Me'naan felt in his bones the unknown he was heading into. Since he had learnt two days earlier that his destination in his resettlement country of Norway was a reception centre for asylum seekers located in an out-of-sight, remote countryside with few residents somewhere in the northwestern part of Norway, he was not sure whether all he went through was worth this kind of last-minute revelation. Why? Another screening again? How long should his family wait to be rescued?

He recalled, however, his was a relatively quick process in Kenya. The time he spent in a relatively well-furnished refugee centre in Nairobi waiting to be resettled in a third country was a tiny fraction compared to those refugees who spent years or decades in the most remote areas in Kenya under most unbearable living conditions in refugee camps.

How was this possible?

David Ochieng, the journalist Me'naan became acquainted with at a journalistic workshop held in Addis Ababa, received a phone call from his fiancée one late evening.

"Guess who I met today?" She was full of smiles.

"Don't tell me you met a gentleman that would replace me in that remote area you chose to hide yourself in."

"Dave, don't say that. I am not hiding. I am doing a service to my country and my people, and that includes you, too."

Ochieng laughed and excused himself. "Okay, tell me."

"A person named Me'naan, who happened to be acquainted with you in one of your sojourns in Addis

Ababa months ago. I think he is on the run, my dear. He directly approached me in a cafeteria where I was having my afternoon espresso and asked me in Swahili whether the seat at my table was free."

"Oh...?"

"Yeah. Then, after a short while, as if you had put a hidden stamp on my forehead that tells strangers that I have a relationship with you, he asked me to help him find your phone number."

"What...?"

"Yeah, that was the same way I felt at first. But then I saw how desperate he was and promised him at last that I would try my best. Tomorrow, early in the morning, he is travelling to Nairobi riding one of the lorries of that Boran livestock merchant. I once helped his pregnant daughter with that life-threatening complication I told you about."

"Is he with you now?"

"No, not with me. He is staying overnight in the house workers' service-house, outside the main house. Even those who are living with me didn't see him. I just didn't want him to have to explain himself, you know. I promised I'd drive him to the old man early in the morning. I didn't tell him our relationship."

"That is the woman I love, highly adore and respect." Ochieng blew a kiss to her down the phone.

"I paid the old man for the trip and asked him to see to it that Me'naan comes into contact with you as soon as possible."

"I look forward to meeting him, Mary. By the way, I miss you at a time like this. You know for sure what I would have done to you after hearing such an amazing story."

"If you miss me, come to me."

"Soon, my love, soon."

A few days after he met Me'naan in Nairobi, Ochieng arranged the first meeting between Me'naan and the reporters from the *Kenyan Nation* newspaper on 1st May, the international Labour Day. The meeting took place at the office complex of the *Nation* newspaper in the heart of Nairobi. The security check, the registration process to enter the compound, and the huge office complex with all the gadgets of modern technology were unimaginable for Me'naan. He had seen no equal establishment of this kind in his own country.

A day after the interview, the *Nation* newspaper published Me'naan's story. A day after that, *Sunday Nation*, in its editorial about the Press Day and the ideals of liberty, discussed Me'naan's issue at length. Right after that, Ochieng was contacted by various people from the Ethiopian Embassy and the Ethiopian community in Nairobi with a demand to help them get in touch with Me'naan. Me'naan became terrified and told Ochieng that he didn't want to come into contact with anybody, either from the Ethiopian Embassy or the Ethiopian community. He reminded Ochieng about refugees who had been targeted and deported out of Nairobi by the Ethiopian Embassy, and pleaded with him to help him get protection from UNHCR as a refugee.

Two weeks later, Ochieng drove Me'naan to the office of the Kenyan Union of Journalists at Chester House. There, Me'naan was received by the secretary general of the Kenyan Union of Journalists and they discussed at length the problem he and fellow journalists in his home country were facing and the challenging situation he was in. After their more than an hour-long discussion, the secretary general agreed to send a letter to the United Nations Higher Commission for Refugees (UNHCR), Jesuit Refugee Service (JRS), the International Federation of Journalists (IFJ), and to the Committee to Protect Journalists (CPJ), describing Me'naan's situation.

Again, two weeks later, Ochieng brought to Me'naan the letter the general secretary of the KUJ wrote to the UNHCR protection officers' office. Me'naan took the letter and went to the UNHCR head office in Westlands, Nairobi. It was not easy for Me'naan to meet in person the protection officer the letter was addressed to. Instead, a Somali woman working there promised to hand over the letter to the office of protection officers.

The next afternoon, Ochieng met Me'naan and told him that the UNHCR protection officer had sent a message to the KUJ telling them that they wanted to meet Me'naan the next day. It was good news for Me'naan. Ochieng handed over to him the letter he was supposed to show at the gate of the UNHCR office in Westlands the next morning. The interview at the UNHCR office took hours. He documented his case with pictures and excerpts from newspaper publications. He identified himself with the ID-cards he had with him. He even had been given the opportunity to call his wife at their home in Addis.

He left the interview room at three thirty p.m., and was told to wait in the waiting room. Half an hour later, another protection officer received him in her office and told him that they had arranged a car for him and that he would be taken to a refugee rehabilitation centre in Nairobi, where he would stay until he obtained resettlement.

Me'naan, cut off from the outside world, accustomed himself step by step to the life in the Kangemy rehabilitation centre. While waiting for the day he would be summoned to process his travel abroad, he became acquainted with refugees who had survived genocide in Rwanda and Burundi, civil wars in Somalia and Congo. He sat down with people limping around with body parts badly damaged, and who were there in the centre to get both medical and physiotherapy treatment, and he listened to the horrific stories of human atrocity that traversed both national and international borders. He kept jotting down in his diary from the first day he started his conversations with these marvellous people, how their extreme willpower to survive and move on kept them alive. They became his mentors in a very different way. He admired their dreams, no matter how precarious it sounded. He applauded those who made it possible for these people to dream again.

It also happened to be one of his daily routines that he, after lunch, directly went to the relatively big room he was living in, sharing with dozens of other refugees from various African countries, to take a half-hour siesta lying on his bed, and then to come out and sit together with the doorman, a Kenyan named Simon Wanbugu, one of the attendants to the entrance of the Kangemi rehabilitation centre. Simon was often kind enough to allow him to step out of the compound and sit under the shade of the big tree on the right side of the entrance gate, just leaning to the fence separating the centre from the outside world.

Most of the time he sat there alone and contemplated about everything: his wife, his small boys, his friends, his trip to Nairobi, his contact with Ochieng, his current life and his future. What an endless review. Sometimes, when the Kenyan ladies were passing by, he kept his eyes following them, while wondering and admiring their gorgeousness, their grace, and their seemingly very loud conversation.

Me'naan had shared this tree-shade a couple of times with an outstanding person, a medical doctor with twelve years of experience working for the United Nations, who also spoke five languages fluently: English, German, Arabic, Somali and Swahili. He was a Somali citizen whom he was acquainted with on the first day he arrived at the rehabilitation centre. The doctor was once badly injured, while working with medical professionals from three European countries in a place called Jazeera, some twenty kilometres to the south-west of the capital city Mogadishu, when Somali rebels shot him in his chest and arms and left him for dead. Against all the odds, he survived. Under the protection of UNHCR, he received treatment that helped him to function again in the rehabilitation centre. Three days ago, through the travel arrangement organised by the International Organisation for Migration, IOM, he travelled to New Zealand to be resettled in the country located in the south-western Pacific Ocean.

He remembered, it was he, Me'naan, who first told the doctor that the UNHCR had found a third country for him where he could soon be resettled. The doctor congratulated him and told him that Norway was the country most favoured by so many worldwide to live in. At that time, the doctor didn't have any information at all about his and his wife's resettlement. But then, bloody bomb explosions occurred in front of the American Embassy in the centre of Nairobi, Kenya, and in Dar es Salaam, Tanzania, in the late hours of that cloudy Friday. The damage caused by the explosion in Nairobi, Kenya, was so huge that the rescue work to save the lives of those buried under debris took more than five days. The death toll jumped over three hundred, and more than five thousand people were injured. The material damage was estimated to be around thirty billion Kenyan shillings. The bomb blast was undoubtedly masterminded by terrorist groups, and that occurrence impacted very much on the UNHCR plan to resettle refugees in other countries.

While the UNHCR in Kenya postponed its plan for refugee resettlement, the USA conducted an air raid in northern Sudan and on the border between Afghanistan and Pakistan in punishing the terrorists who had masterminded the blast. The air raid happened about two weeks after the bomb blast occurred. Three months and three weeks after this bloody incident, the UNHCR resettlement processes resumed by screening anew all the refugees who had already been granted resettlement in a third country.

A day after his Somali friend left for New Zealand, Me'naan spent the whole day at the UNHCR office at Westlands, Nairobi, Kenya, attending the interview process conducted by the Norwegian immigration officers who came direct from Norway. He was interviewed by a very decent and quiet person, apparently in his late fifties, with golden grey hair and beard. Me'naan was presented to this immigration officer by the UNHCR protection officer, a young Kenyan law-school graduate named Florence

Mugenda, who interviewed Me'naan almost five months earlier, after which the UNHCR granted him protection as a refugee and sent him to the Kangemi Rehabilitation Centre. The interview went smoothly. At the end, the Norwegian advised Me'naan to be prepared for every possible thing he might encounter. He told him that he would hear the result in a week's time and wished him good luck. The next day, the lady in charge of the protection office at the UNHCR head office in Nairobi, a Danish woman named Anne, came to Kangemi Rehabilitation Centre. On her way out of the compound, she saw Me'naan sitting under the shade of the tree. She stopped her car, rolled down the window and greeted him. He stood up, hurried towards her, and greeted her warmly. After a few exchanges of good words, she told him that he had made a very good impression upon the interviewers from Norway. She motivated him by telling him that it could be a matter of weeks to get resettled in his new country. Then she, too, wished him good luck.

Me'naan yawned, then stretched himself out against the trunk of the big tree, his hands clasped behind his head, looking up into the gorgeously formed branches.

'I do need that good luck all the way!' he said to himself.

"I was fortunate to have luck all through my escape journeys that brought me to this junction. And I want to continue having that unbelievable experience."

He smiled and remembered all that had happened to him since his arrival in Nairobi. His experience with Mary was especially extraordinary.

The day Ochieng told him that Mary was his fiancée, Me'naan couldn't utter a word.

He looked at Ochieng with his eyes bulging in sheer surprise. "What a coincidence!" Me'naan shouted. "My goodness, as desperate as I was, I went to where she was sitting, talking to her in Swahili, using my few picked words to start a conversation, then asking her to help me find a phone number to a man who is her fiancé?... Wow!"

Ochieng laughed and acknowledged how lucky Me'naan was.

Now, here he was again, at Jomo Kenyatta airport, standing at the boarding gate, an hour before midnight, gazing at the IOM field officer talking to a female boarding assistant, and wondering what to expect when the plane that was taking him to Norway landed at its last destination.

He landed at his last destination, Kristiansund Kverneberget airport, after eighteen hours and three in-between landings and transfers.

It was an hour after midnight. There were few people in that small Dash 8 airplane, bearing the name Widerøe, the Norwegian regional airline.

"What darkness, and what cold!" he whispered to himself as he stepped out of the airplane. Going down the stairs, the IOM paraphernalia in a plastic bag containing his travel documents hanging on his wrist, he thought about his wife, his children, and his life.

'They might celebrate if they knew that I have safely arrived in Norway. But I cannot celebrate because I don't know what is waiting for me.'

Then, as he entered the well-lit waiting room, he saw his welcoming Norwegian officials holding a sheet of paper upon which his name was written, ANAATOLI, Me'naan Tuuji. They put his grandfather's name first, reciprocating to the family name hierarchy in Norway, in block letters.

It was a short welcoming ceremony. First, a bouquet of flowers was presented to him. Then the older man addressed him in English.

"Welcome to Norway, Anaatoli Me'naan Tuuyi. Correct me if my pronunciation is incorrect."

"Tuuji! You can call me Me'naan," Me'naan responded.

The old man smiled.

"Right. My name is Dahlem Tor. I am the CEO of the Tingvoll Refugee Reception Centre. Our centre is located fifty kilometres away from here at Tingvollvågen. It is about a forty-five-minute drive. We have a minivan, so if you are tired you can take a nap on the way to our centre. We have some sandwiches and mineral water in the car. Formal briefings you will receive tomorrow in my office. Shall we go to the baggage reclaim for your baggage?"

"No, I have no baggage except these ones."

He touched the backpack hanging on his shoulder and pointed to the IOM plastic bag hanging on his wrist.

"Okay, then, let us go to the car."

Me'naan thanked them and followed them to the car.

Tingvollvågen, or Tingvoll, is a very quiet village serving as the administrative centre for the Tingvoll municipality that belongs to Møre and Romsdal county in western Norway. The population size in the whole municipality was about three thousands. The number of residents in the Tingvollvågen village where the refugee reception centre was located was about three hundred persons. There were two hotels, two supermarkets, a bookstore, and other facilities, clustered in the centre of the village. The one bookstore in the village was owned by the CEO of the Tingvoll Refugee Centre, Dahlem Tor. Me'naan gathered this information from his first-day briefing by Dahlem himself, and from repeated tours he had conducted to the village to buy some necessities.

A few hundred metres away from the refugee reception centre, the Tingvoll church stood tall. It was a young asylum seeker, one of those from Africa he met in the refugee reception centre, who brought the church to his attention. On the first Sunday after his arrival at the reception centre, around lunch-time,

Me'naan was making coffee in the shared kitchen for the residents of the centre.

The young man greeted him.

"Good morning? How do you feel the cold? February is the coldest month in Norway, especially in this area."

"I am feeling it all right. I assume even the people seem to be very cold. And that might be because of the impact of the weather. Those few people I happened to meet on the street, they don't have any hint of a smile on their faces."

"You are right. When outside at this time of the year, people are more concerned about protecting themselves from the cold. They don't seem to bother to give or take a smile. But inside, it is a different story."

"Inside where? Is there anyone who would open his/her door for you?" Me'naan looked at the young man with curiosity.

"For example, the church," the young man smiled.

"You go to church? How long have you been in this centre?"

The young man shrugged his shoulders expressing indifference. "Over three years now, or maybe more."

Me'naan was about to shout out his anger when another man, an asylum seeker living in the centre, seemingly from the Middle East, came into the kitchen.

Me'naan counted to ten and calmed himself down. This had become his anger-control procedure since the first day he ran away from his country.

He poured himself his coffee and took a seat at the table in the corner of the kitchen.

"No way would I stay here for so long. It is just unfair. I shouldn't be here in the first place. Norway brought me here to give me protection, not to keep me inside an asylum seekers' refuge."

He felt exhausted and couldn't find peace with himself.

Unwillingly, he turned his attention towards the figure approaching him.

Politely, but earnestly, the young man asked him if he would join him going to church. Me'naan smiled and shook his head.

"I don't do a church thing. I have my God everywhere with me."

"That is good. But being together with others, listening to God's words, gives you hope and strength. That is how I cope with the painful tension I am living with each passing day."

"That is what it is, religion. It encourages you to be submissive to unfairness, rather than acting on your own to fight it and solve it. You must know that it works on you like anaesthesia works on an injured body, to make you able to tolerate the intolerable."

The young man failed to see his point. "What is wrong with that? To be able to tolerate the intolerable is the power you need to conquer the devilish cruelty through time."

Me'naan raised his arms. "Okay, brother. We will never come to an agreement because we both argue based on our conviction. However, I think it is a good idea to be somewhere than to stay confined in my room all day. But remember this, I don't need you to tell me as if you know my God better than me. I rather want to see how people are inside the church – warm or cold. Okay?"

The young man smiled and praised him.

"That is okay with me. God bless you."

The interior of the church was breathtakingly beautiful. The high walls of the church, built from rocks and stones, fused with the shiny brown benches; the raised altar where believers received the blessings of God during the mass by taking the sanctified bread and wine from the priest; the beautifully clothed lectern from where the priest read his bible and conducted the religious services; and all the pictures lined up on the wall as reverence and memorial to those who certainly had paid decisive roles in establishing and leading this parish church originating in the eleventh or twelfth centuries; and the purposely dimmed lights all together created a sort of sacred tranquillity that indeed tempted a person to assume divine calmness.

Sitting there in complete quietness, Me'naan thought solemnly about religion and religious activities, about belief and veneration, about adoration and devotion that had for many centuries devastated human lives rather than blessing them. Even in the church the sword was the effective weaponry of subduing people to the so-called words of God, not the pure preaching of those who insisted the almighty God had revealed himself to them. He thought also about how the power of devotion to any kind of religion made someone less mindful to pain and hardship, to the man-made tribulations and sufferings, and to all the discomforts that otherwise could have been solved by using the one especial gift God had given to humans, that is the human mind, the human brain.

He moved in his seat and watched the proceedings in the church. He tried to locate smiling faces and warm receptions. He found none until a woman, followed by her two teenage sons, approached him and asked him with such a gorgeous smile to let them pass to sit on the very bench he was sitting on. He smiled back quietly and stood up and let them pass.

"God has many ways of answering your call. Me'naan, it is your decision to acknowledge it or not."

He shook his head to get rid of the sentences he felt reverberating in his head.

"What a joke, God sending me a smiling woman with her two children? What poor thinking!"

Me'naan turned his head slightly and looked at the woman with her two children.

"Is it?"

Another question echoed in his head immediately. Me'naan became restless.

"Wow, this must be the kind of revelation people are talking about." He smiled. He shook his head again.

'Calm down, man. Calm down. You didn't come here for this.' He tried to jump out of the situation he had immersed himself in.

'What did you come here for? Isn't it to find smiling people? Don't run away from the truth.'

Me'naan rested his head on his palms.

'Oh my God, what is going on in my head?' He slowly stood up and left his seat.

At the coffee break, while intermingling in the foyer of the church, the sons of the woman with the gorgeous smile approached him and greeted him politely and asked him where he came from.

'Not again!' he said to himself.

He smiled to them hesitantly.

He told them where he came from.

Then, for a minute or so, he stood there dumbfounded, failing to react properly to the fluent greetings communicated to him in Amharic, the broadly spoken language in Ethiopia, by those teenagers. He put his hands on his mouth and took time to work out what was happening.

The boys smiled and took his reaction as a positive surprise.

"Oh, sorry, boys. Meeting a child speaking the language of my country in this remote part of Norway is not something I was expecting."

He smiled widely and gave them a hug. Then he approached their mother.

"You, too, speak Amharic, am I right?"

She answered him in a dialect he was aware of, having its origin in southern Ethiopia. He looked into her eyes and smiled.

"How come you people speak the language so fluently?" Me'naan asked.

"Well, I am a nurse by profession and worked as a missionary in Arba Minch for over twenty years. My children were born there."

She, too, looked into his eyes and smiled.

He took her hand into his hands and smiled back.

"Oh my God, what an amazing coincidence. I came to this church today looking for smiling souls in the church, and my God sends me you with your children and the most gorgeous smile I no longer remember when I have seen last, and above all, speaking the language of my country."

The young man from the refugee reception centre approached from behind and smiled widely.

"Be grateful, Me'naan. This is the house of God, where you can find what you are looking for."

Me'naan silently released the hand of the woman.

The young man greeted the two boys and their mother in English and turned his face to Me'naan.

Me'naan stopped him short.

He stretched his hand to the mother of the two boys again.

"My name is Me'naan. I am staying at Tingvoll Refugee Reception Centre. I am new around here and don't know how long I am staying in the centre. It was nice meeting you and your boys."

Me'naan didn't wait for her answer. He gave her a strong handshake and left the church.

On his way back to the centre, he thought seriously about his experience in the church. Such a revelation was mysterious, of course, he argued. But it could not be in any way related to God's miracle whatsoever, he assured himself.

Then he thought about the incidence in Moyale, how he met Mary, the very first day he crossed the border to Moyale, Kenya, the fiancée of the journalist whom he planned to get in touch with when he decided to leave his country.

That was another coincidence again. No more, no less.

'Another lucky occurrence in the middle of nowhere? To what end? Why is this happening to me?'

Me'naan started jogging towards the centre. He denied himself the chance to confront the ideas reverberating in his head again.

'I am far away from danger now. I can sort out on my own the reason why I ended up in this asylum seekers' centre. I don't see any need for me to recheck my understanding of divine power.'

He abruptly stopped. He shook his head.

He was not entirely convinced. 'Whatever!' he said to himself.

A week after his church visit, Dahlem Tor invited Me'naan to his office at the refugee reception centre, poured him a cup of coffee and asked him to sit down.

"As I told you, Me'naan, my responsibility here is only an administrative one. It is all about securing accommodation, providing basic information and necessary daily services to the residents of the centre. I have no way of knowing or impacting asylum seekers' cases."

"That is where the core of the misunderstanding lies. I am not an asylum seeker. I am a refugee sent by UNHCR in Nairobi, Kenya, to Norway to be resettled. That is why I think you are entitled to ask the authorities in charge what a quota refugee – that means a resettlement refugee – is doing in this reception centre. Because UNHCR couldn't give me a permanent solution in Kenya, I was offered resettlement in a third country, that is Norway."

Me'naan tried to vent his frustration in a more decisive and persuasive way.

"Yes, you have told me these things so many times. I have forwarded the very point you raised to the authorities at the Directorate of Immigration, UDI, from the day you told me. At last I received an answer today and that is why I have invited you to come to my office."

Me'naan was curious.

"UDI wants you to contact the sheriff's office in Tingvoll for further clarification, and the sheriff told me that they have reserved an appointment for you on Wednesday at ten a.m."

"Sheriff's office?"

Me'naan felt alarmed. The adrenaline blast in his blood started wetting his forehead. Slowly, he put down on the table the coffee cup he was sipping from.

Dahlem continued with his explanation.

"Yes, the UDI people say they want you to be interviewed at the sheriff's office."

Me'naan couldn't hide the fact that he was upset. Although he had been restlessly waiting for messages from UDI for weeks, he was more confused now after he had heard what Dahlem told him.

"Why?" he uttered to himself. And then smiled.

He reminded himself that Dahlem Tor had absolutely no knowledge about what was going on. Therefore, it didn't help to argue with him.

Me'naan breathed deep and stretched himself in his seat.

"By the way, Norway has sheriffs in the city? I thought sheriffs belong to the West, especially the USA?"

Dahlem smiled.

"No, it is a Norwegian thing. In the olden times, governors in various counties established the farmers' ombudsman as an agent of law-keeping, to be able to collect taxes and fees from the peasants. Today's sheriff's office, Lensmannskontor, is the continuation of this development with the responsibility of a police authority. We have sheriffs in small villages like Tingvoll all over the country. Does it make sense?" Dahlem laughed.

Me'naan smiled.

On Wednesday, Me'naan arrived at the sheriff's office ten minutes ahead of time. The receptionist, a young lady with shoulder-length golden hair, asked him to wait in the waiting room and said that he would be contacted when the time came.

The sheriff, very young looking, came to the waiting room on time and called his name. "Me'naan?"

Me'naan stood up and answered the call. "That is me."

"Welcome to Tingvoll Lensmannskontor!" the sheriff greeted him warmly.

"Thank you."

"Follow me, please!"

Me'naan followed the sheriff back to his office.

The sheriff let Me'naan get into the office and closed the door. He directed him to where he was supposed to sit.

There she was, the woman he had met in the church. This time, her face was without the hint of a smile. She was as earnest as a woman could be.

She stood up and greeted him coldly.

"Good morning."

Me'naan was speechless.

He greeted her, bending his head.

"Please, sit down Me'naan!"

The sheriff smiled. "Let me introduce myself. My name is Eirik Olsen. I am the sheriff of Tingvoll. This is Anne Marit Henriksen. She is Norwegian American and speaks Amharic, too. The Norwegian directorate of immigration assigned her to conduct today's interview. I am here to keep the record of the interview. Since you registered that your mother tongue is Afaan Oromo and that you can speak English, we thought it might be comfortable for you to give your interview in English."

Me'naan felt a stomach-churning disgust for everything that had evolved since he entered the sheriff's office. He hated himself. He regretted silently his choice of the third country he was supposed to resettle in. He chose Norway as it was suggested by UNHCR in Kenya and because he was afraid to wait indefinitely for another chance to surface.

He threw a sigh.

"Why are you interviewing me? I didn't come to Norway to seek asylum. I have been sent here for resettlement. I have gone through all the necessary interviews in Nairobi, Kenya, by your own immigration officers. I was screened twice before those officials decided to send me here. Then, why do you want to interview me again?"

The more he spoke, the more he became furious.

"My family is waiting to be rescued. That is why I said yes to the first choice given to me to be resettled in Norway, to be able to rescue them. They are suffering because of me. I was happy coming to Norway as I was visioning to be able to reunite with them quickly after my arrival here."

He had tears in his eyes, but refused to let them run.

The sheriff seemed to be confused with all that he was hearing. He tried to comfort Me'naan.

Anne Marit Henriksen was indifferent.

"It is up to you, Me'naan. Look, the authorities think you have not told them everything you should tell them. That is why they want you to be interviewed again. So, I advise you to tell them everything. Answer the questions they have for you adequately and you will be seeing results in no time. I mean it, it is up to you."

"You are not serious, are you? First and foremost, you sound like those cruel interrogators who made my life unbearable in the country I was forced to run away from. You don't seem to be part of the Norwegian history I have been told about: fair and justice-loving people and a democratic country with the rule of law."

He looked at her with bulging eyes.

"Tell me who these authorities you are talking about are. Who are they? Are you saying Norwegian authorities think I am not telling them the truth?"

She kept her earnest look and answered him sarcastically, "Those authorities who were facilitating your resettlement, Me'naan."

Anne Marit seemed to be from another world, very resolute and unsympathetic. Suddenly, the clouds in his head started to clear up.

'Who are those who think I haven't told them all my story? Why do they think so? What has been told about me in my absence that they need authentication for?'

He breathed deep. He shook his head.

"You know what, I am tired of being suspected. Believe it or not, I am who I say I am. No matter what people were telling you about me, I am just who I am. I told them before, and I am telling you now. Unless you stop following the definition of those transgressors I am running away from, you will never stop asking yourself whether I have told you all or not. Believe me, I don't fit into that definition."

8

He breathed deep and he looked at the two ladies with a half-smile. Then he focused on Ingrid.

"It was a month after that almost four-hour-long interview at the sheriff's office in Tingvoll, that UDI approved my resettlement in the Lenvik c ommune." He sighed. "The time I spent in the Lenvik commune, Ingrid, you know much of it!" He took up his beer.

The two ladies kept quiet for some time, sipping on their beers. It was Ingrid who found her words first.

"Truly speaking, Me'naan, it is a novel that you have presented to us here. This is a story worth telling, of course. My goodness, I have never listened to someone telling their story with such undivided concentration. It is indeed a captivating story, and you are damn good at telling it. Yes, at times I was able to feel your sadness and sorrow, and helplessness. And…"

She looked at her friend Solveig and smiled.

"I would have loved to hear the continuation of your experience after you were resettled in the Lenvik commune. It might have mirrored all of us who came to know you in one or the other way."

"You bet it might have!" Solveig exploded in laughter.

Me'naan seemed to be confused.

"How much of that life in Lenvik does Solveig know?"

He fell deep into his thoughts and unknowingly started running his eyes all over Ingrid. She smiled and batted him on his shoulder.

"It is enough storytelling for today. We really appreciate your trust in us. And you know what? I have my own story that I want to share with you. But that must wait until tomorrow. That is if you might have time for me."

She stood up and started removing empty bottles and glasses from the table in their two single-bed room. Solveig accompanied her cleaning.

Me'naan understood that the ladies wanted him to go.

"Thank you for your patience and I'll see you tomorrow, then."

He left their room without much ado.

The next day, right after breakfast, Solveig excused herself, saying that she had slept badly the night before and that she wanted to go back to their hotel room and get herself some extra rest. Ingrid and Me'naan went for a walk in the neighbourhood.

Ingrid started the conversation after she suddenly turned to him and gave him a quick kiss on his lips.

"Do you believe me if I tell you that I never kissed a man after my adventure with you, Me'naan?"

Me'naan was not sure how to respond. This was not what he was expecting.

"Is this the story you want to tell me, Ingrid? You remember what we agreed upon the last time we were together?"

He looked at her with distressed eyes.

She smiled and took his hand into her palms. "No, that is not the story I want to tell you."

She released his hand and moved one step to her right.

"Sorry if I have offended you, Me'naan."

They walked a few steps together, feeling an exhausting stillness in the air. Me'naan was about to say something, but she started first.

"It is about this foster child I have in my care that I wanted to talk with you about. He is such a lovely child, bright and very smart. He is an Oromoo."

She looked for Me'naan's reaction.

He raised his eyebrows with visible surprise on his face.

"Yes, he is a very sophisticated young man. I am so happy for being able to be there for him."

She looked at him seriously. At first, he hesitated.

He couldn't remember whether he had told her about his real perspective regarding white foster families for black kids. And then he thought how genuine and strong Ingrid's emotion could be. He remembered her straightforwardness, that she said what she truly felt.

"How did you get into this? Wasn't it too much in addition to your work?"

"At first it appeared to be a challenging endeavour. Through time, I managed both my work and Latiinsaa."

She looked into his eyes.

"Two or three years after you left our city, Solveig got a new job in Trondheim. After ushering her goodbye, I couldn't find either the energy or the calmness to proceed with my life as usual. Two years after Solveig moved to Trondheim, I got an offer to work at Trondheim Police Department's immigration office. I accepted it immediately and moved there two months later."

He interrupted her. "I have been in Trondheim so many times. Had I known you were there, I would have paid you a visit. As a good friend, of course."

He smiled.

She smiled back.

"Stop kidding, Me'naan, you wouldn't do that."

"Maybe not." He smiled. "Now to your Latiinsaa; when was it that you decided to be a foster family?"

She looked into his eyes. "You want to hear the truth?"

Me'naan raised his eyebrows.

"Yes, of course."

"All of it started after I had participated in a two- day seminar organised by the Trondheim municipality for people with an immigrant background. I had a presentation myself regarding what services our immigration office offers. Among those who took the podium were people from the child welfare service who explained how very difficult it was to register families who were ready to give a home to needy children. Then, I think it was some two weeks after the seminar, the case of Latiinsaa and his family came to our attention at the police department."

Then she paused. She looked into his eyes.

"When I heard this child belonged to an Oromo family, I thought about you. I mean it. Me'naan, I would certainly be lying to you if I say it was simple to forget that wild adventure I had with you."

She took a couple of strides without saying a word. Then she turned to him.

"While you were celebrating your family reunion, I was crying my eyes out, cursing the day I met you. When I found out that you had moved out of Lenvik municipality without saying goodbye to me, I was overwhelmed by sadness. Everybody around me noticed my sadness."

He took her hand in his. He tried to soothe her in silence.

She took her hand back.

She rubbed her eyes dry and inhaled deeply.

"Two years after I attended a course for foster care as a single person, the regional head of child welfare service wanted to have a meeting with me. At the meeting, she mentioned the difficulties they were having to be able to give this immigrant child a permanent foster home where he could truly feel safe and start trusting people. She told me that sometimes weeks, sometimes days after his placement with foster families, he started quarrelling, most of the time using some minor issues as an excuse, fiercely fighting either with grown-ups or their children. Then she directly asked me if I wanted and could take care of him."

Ingrid smiled and looked into his eyes again.

"That is how my adventure as a foster family started. It took me months to win his trust and to figure out how I could communicate with him without driving him crazy, or without losing focus to play the right role of a parent. I was lucky, and at last Latiinsaa accepted me."

Then she let her tears drop freely. Me'naan gave her a strong hug.

"Because it is you, Ingrid, a decent and loving woman. He found the right person to trust and love. That is why he accepted you."

She stayed in his arms for a while and then she removed herself.

"Solveig encouraged me to take this short vacation right after Latiinsaa had made a truce with his parents and went to them for his first week-long stay away from me. Before we reached this agreement, he confessed to me that his real parents were in Ethiopia. He shared with me that what his child mind had registered why they, his parents, wanted him to go with his uncle as his own son. One of the reasons why he ended up being an institution child was his bitter longing for his real parents and the revolt that this feeling created in his mind."

She suddenly took Me'naan's arm and stopped him.

"That child has lived through hell, Me'naan. The system couldn't decode his longing, and the reason that constitutes his rebellious action, and therefore couldn't protect him. I could never come to know about it on my own if he hadn't told me. He was determined to find out what had happened to his real parents, and I have sworn to him to help him."

She looked into his eyes.

"You know, before I met you yesterday evening, I told Solveig while we were eating our dinner the first day we arrived here, that I wished to find you around here to consult with you about this problem, and she laughed at me and reminded me to get old."

She smiled.

Me'naan smiled back. "Your wish came true, didn't it?"

"Indeed, miraculously."

She wanted to jump on him and kiss him, and she hesitated. Me'naan read her mind.

He gave her a strong hug.

"Don't you think the right person for this is his uncle who brought him here as his child? Why don't you talk to him and find out whether he has contact with them or not? For sure there must be communication between them. It is a normal procedure that he gives them feedback about the child."

"Yes, that was the first thing I thought about when Latiinsaa confided his secret to me. But I changed my mind when he begged me not to tell his uncle that he had told me the truth. He didn't want them to suffer more. They just wanted to help him, according to Latiinsaa. What Latiinsaa is very much interested in is to find out why his parents couldn't safeguard his upbringing and why they went so far as to have decided to send him away as someone else's child. His child brain couldn't figure out this puzzle for him then. But now, I think because he has trusted me and even called me mum, he wants to find out, without anybody knowing. He said to me that he would never stop until he found out what made his real parents take that awful decision." Her tears started falling again.

Me'naan put his hand on her shoulder and tried to soothe her.

"Okay, Ingrid, who knows, we might be able to find a way to help him. But you must know, looking for somebody who might be in a bad mood with the government could bring you to a dangerous territory. Our country has a reputation for preferring to solve their internal problems the way they think is proper. They do not appreciate interference, especially from foreigners."

She smiled and rubbed her eyes dry.

"I do understand what you are trying to tell me. I will work on it."

On their way back to the hotel, Me'naan explained to her the politically motivated problems she might face and the cultural shock she might encounter, in case she got ahead in accompanying Latiinsaa to his real parents. It could be a possibility that one or both parents might have been thrown into jail, or killed, or forced to leave their country. He also explained that it might be very hard for her to fathom the reason why people get arrested, killed or maimed without having committed any wrong. He suggested she should make Latiinsaa wait for a few years and then put him in the driver's seat in his search for his parents. He advised that Ingrid should thoroughly organise this project by getting advice from the Norwegian Embassy in Addis Ababa.

"Do not worry, Me'naan. If you could survive the cultural shock you have encountered coming to Norway, there is no way I couldn't. Don't forget, it was not too long ago that Norway also had a countryside life that was like most of the developing countries today. My goal is clear. I want Latiinsaa to find his parents without making loud noises. Nothing is political in this."

Ingrid stopped suddenly, her eyes focusing on a woman standing at the entrance gate of their hotel. Me'naan stopped, too, reacting to Ingrid's sudden halt. He followed her eyes. Just then, he saw her, too. He smiled and quickly advanced to the woman in front of the entrance gate.

"Bliss, I almost forgot our appointment…"

She didn't let him finish.

"No problem; take your time and go ahead with what you are doing. Our appointment can wait."

Though he didn't appreciate her sarcastic comment, he smiled and introduced her to Ingrid.

"Ingrid, this is the woman I told you about. Bliss, I want you to meet my Norwegian friend here."

While the two women shook hands and exchanged small comments, Me'naan remained calm and tried to figure out his next move. He knew very well that Bliss never showed her real disappointment if she suspected something. He didn't want to get into the idea that Bliss might suspect him of having an affair with Ingrid here in Rome, right behind her back, after he told Bliss he came to Rome to see and rediscover her. Rather than speculating about what was going on in Bliss's head, he decided to be frank.

"I met Ingrid and her friend at the hotel right after I came back from sending you home yesterday. I was acquainted with Ingrid the first time I was resettled in Norway, many years back. They, too, came to Rome for a vacation yesterday, and they, too, rented a car from the same car rental, and they, too, have booked a room in this hotel."

Bliss smiled. "What a coincidence."

It was like a whisper, but both Ingrid and Me'naan heard her.

"Yes, indeed," Ingrid smiled. "Now it is time for you people to keep to your appointment. Okay? Nice to meet you, Bliss." She stretched her hand to Bliss.

Bliss responded. "Nice to meet you, too."

"Me'naan, we'll proceed with our discussion some other time. Okay?"

"Okay, Ingrid."

Ingrid opened the entrance gate and disappeared through the main glass door of the hotel.

Me'naan gave Bliss another hug and looked into her eyes.

"How are you, Bliss?"

"I am fine. What? I am fine."

She tried to smile, but couldn't recover from the sudden shock seeing Me'naan with another woman created inside her.

This innate feeling of psychological ownership, when it came to her love life with Michael, had forced her to do ridiculous things so many times in those old days. She remembered incidences whereby she forced him to greet girls who stared at him while he walked with her, suspecting there must be something he had with them. The need to have control over him to secure her love relationship had, most of the time, backfired and made Michael very angry.

Her memory brought a smile to her face.

Me'naan responded by cheering her up for a ride. "Okay, then, let us drive out and spend time together."

He guided her to his rental car. Bliss followed him willingly.

"Believe me, I want our relationship to have a future." She said it with such a calmness that made Me'naan drop his lower lip.

He looked at the red traffic light that had stopped them for a while and turned his face towards her.

"What kind of a future, Bliss?"

"A beautiful future, a future that will give us another chance to be true to our feelings. I myself have rediscovered how much I still love you from the first day I talked to you on the phone. But yesterday, after you sent me home, it became clearer that I want to keep your love as my treasure. You were the first man in my life and the first man who willingly ran away from me. But you came back and helped me to decipher the true story behind our separation. It didn't turn out as I feared. I never thought I could confront my past so easily. You also helped me to find out that even now, after I have got my husband, my kids and my life, that you are the one I truly love. Look, I just dropped an important family appointment and decided to come to you and have time with you. True love has nothing to do with marriage or child-bearing. Neither is finding your way back to somebody you love so much a transgression or a sin. I want to have a chance again to love you, to be touched and caressed by you. I want to show you my love as a matured woman. Yes, I want you to rediscover me, and then let me have you in my life so that I can run into your arms whenever I get the chance to do that."

She placed her left hand on his right thigh.

"If you still love me as I do love you, there is a way to give our relationship a future. Believe me."

He stopped the car on the right shoulder of the road he was driving on. He released his seatbelt and pulled her towards him. He kissed her on her forehead.

He went out of the car, he stretched himself and took a deep breath. He moved back and forth for a while. And then he abruptly opened the car and dropped himself on his driver seat.

Bliss looked at him cautiously.

"What is happening Michael? Did I say something wrong?

"No, Bliss, not at all."

He sighed.

He looked into her eyes.

"You have no idea how many times on my way to you, to Rome, I have argued with myself using the same logic you have just brought up; that finding your way back to somebody you truly love so much cannot be a transgression or a sin."

He placed his right hand on her thigh and caressed her with his finger.

"Last night, I thought about us, about our relationship in the future very seriously. Just as you are saying, I thought about having a chance to love you and discover you anew."

He looked into her eyes.

He tried to read her feeling. He wanted to be cautious not to hurt her.

"One thing that became more obvious to me through my thoughts is the fact that I do love you and that you, too, love me. But the years we spent apart and the decisions we made had brought a radical change in our life. We are no more you and me alone. Finding our way back to each other and doing what we loved to do in those olden days, will become a transgression and a sin because of the impact it might have on the innocent souls we have established as our families. We must weigh the satisfaction we get from our new adventure against the possible damage we inflict upon the people we hold dear."

He turned his face toward her, and he felt insecure by the earnestness he saw on her face.

"I am ready to be your best friend, and to show my love for you in a very different way. I know Bliss. Discovering the intensity of my feeling for you, this was

not an easy decision to make. But I hope you understand me, and you will help me."
She kept quiet for a while, and she smiled at last.
"We will see!"
She said, and yawned.
"Drive the car now. It is better to talk over this matter at your place. I want you to hold me in your arms and tell me all your reasons one more time."
She smiled.
Me'naan didn't.
Reluctantly he started the car.

9

Ingrid woke up early. The six-floor hotel they were booked in through their contact at the Embassy in Addis Ababa was beautifully furnished. She came to the breakfast room to find out how it was before she woke up Latiinsaa and Solveig. They had arrived in Ambo late in the evening the day before.

The project that helped them to reach this last destination of theirs took almost two years of planning and organising after Ingrid discussed the case with Me'naan in Rome, Italy. Me'naan telephoned Latiinsaa's uncle right after he came back from his short vacation in Rome where he had met Ingrid and Solveig. His phone call had at first created emotional breakdowns. Latiinsaa's uncle himself had a lot to talk about, things he couldn't share either with Latiinsaa or with appropriate officials. The pain he was trying to ignore was not only bothering, but it had brought him to the verge of collapse, if it had not been for the solid support he received from his wife. A lot of things happened and kept happening both in Norway and back home in Ethiopia, of which the most painful was the letter he received from Latiinsaa's real mother. It was a long letter describing what his brother was forced to face in prison, how dwindling his health had become, and how helpless she was to be able to rescue her husband, the father of her only son, the son they both decided to send abroad with his uncle, hoping for a better future for him. She wrote begging him and his wife to be the true parents of her son, for her hopes to see him again were vanishing. Latiinsaa's uncle responded to her plea by sending her money and comforting words, while he himself was suffering untold helplessness in fulfilling his own promise to take care of Latiinsaa. The conflict he experienced with Latiinsaa was something he couldn't foresee and understand and solve on his own. It went out of his control without even knowing there was a conflict. He lied with the best intention of helping Latiinsaa, and that lie drowned Latiinsaa's tolerance and trust, both in himself and his uncle. He became unable to continue living as if his real parents were not existing. That same lie hindered Latiinsaa's uncle to open up and tell the truth. As a result, he became a moving host of permanent sadness and sorrow.

When Me'naan confronted him with the fact that he was denying reality on the surface through all these times, Latiinsaa's uncle grieved, cried, and at last spilled his guts out confessing to Me'naan. After an hour-long sincere discussion, they came to an agreement as to how they could help Latiinsaa and Ingrid without disclosing that they knew what had happened between Latiinsaa and Ingrid. Me'naan asked

Latiinsaa's uncle to share with him any information he received about Latiinsaa's real parents so that he could share it with Ingrid and assist her in planning her project of helping Latiinsaa find his parents.

When Ingrid asked Solveig to accompany her and Latiinsaa to Ethiopia, Solveig's answer was a big 'No'.

"You are about to mudding someone's water, Ingrid. Political life in Ethiopia, as far as I learned from people I have talked to, is a very dangerous domain to enter, particularly as a foreigner. You are not going there to adopt an orphan, for which the government would have sympathised with you and therefore have facilitated things so that your dream could come true. But you are heading there to find out about the truth regarding Latiinsaa's parents. What if they have been thrown into jail and your enquiry about them as a white woman could create suspicion? You do remember the news about the arrest of the two Swedish journalists who entered the country to report the bloodshed in the eastern part of the country? Yes, you do remember. They just narrowly escaped capital punishment. The government does not like to wash its political dirty linen in the open for the entire world to see."

Ingrid was not in agreement with her friend. She was not totally against what Solveig was saying, either.

"My dear friend, I know that power, State power, is more sacred than human life in countries like Ethiopia. The rulers are authoritarians who do not want to be governed either by their own constitutional law or by the international laws and regulations. For the power people to feel secure, suspects are made overnight in this corner of the world. Then they get investigated, not to unravel crimes or wrongdoings, but to wear down, weaken and to drive them to the confession of a crime they might never have committed. This is because killing, maiming, arresting, and torturing are part and parcel of the daily political business the power usurpers are transacting to stay in power. But that shouldn't be something you should use to make me feel helpless, Solveig."

Ingrid became very serious.

"Thanks to my profession, to our profession, I have developed a thick skin resisting the abusers who always try to mislead their victims by creating a false narrative and making the victims themselves question their judgement and reality and at the end plead guilty. I do not want to allow anyone anywhere to have a monopoly of violence and manipulation. Therefore, I cannot see any viable reason that can stop me from muddying someone's water for the sake of truth and justice."

She looked around and focused on Solveig.

"Look, the one thing I know for real is that right now there are many Norwegians who travel to and out of Ethiopia without any problem. So, no reason for me to be suspected in Ethiopia because I am a white woman. In addition, I am not entering Ethiopia holding a banner that says: 'Justice for Latiinsaa's parents'."

She stopped herself from smiling.

"The other thing is, Solveig, our Embassy in Addis Ababa was informed about our trip, and we have already got a contact person at the Embassy in case we face complications. Furthermore, Me'naan and Latiinsaa's uncle have already established a trusted courier who will help us to meet Latiinsaa's parents."

She looked deep into Solveig's eyes and breathed deeply.

"There is no reason for me, Solveig, to jump the gun in Ethiopia and start condemning the rulers of the country so randomly. That is not my mission, and you know that. Your presence, as a friend and colleague of so many years, would have helped me to stay on track, but you are very scared, so I don't want to force you to accompany me."

She waited for Solveig to interrupt her. That interruption didn't come immediately.

It took Solveig more than forty-eight hours to make her decision. She made her decision not because she was convinced, but because she wanted to be by the side of her friend and colleague at a time like this when she needed her most.

Ingrid went to Solveig's room and knocked on the door. The answer came from behind her in the corridor.

"Good morning, Ingrid."

Solveig was full of smiles when she introduced to Ingrid a young Swedish girl whose hand she was holding.

"You know what, we are so lucky. She does know the city very well. She is teaching at the sister school which is linked to one of the junior secondary schools in Stockholm, Sweden. I met her at the reception while she was waiting for the new arrivals from Sweden who came yesterday to visit her school and who spent the night here at this very hotel."

The introduction was quick, and the young Swedish girl went back to the reception promising to look for them in the afternoon.

"Wasn't it interesting, Ingrid? She might make our sojourn in Ambo city very smooth by giving us an alibi. If there is some tailing issue, we could easily fade into the people who came to this elementary school for a visit."

Ingrid seemed not to be sure about it.

"We will see. Now, first things first. Let me wake up Latiinsaa and let us have our breakfast together. I was down to the first floor to check out where we eat our breakfast."

"Oh, I did the same, you know. When I saw this young lady entering through the main door to the reception, I left the breakfast room and went there to find out more."

"You did find more all right, Solveig. Now let us have breakfast." Ingrid went to Latiinsaa's room.

The city was overcrowded with people. The main road that dissected the city was equally used by pedestrians as by car drivers, and by some horse-pulled carts. Though it was the rainy season, youngsters on the street were dressed well and looking good. As to the mood in general, there were abundant smiling faces out there, moving in every possible direction. The images from news reporting that were, some time ago, imprinted somewhere in Ingrid's mind relating to the starving population in Ethiopia, were nowhere to be traced in this city.

The scene at the school they were invited to visit by the Swedish girl they met at their hotel was more of an indication of a vibrant and pulsating social life than the hazy picture the narratives from the asylum seekers' perspective used to paint. The pupils were full of excitement and were oozing such an infectious joy and self-confidence, accompanied by celebratory ululation coming from the attendees that it was impossible for newcomers to trace the chronic shortcomings outsiders were talking about.

Ingrid, Latiinsaa and Solveig were sitting in the first row of the seats prepared for the occasion at the junior secondary school to welcome the visiting guests from the sister school in Stockholm, Sweden. After the welcoming committee chairman opened the ceremony, the colourful choir of young girls and boys entertained the attendees, most of which were parents of the pupils of that very school. Ingrid found herself motivated after listening to how the sister-school relationship between this school in Ambo city and the one in Stockholm came to life. While sitting there and following the presentation from various people in charge of the relationship, Ingrid started envisaging what her son Latiinsaa and she might do in the future for the community she was going to learn more about.

"That is not, however, my priority right now," she whispered aloud, and that made Latiinsaa swiftly turn his face towards her.

"What?" He raised his eyebrows.

"Oh, no, I was thinking aloud. Sorry."

He smiled and turned his attention back to the presentation.

Hidden from the eyesight of Latiinsaa and Solveig, a young man in his mid-twenties, wearing blue jeans, encroached to the seat directly behind Ingrid and whispered, "Don't look back. Take the notice paper I am stretching to you now, on your left side."

Ingrid found herself paralysed by the voice she had just heard. It took her an eternity to trace the notice the young man was talking about. With her heartbeat gradually decelerating, she at last managed to look at the notice. She read it.

"I am your contact person you were told about. I was at your hotel. I heard someone calling you and found out who Ingrid in person is. Then I followed you to this event. I will stay here until the end of the ceremony. After that, you will allow me to introduce myself to you three as one of the guest-attendees here at the school. Then we will have dinner together at the restaurant at your hotel. Don't be scared. Everything is happening according to plan."

At first, Ingrid was not sure whether to trust or not to trust. She weighed the choices she had. She had none. The one thing that crossed her mind was to make the best out of what was transpiring in front of her own eyes.

When the children's singing group finished their song, she clapped enthusiastically and smiled to Latiinsaa and Solveig.

"What a beautiful melody. My gosh."

"Yes indeed, beautiful," Solveig responded.

Ingrid turned around and smiled to the young man sitting behind her.

"Are you a teacher or one of the parents? Congratulations. It is quite a performance here. You have talented children."

The young man smiled.

Ingrid smiled back, wondering what she was doing.

"I am a substitute teacher in my free time from the University of Ambo. I am a full-time third-year student there."

"What are you studying?" Solveig wanted to know.

"Business administration."

Ingrid stretched her hand out. "Wow, that is awesome. By the way, my name is Ingrid."

He gave her his hand. She shook his hand and released it.

Then, without waiting for his response, she turned to Solveig and Latiinsaa.

"My friend here, her name is Solveig. Here is my son, Latiinsaa."

"I don't know the meaning behind the names of the two of you, but your son's name is beautiful. Getting an Oromo name from foreign parents, that is splendid," the young man responded.

Latiinsaa lifted his shoulder in disagreement. But he didn't utter a word. He was not supposed to do any talking to anyone other than Ingrid and Solveig, according to the instructions they received from their contact person at the embassy in Addis.

The young man registered Latiinsaa's reaction and smiled.

"My name is Fayyeeraa. It is so nice to meet you."

"It is our pleasure. We came to your city yesterday. We were so lucky to be invited to this ceremony by our neighbours from Sweden. And, as a result, we happened to meet one of the city's future generations, the young student, that is you. Thank you for being here. I wonder if you have time to accompany us to our hotel when we are done here so that we might ask you about your city."

Solveig raised her eyebrows and stared at Ingrid.

'We are on a mission!' she told herself.

The young man smiled.

Deep inside, Fayyeeraa thanked Ingrid for facilitating his introduction. He was not so sure how to contact them after he received a call from his friend in Finfinnee, working at the Norwegian embassy, to immediately get in touch with them after they arrived in Ambo city. He was informed in which hotel they were going to stay and that they were told they would be contacted by him. They arrived late in the evening, and he dropped the idea of contacting them right away. In the morning, he observed them with a young Swedish lady who came to the junior secondary school where he was a substitute teacher two months ago and other foreigners he was not told about. He felt a relief when he overheard that they were heading to attend the event that was taking place at this very school he was working at as a teacher. It was a good cover for him to get in touch with Ingrid at this event than anywhere else. Now, with Ingrid starting their conversation right there while the celebration went on, rather than waiting until the end, everything seemed to be perfect.

He cleared his throat smoothly and focused his eyes on Ingrid.

"I have time today. My afternoon class is cancelled because most of my pupils are participating in the singing group here. And again, it is my pleasure to meet you all."

Two days after they talked to Fayyeeraa and had dinner with him at their hotel's restaurant, the three of them hung a 'do my bed' sign on their door and went to the breakfast room earlier than they usually did.

"Where are we going so early?" Latiinsaa asked Ingrid.

"Nowhere; we are just going to have our breakfast."

"Isn't it too early for that? And I don't understand why you insisted we all need to hang on our doors the 'do my bed' sign."

"Trust me, it is also part of our mission."

She smiled and gave him a push towards the breakfast room. Solveig pulled her back.

"Latiinsaa, go and fix yourself your breakfast. I want to have a word with Ingrid." She gave him her biggest smile.

"Don't you think it is better to keep an eye on what is going on from nearby? I do want to stay in my room and…"

"No, Solveig, you don't need to do that. Until now, everything has gone according to our plan. We have no reason to do it differently now. For whatever reason, Fayyeeraa insisted we all three should hang up the 'do my bed' sign and remain at the breakfast room for at least the first forty-five minutes."

She looked at her watch and pulled Solveig towards the breakfast room.

"Don't forget, we are in a foreign country. Besides, I suspect the situation is more volatile than what you observe on the surface. We have no choice than to stick to the direction we have been given."

She couldn't hide her fear.

Solveig registered it and tried to calm her down.

"You are right, Ingrid. We must stick to the direction we have been given. It is the best choice when you don't know or have no idea about the rules of the game."

She smiled.

"Let us fix our breakfast, then."

Dheeroo, an army colonel in charge of the detention centre located some ten kilometres north-west of Ambo, was not alone that Wednesday morning. Daansoo Margaa, Latiinsaa's biological mother, had arrived early in the morning to accompany her husband, Miidhagaa Mijana, to meet a specialist in the city for health check-ups. The colonel greeted her without any sign of facial expression that he was under duress. She tried to reciprocate his smile with a smile. But she couldn't make it.

She looked very exhausted and miserable. The prison time her husband had been subjected to, without any kind of court ruling, final or non-final; the derogatory interrogations he was forced to go through; it had all broken her spirit of resistance a long time ago. The first two years she had kept hoping for his release and visited him daily. She came to him with home-made food so that he could totally drop the hogwash food the detention centre provided. This last year, however, watching how her husband's health kept deteriorating each passing day, and how he was giving up on life by saying goodbye to making sense of things, she found herself depressed and traumatised.

She knew that the investigation her husband was exposed to had nothing to do with the unravelling of the possible crime committed. Rather, it was aiming to break him as a person, to wear him and his resistance down, to weaken his determination; and she couldn't do anything about it. It seemed to her the entire community was aligned with the devil. That revelation did hurt her through time. She lost her energy and became totally exhausted and numb, divorcing herself from the idea that for so long had reverberated in her mind, amplifying the need for endurance and commitment to at last win over all the wrongs and injustices.

'How can he simply endure when he is not wanting to live? Why, for God's sake, is he not willing to work for them rather than suffering endlessly? What is the meaning of crying for justice and freedom, when the entire mankind seems to be foreign to that very outcry?' These questions and others she asked herself so many times, but she never came to the decision to ask him, her husband, directly.

The aggressive refusal of the detention centre officials to let her see him when they kept him in those dark rooms, in those infected holes in the ground, for weeks, left her nothing but suffering, both emotionally and physically. On top of all that, the lack of satisfactory information about her son living in Norway drove her crazy. On many occasions she broke up her visit and ran away from her husband whenever he was starting to suggest that she should forget him and rather work hard to be reunited with her son. Listening to him saying his days were numbered was like experiencing a hard punch in the stomach. Not only once, but on many occasions, this talk of his knocked all the air out of her lungs, resulting in such an intense cramping feeling in her belly that she needed to leave him and run to the toilet and vomit.

Then, suddenly, her hopes came alive again. The reason to live and to hope returned to her when she heard her son was planning to visit her, accompanied by his Norwegian family friends. She had been told that because Latiinsaa's uncle couldn't travel to his home country, these family friends offered their support to accompany him to Ethiopia. That news made her cry all day and all night long with joy. The constant sorrow her husband and she were living with, however, became a burden she wouldn't know what to do with before her son arrived. But she didn't want her son to see and feel that sorrow, coming to see her after all these years. She therefore wanted to do something about it.

She remembered how many times Colonel Dheeroo had suggested to her that her co-operation would certainly ease the conditions her husband was living under. She remembered also that she kept asking herself every time she visited her husband, 'What kind of co-operation is he talking about?"

Some six months ago, when she first heard from Latiinsaa's uncle about the possibility of Latiinsaa visiting them, she thought about this very question a little more seriously.

"What is it that they want me to do for them to ease the circumstances around my husband in their prison? Is that maybe some sort of political campaign? Is that maybe an indication that they want to recruit me so that I will try to convince my husband to co-operate?"

Bearing all these questions in her mind, one Friday afternoon, after visiting her husband, she asked Colonel Dheeroo if he minded talking to her.

Entering his office, she immediately figured out what the said co-operation was all about. The way he rolled his eyes, the way he talked to her, his attempt to put his hand on her shoulder while inviting her into his office, all of it unravelled his intention.

She smiled and she sat down on the sofa he pointed at for her to sit on.

'What a dangerous situation I have let myself get into by playing along and not seeing this coming,' she mused.

She fearfully thought about it and looked around the office of the colonel. It was a well-furnished office.

She cautiously followed every move the colonel was making.

He took off his heavy military overcoat and hung it on one of the coat hangers placed inside the open mahogany wardrobe. He took some steps towards his huge office desk and sat on the edge of it. He looked at his watch and then looked at her.

"Have you eaten lunch today?" he smiled.

"Yes!" she answered quickly and aggressively.

He smiled. 'In my world, the first aggressive reaction of a woman is a good sign,' he told himself.

"Well, I was about to invite you to dinner. You know there is this newly opened restaurant on the outskirts of our city. They care for privacy so much. One can easily order a secluded place to dine in peace."

She smiled again. She tried to control her nervousness. She thought about her son, their son. She imagined his sadness if he could not find his parents.

"I would have said yes to becoming a member of their party and to advocate for them if that was the price that I must pay to save my son from experiencing this sorrow. But this…? Sorry, my son!"

Abruptly she stood up.

She looked into the colonel's eyes and smiled a bitter and lifeless smile.

"It is so kind of you, Colonel. But I have to say no, thank you. It could be an honour if the circumstances were different. My husband is suffering in the detention centre you are administering, so how can I make it to dine with you? No, thank you."

He went to the back of his desk and sat in his chair.

"As I told you, your co-operation is the one thing that could save your husband."

"What sort of co-operation, if I might ask?"

She wanted to hear it from his mouth.

He smiled. "I thought I had clearly expressed it."

He looked into her eyes and pointed his finger at the door.

"If it is so hard for you to see my point, please, you can go."

She hesitated for a while. Then she said it. "Ask me for anything I can do to save my husband, but not this."

She opened the door and disappeared behind it. She resisted crying. She knew if she was going to take a taxi, she would explode emotionally. So, she decided to hit the road on foot the ten-kilometre distance to Ambo city. A few kilometres along the street, she couldn't stop her tears. Deep inside, she burned with anger. She wanted to cry aloud, to vent her anger. She stopped for a while and asked herself, 'How can I possibly fight alone against such a shocking abuse of an office, an institution? How can I singlehandedly impact the bad behaviour of irresponsible office-holders in such an institution?'

She thought about the people she had talked to all these years, looking for help to rescue her husband.

'How is it possible for so many people to be so indifferent to the sufferings of fellow citizens? And how long can I stay non-reactive to all these injustices while waiting for a solution from the abusive system itself? Is there any possibility to do otherwise …?'

The honk from a passing car brought her back to herself. She hadn't realised she was walking in the middle of the road. She returned to the unpaved and dusty pedestrian area.

A short while after, she arrived at the campus of the university in Ambo. As she approached the majestic entrance gate to the campus, she spotted the person she wanted to talk to. Fayyeeraa was one of the students at Ambo University whom her husband, Miidhagaa, was working with before he was detained. She knew about the various cells they had organised clandestinely, though she was not a member. She knew about the assistance they were able to provide to those who had been arrested. Ambo city was and is the hotspot of the protest movement against political oppression and discrimination. She knew that they had developed a way to intervene and stop or minimise the abuse of their incarcerated members. But that knowledge never gave Daansoo a sense of security regarding her husband. She hadn't seen any help coming from them to rescue him, though she had been told by her husband, every time she visited him, how successful the underground movement was. Her desperation forced her to think otherwise.

'The existence of such illegal cells was the sole reason why the officials determined to break down inmates like my husband,' she reasoned with herself so many times. She did choose to look for excuses why her husband had ended up where he was these days, denying herself to see and understand the real situation on the ground, the extreme brutality of the political office-holders. Though she never dared to pronounce it openly, she did tell herself, more than once, that her husband was 'foolish to line up with the intolerant youth movement'. She kept registering sadly that through the clandestine undertakings of those young community members, things were radically changing for the worse. The tit for tat actions both sides willingly employed terrorised the whole community. The youth, once known for their lively presence, had become a liability to their family because they were randomly targeted by the government. Gradually, when their clandestine movement became a force to reckon with, the government enhanced its brutal undertakings. She was convinced, because of the actions of the youth movement, that State violence kept raging, and the young people in the city and all the community members harbouring them were brutally targeted. She was equally convinced that despite the brutal undertakings, the youth movement in Ambo city and in the surrounding areas couldn't be subdued. Rather, the opposition to the injustices committed kept getting networked and structured, and became more powerful and persuasive day after day.

But now, the revelation of the intention of Colonel Dheeroo changed her cautiousness towards the underground movement. She regretted not trusting them for so long. Suddenly, she felt tormented by an overwhelming appreciation for the actions taken by these groups so far.

'It is time to be part of it!' she told herself.

Approaching Fayyeeraa from behind, she whispered,

"Do you have some spare time? I need to talk to you."

Two weeks later, Fayyeeraa paid her a visit. It was in the late afternoon. She was doing the usual chores inside her compound when, standing at the entrance of her compound, he called her by her locally acknowledged custom name, "Haadha Latiinsaa", meaning "Latiinsaa's mother".

She didn't answer his call immediately.

She had come home a few hours ago after she visited her husband at the detention centre. She didn't like the way she was treated there by the guards and the receptionists.

They were too respectful and considerate towards her, something she had never experienced before. She found it very unusual, and she didn't like it. When she told her husband what she encountered, he looked into her eyes and kept quiet.

Now, Fayyeeraa's sudden arrival caused waves of both anxiety and excitement inside her. The anxiety wave took over and her heart started pounding. She couldn't move herself towards Fayyeeraa. She gave him a sign to come to her and slowly sat down on the dusty ground of the cabbage field she was working on inside her compound.

"What is it, Fayyeeraa?"

She didn't bother to greet him.

Fayyeeraa smiled and tried to calm her down. "No worries at all, my sister. I came to you with good news. We reached an agreement with the colonel. Though it took days for him to take the bait, and for us to get him cornered. The rest is history, my sister. For now, he has agreed to collaborate with us by letting Miidhagaa go to the specialist in the city for a health check-up. He agreed that you can accompany him right from the detention centre. The guard will be instructed to wait for you at the specialist's workplace while you and Miidhagaa will be away to spend some time together. There will be some security routines to be followed cautiously, of course."

She stretched her hands out to hug him, with her eyes turned red and her sight blurred because of her tears running nonstop. Fayyeeraa knelt and took her hand and helped her to stand up on her feet.

"Now listen to me, Daansoo. You must stop crying and get ready for the challenges ahead of us. We took the risk, and we played the card you provided us. If we hadn't heard from you about the dirty behaviour of that officer, it wouldn't have been easy to catch him and corner him. These criminal officials are only powerful if their secret is kept away from their bosses. I can tell you this, we have tailed him for so long with some limited success. The breakthrough came with the information you gave us. We pieced together his behaviour and his relationships with various people. He couldn't gamble his position by saying no to our demand. We know that he might plan how to retaliate in the future, but now he is completely abiding by the conditions we set up for him."

"He will really let Miidhagaa see his son?"

"Be careful, Daansoo. We didn't tell the colonel that part of the story. The one thing he was made to know is that Miidhagaa should attend a health check-up. After that, he would spend some time with you at the hotel without being bothered. No word about you meeting your son. Okay?"

"Okay, Fayyeeraa. Thank you. What more can I say? Except that, may your prize be your freedom and the freedom of all our people."

"You might need to be ready and prepared to be free, too!"

He smiled.

She smiled back.

On Wednesday morning, Daansoo Margaa arrived early to accompany her husband to visit the specialist in the city for a health check-up. Though she looked very exhausted and miserable, she was feeling good. As she was brought to the colonel's office, she saw a different person. Although he greeted her without any sign on his facial expression that he was under duress, she knew he was not that same person now. He smiled. But she failed to reciprocate his smile with a smile. Thereafter, her husband entered the colonel's office accompanied by two well-trained and hugely equipped guards, and a corporal without any kind of armament.

Very surprisingly to Daansoo, the colonel warmly welcomed Miidhagaa. Miidhagaa ignored him and ran into his wife's open arms. His exhaustion was visible. Daansoo helped him to sit on the sofa.

The colonel came to the front from the back of his desk.

"I heard it is time for you to get thorough health check-up, Miidhagaa," he said.

Then he turned his attention to the guards and the corporal.

"Corporal, it is your lucky day. You remain in Ambo city until Miidhagaa is done with his medical check-up. He also has permission to spend some time privately with his wife after his medical check-up."

The colonel turned his eyes towards Miidhagaa and Daansoo and smiled. Immediately, he turned back to the corporal.

"So, arrange with them what time they will come back to the physician's compound, and call me and tell me what time you want the driver and the guards. Sergeant, you come back with your soldier and the driver immediately to the centre after you have taken them to the specialist. Good luck."

He randomly ushered them all from his office.

Kumsaa General Medical Clinic was the best health centre in Ambo city. It was located a few hundred metres away from the centre of the city named Arada, bordering the huge Hulluuqaa river that dissected the city. The ground plus t two buildings of the clinic were very modern, and it housed primary health care and outpatient services.

Half an hour after the old Land Rover station wagon transporting Daansoo and Miidhagaa arrived at Kumsaa General Medical Clinic, another car, a five-seat grey Volkswagen Beetle, driven by a young Swedish woman, entered the compound of the clinic through the back gate that was hidden from onlookers. Fayyeeraa climbed out of the car quickly, collected the suitcase Daansoo had given him the day before, and disappeared into the clinic. A quarter of an hour later, he came out of the clinic, accompanied by Miidhagaa and Daansoo, their clothes shifted, and they entered the car. A moment later, the attendant of the back door of the clinic slowly opened the gate, and the grey Volkswagen Beetle, with the two new passengers on the back seat, disappeared into the morning hustle and bustle of Ambo city.

After about five minutes on the street, Miidhagaa broke the ominous silence in the small car.

"Excuse me, madam, is it you who brought our son to us?" He sounded stiff and sad, like he was about to cry.

The Swedish lady tried to locate him in the car's rear-view mirror.

"No, sir. My colleague Fayyeeraa asked me to do him this service of driving you to where you are going to meet your son."

She smiled.

"I am a guest teacher at Awaaroo junior secondary school here in the town, where Fayyeeraa is also a temporary teacher."

"Very kind of you!" Daansoo whispered.

"Yes indeed!" Fayyeeraa amplified Daansoo's comment.

Then the ominous silence held sway again in the small car. No single word was communicated until they reached their destination.

The colonel became restless and started walking around in his office. He was supposed to receive a call half an hour ago from the corporal who followed Miidhagaa and Daansoo to the specialist in the town. His plan was to re-arrest Miidhagaa, this time together with his wife and Fayyeeraa. He had been planning this ever since he was threatened by Fayyeeraa and his friends. At first, he was shocked by the audacity they displayed to disrespect his uniform, his rank, and his position.

He was feared and saluted by almost everyone because of his uniform. His uniform and his rank had made him feel untouchable for so long. He never considered himself a service man, who took an oath to serve his people and his country to the best of his ability. He was a con man, who made a choice to cheat and deceive. He had a talent to persuade people to believe that what he was telling them was true. In his world, weak people were there only to help strong men achieve their dreams. He had occasionally offered himself to be a victim so that his superiors could freely step on him to climb up the ladder of military promotion, while he made himself a reputation by asserting utter dominance over his minors. He found a way to downplay complaints that reached his superiors about his work ethics and his naughty behaviour towards female employees. His systematic disobedience to pay attention to the directions given to him by his superiors created at times furious reactions. There were times when he was forced to lick boots to escape incarceration.

That these hidden vices of his had fallen into the hands of these so-called vigilantes had infuriated him. He couldn't figure out how they found out about his fallout with his superiors because of repeated disobedience, and on top of that his sexual intimacy with the spouse of one of his superiors. He immediately saw how vulnerable he was, and he decided to surrender for the time being. Not knowing how far they would go with the information they gathered on him, he chose to co-operate and to treat all of them delicately.

When he came to his office that Wednesday morning, he had already assembled in his mind how and when he was going to make his move. He summoned to his office the two soldiers whom he had chosen to escort the prisoner and his wife, and cautiously oriented them about his plan of action. Later he ordered the corporal whom he suspected to have leaked information about him to the vigilante group, to stay with the prisoner and his wife at the Kumsaa General Medical Clinic.

According to the intelligence he had received from the police department, among the list of the people staying overnight at Ambo Central Hotel were Norwegian and Swedish guests. Fayyeeraa was observed dining at the restaurant of the hotel together with two of these foreign guests whom the police didn't identify as Swedish or Norwegian. Neither did the police provide him with information regarding the young boy in the company of the two foreigners.

Convinced that there was something bigger in the making, he worked out his own theory. Fayyeeraa and his friends wouldn't have taken such a dangerous path of blackmailing him to only help Miidhagaa to get a medical check-up and spend some time with his wife. Key to unlocking this mystery were these two foreigners whom Fayyeeraa dined with, and who arrived in the city a few days ago. However, he couldn't go as far as taking them into custody. It would have exacerbated his vulnerable position. But he could safely get help from the police to re-arrest Miidhagaa along with his wife and Fayyeeraa, accusing them of helping the prisoner to escape. He hoped to catch them red-handed after they left the clinic and entered the hotel where they were to supposedly meet with these foreigners.

Now, the phone call he was waiting for was not coming. He wondered why it took so long for the corporal to call him. He was not sure whether he could tip off the police to go to the hotel before he knew his suspects were moving there.

"Yes, I can tip them off," he decided at last.

A few hundred yards away from Ambo Central Hotel, Fayyeeraa asked the Swedish lady to stop the car and park alongside the road. He excused himself for a minute and went to a taxi that had stopped right behind the grey Volkswagen Beetle the Swedish lady was driving. He went to the driver side and handed over an envelope to the driver.

"You go to the breakfast room and give this to the lady you saw me talking to at the school. I am sure you remember her. Her name is Ingrid."

"I remember her. I saw the three of them eating their breakfast fifteen minutes ago. I went into the hotel to check whether those cleaners were in the rooms as they were told."

"And?"

"Perfectly on time with their housekeeping cart full of towels and bed sheets. I don't think anyone can suspect the guests are inside."

"There is a change of plan. We are not going into those rooms. I suspect the colonel might try to ambush us there. Instead, you drive them to this address."

He gave him another piece of paper.

"After you give her the envelope, tell her that your taxi is waiting for them at the parking area. Tell them to use the back door. Hurry up."

Fayyeeraa went back to the car that was waiting for him and they drove away.

Solveig couldn't hide her irritation. She had never been in such a situation where she had constantly been dictated to about what to do and where to go. The way Ingrid simply slid into the constantly changing plans of their guides was driving her crazy. It was Solveig who first saw the young man in his twenties coming to their table with such purposeful strides and an atmosphere of having control over the whole surroundings. He approached them with a big smile and directly addressed Ingrid.

"Good morning, Madam Ingrid. How are you this morning? How is the breakfast?" It seemed as if he had met her before.

Then he turned his look towards Solveig and Latiinsaa.

"Good morning to you, too!"

Stunned as they were, both greeted him back simultaneously.

"Good morning."

Then, Solveig saw the way he shoved an envelope under Ingrid's plate and whispered into her ear.

"Read the message and follow me to the hotel's parking area through the back door."

The young man smiled and went to the coffee stand, pretending to be pouring coffee for himself.

Ingrid pulled the envelope from under her plate, put it on her lap and cautiously opened it while watching Solveig and Latiinsaa. Then she looked down and up again quickly. It was a half-line message: *"Trust me – and do what this man is telling you! Fayyeeraa!"*

"What?" Solveig wanted to know.

"Change of plan!"

"What? Ingrid? What is going on?"

Ingrid ignored her for a while and put the piece of paper back into the envelope and the envelope into the pocket of her trousers. Slowly, she stood up.

"It is part of the mission, Solveig. Just follow me!"

She looked at Latiinsaa. He smiled widely, and she felt encouraged. She turned around and made eye contact with the young man.

The young man turned around and gave a sign to one of the woman helpers in the breakfast room. She conveyed the sign further to a woman standing at the other end. The young man, after assuring himself that the cleaners had received the message to abort their undertakings, went to the back door. Ingrid, Solveig and Latiinsaa followed him.

A few minutes after Ingrid, Solveig and Latiinsaa left by taxi, two uniformed police officers and two in civilian clothes came to the reception area of Ambo Central Hotel. The two uniformed police officers sat on the sofa in the lobby, and the two in civilian clothes went to the breakfast room. They came back after ten minutes and reported to the uniformed police officers that there were five foreigners – three women and two men – in the dining room. They hadn't spotted a young boy with any one of them. The information was conveyed to the police department that sent them on this mission, and the police department contacted the colonel.

The colonel called the corporal at the clinic for the sixth time, and the phone was answered immediately.

"Corporal, where have you been? Why is it that I was not able to get through on your phone?"

"Sorry, Colonel! My mobile died on me. I had to ask the gateman here to help me charge it. It is not fully charged yet, but it is back to life now."

"Where are Miidhagaa and Daansoo?"

"I think they are inside the clinic. I didn't see them come out."

"Are you sure they are inside?"

"Where can they be, then? Nobody came out. I never left my post since we came in. I charged my phone here at the gateman's post."

"You fool! Go inside the clinic and ask the receptionist where they are and call me back soon."

"Okay, sir!"

The corporal showed his middle finger to his own phone, thinking of the insult he had received from his boss. Then he smiled. Instead of going into the clinic, he started dialling a number.

The grey Volkswagen Beetle entered the school yard and Fayyeeraa jumped out of the car. He approached the gateman, leaned towards him and whispered, "There is a taxi coming soon after us. Let the foreigners with the young man enter the compound and bring them to the guest house, closing the gate immediately behind you."

Then he hurried back to the car and they drove the few yards to the guest house where the Swedish lady was residing. She opened the main door and invited all of them to come inside. The sitting room was moderately furnished. Daansoo and Miidhagaa sat on the couch and Fayyeeraa sat in one of the armchairs.

"Welcome and feel at home. I don't know what a situation Fayyeeraa has put me in, but I do hope it must be for a good cause. I have a class now, so I leave you to Fayyeeraa, and say goodbye in case you leave before I come back."

She offered a lifeless smile.

Fayyeeraa stood up and gave her a tight embrace.

"I don't know how to thank you. You did a lifesaving job today. No, we won't wait until you come back. And don't worry, the school administration is part of this smooth undertaking. You don't need to know more. But don't forget, no mentioning of what happened today."

"I understand. If somebody has spotted me and my car at the clinic, I was there to talk to my husband working there."

"Exactly. Thank you so much."

After the Swedish lady left, it took the three of them more than a quarter of an hour to agree upon what they should do next.

"Daansoo!"

Fayyeeraa looked into her eyes.

"Miidhagaa is not going back to the detention centre. We have arranged everything to take him away from all the tribulations. Don't worry. He is not alone. I am with him. I am not staying here. Now, you have a decision to make. You remember? I told you to be ready to be free. Either you follow us, or you travel to Finfinnee and hide there. I know you have connections, and even relatives there. This is better than to end up in the colonel's detention centre."

She didn't utter a word. She cried silently.

"Daansee tiyya, we don't have time to cry now. We have done that all these years." Miidhagaa put his hand on her shoulder.

"The very important thing right now is to meet our son and wish him good luck and bless his future with this unimaginably good person who took all the risk to come to this Godforsaken country to help him find his real parents."

He kissed her on her forehead.

"I want you to travel to Finfinne and stay there. Fayyeeraa has already talked to my uncle to take care of our place. He has always been our supporting hand, you know that."

She looked into his eyes.

She wanted to ask him a lot of questions. She wanted to have him alone. She wanted him to hold her in his arms and whisper to her the way he used to in those good old days.

"Oh, my goodness, Miidhoo, you are telling me we are running out of time for everything."

She turned to Fayyeeraa.

"You should have told me this earlier. I never thought you were telling me this when you spoke that sentence: 'be ready to be free'. I feel helpless right now. A sudden flight is just like a sudden death to me. You people are telling me to leave behind everything that kept me alive all these years."

"Daansee tiyya, think realistically. Me running away, there is no way for you to remain at our place.

They will come for you. I asked Fayyeeraa to pack things you will need and some money, too. He has done that."

Miidhagaa turned to Fayyeeraa.

"Yes, you will find it in the car that will take you to Finfinnee right after we are done with the meeting."

Daansoo grabbed her own hair and wanted to shout. She swallowed hard.

"Do I have a choice?"

Miidhagaa took her face into his hands and looked deep into her eyes.

"No and yes. No, if you are asking to stay back. But yes, if you are asking about staying determined, hopeful and committed to the end. You were crying all those times, witnessing what they did to me in that detention centre. Now I am about to reclaim my freedom, so you should not be crying, Daansee tiyya. You should be ready to reclaim your freedom, too."

He kissed her, softly at first, then voraciously. Fayyeeraa left the sitting room. He wanted to tell Olivia before he leaves.

Unknowingly Daansoo repeated the way her husband called her; 'Daansee tiyya! – My Daansoo.

It was Ingrid who entered the house first. Latiinsaa followed her. Solveig stayed outside.

Daansoo and Miidhagaa jumped to their feet.

For over ten years they had dreamed of this moment happening. Now that the moment was here, they felt dumbfounded. The picture they had in their minds was always that little boy, smart and happy, searching for answers to everything he encountered, never getting tired chasing around baby goats, chickens, calves in that well-kept garden compound of their homestead.

Miidhagaa approached him first. He stretched his hand to Latiinsaa carefully, controlling his pushy feelings, his desire to pull him towards himself and hug him as hard as he could. Latiinsaa was careful, too, having a blurred picture of his real parents. They were changed. His memory was all about a young couple, beautiful and handsome, always smiling. He never expected to see them so drained and exhausted. He had loved their energy and composure, for it was the reason for his happiness.

Midhagaa took Latiinsaa's hand slowly.

"We are terribly sorry, our son, our only son. We didn't mean to let you down. We never wanted you to grow up away from us. We missed you terribly. We never stopped loving you, praying for your wellbeing, day in, day out. Son, please forgive us…"

Daansoo joined him. She took the liberty of embracing her son, crying silently. They held him together in their arms. They held him so tight that Ingrid felt that they might hurt him. Subconsciously, she took Latiinsaa's hand and wanted him to feel that she was there, too.

Miidhagaa saw her. He smiled.

"Son, please sit down."

Latiinsaa slowly disengaged himself and followed Ingrid to the couch. Miidhagaa and Daansoo sat on the other couch.

Miidhagaa was about to say something when Solveig opened the door and went in.

She smiled and took a seat in one of the armchairs at the dining table in the sitting room. All of them smiled back to her.

Miidhagaa let his tears drop while running his eyes over the guests who had accompanied his son to his hometown.

"We are truly grateful if that is the right word. And…"

He stopped suddenly. He wanted to cry aloud. Knowing that he was running out of time, he couldn't figure out what to say and how to say it. That gave him a sharp and intense pain all over his body.

"Oh, God…," he said.

Daansoo shared his agony. She cried silently.

"Latiinsaa, please come and sit between us. We don't have much time."

Latiinsaa jumped from his seat and sank onto the couch between the two of them. First, he hugged his mother and kissed her. Then, he turned to his father. He hugged him and buried himself inside his father's embrace.

"Lubbuun isin argu kiyyaaf baayyen gammade," he whispered in Afaan Oromoo, his mother tongue. "I am very happy to find you alive."

Daansoo and Miidhagaa were extremely stunned by what they were hearing. "You didn't forget your mother tongue, son!" Daansoo shouted.

They all looked at Ingrid. Ingrid felt proud of her son, her foster son. Miidhagaa gasped and huffed.

Grieving deep inside, he wanted to conclude before it got too late and dangerous.

"Dear Ingrid, I heard about you a few months ago and have been told about your determination to bring Latiinsaa home to us. That tells a lot about you. We are so lucky that Latiinsaa found trust and love with you. For us here, this time happened to be the worst time for his homecoming. The problem we faced then forced us to separate ourselves from him. And the situation we are in right now is forcing us to send him back with you again. Don't ask why. You will never understand the causes of our tribulations and the level of atrocities we are experiencing here in this country."

Miidhagaa cleared his throat.

"I always thought about the chance we missed to raise Latiinsaa, telling him our own bedtime stories, singing to him our own songs, Oromoo songs, making him laugh with our own jokes, above all giving him all the love he needed. But now, I see you happened to be more than a foster mother to him. You encouraged him to learn his mother tongue. You gave him love. We see that with our own eyes, and we feel how genuine it was. You were scared, weren't you, that we might hurt him hugging him so hard."

He smiled.

Ingrid smiled, too, trying to stop the tears that filled her eyes.

"What I am saying is..."

He looked deep into the eyes of Latiinsaa. He kissed him on his forehead.

"We say to you goodbye again. This time with the strong confidence that you are in good hands. Don't you forget, we are always your loving parents. The time will come when you truly understand what the reason is for all this to happen to us. I love you, son." He hugged him.

Daansoo pulled him towards her. She kissed him.

"I love you, my son. I always loved you."

They hugged him together.

"We love you so much. Don't forget, you are our only son."

"Wait!" Latiinsaa shouted, and went to Ingrid. "Give me your bag!"

She gave it to him without uttering a word.

He opened it and he found two small packages.

He went back to his real parents and handed each of them one. "Open it!" he said.

They opened it.

They seemed somewhat scared looking at the figures. Latiinsaa smiled for the first time.

"No worries. It is a Norwegian good luck charm troll. It brings luck. It really does!" He looked at Ingrid.

Daansoo and Miidhagaa laughed. "Oh, we need that."

Daansoo kissed him on his forehead.

The corporal started to be restless. He dialled that same number again. After some ringing, Fayyeeraa was at the other end. He was just going back to the guest room.

"Yes?"

"You have got the time you asked for. It is more than an hour now. The colonel wants me to check on Miidhagaa and Daansoo in the clinic and to report back to him. What is your status?"

Fayyeeraa kept silent for a while. He went through his checklists once more. He inhaled deeply and scratched his head.

"Okay then, tell him that you couldn't locate them and that nobody knows where they are. Tell him the way we agreed upon. I don't need to thank you for your co-operation."

He paused. He chased away his hesitation.

"If you didn't change your mind, you know where we meet. Don't forget the passage code. In case you come late, those young people are dangerous. Take care. Bye!"

The corporal sighed.

"Changing my mind for what? To be slaughtered alive? No, thanks!"

"Then you know what to do. Be careful."

Fayyeeraa took a deep breath and talked to himself. 'This is it. The moment of truth has arrived.'

He opened the door to the guest house abruptly. He looked at them, one after another, gasping.

"We must leave now. Daansoo, there is a car waiting for you at the gate. Just go, no goodbyes."

He turned to Ingrid.

"The three of you, you go to Olivia's class. She has already told her pupils that they are getting visitors. You are those visitors. You are here as part of the Swedish visitors at the school from the sister school in Stockholm. I advise you not to stay overnight at the hotel. I have already talked to your contact person at the Embassy yesterday evening and they might send you a car to pick you up. After you have spent some time with Olivia, you can call this number. He is a Norwegian, I have been told. He might be at your hotel right now. You might also encounter some police presence at the hotel. But don't worry, they are not looking for you. In case something inconvenient happens, the man who might be waiting for you should know what to do. No goodbyes for you, too!"

Daansoo left first.

Ingrid, Latiinsaa and Solveig followed her after five minutes. Fayyeeraa locked the door from inside and faced Miidhagaa.

"Are you ready, my friend?"

"Yes, I am ready!"

They hugged each other and went out through the back door of the guest house. Fayyeeraa placed the key where Olivia told him to place it.

The wired fence surrounding the school on this side was almost two metres high. But Fayyeeraa had located earlier an opening through which both wild and domestic animals trespassed.

Before they found their way through the hole in the wired fence, they both looked at the thick bush that ran into the ridge of the Aleltu river and beyond, reaching the forest covering the Wadeessaa chain of mountains.

"The moment of truth, brother!" Fayyeeraa smiled.

"Yes, the moment of truth!" Miidhagaa whispered.

They hugged each other again and quickly found their way through the opening in the wired fence, and disappeared into the wilderness.